THIEVES *of* WEIRDWOOD

THIEVES OF WEIRDWOOD

WILLIAM SHIVERING

Illustrations by Anna Earley

SQUARE
FISH

Henry Holt and Company

New York

For John Cusick—dashing unifier, tamer of chaos

SQUARE FISH

An imprint of Macmillan Publishing Group, LLC
120 Broadway, New York, NY 10271
mackids.com

THIEVES OF WEIRDWOOD. Copyright © 2020 by Wasabi Entertainment Inc.
All rights reserved. Printed in the United States of America by
LSC Communications, Harrisonburg, Virginia.

Square Fish and the Square Fish logo are trademarks of Macmillan and
are used by Henry Holt and Company under license from Macmillan.

Our books may be purchased in bulk for promotional, educational, or business use. Please
contact your local bookseller or the Macmillan Corporate and Premium Sales Department
at (800) 221-7945 ext. 5442 or by email at MacmillanSpecialMarkets@macmillan.com.

Library of Congress Cataloging-in-Publication Data
Names: Shivering, William, author. | Earley, Anna, illustrator.
Title: Thieves of Weirdwood / William Shivering. ; illustrated by Anna Earley.
Description: First edition. | New York : Henry Holt and Company, 2020. | Series: Thieves
of Weirdwood ; Book 1 | Summary: Wally Cooper and Arthur Benton, who resorted to
thievery to pay off family debts, unwittingly find themselves at the center of a battle between
the Fae and the mages tasked with protecting humanity.
Identifiers: LCCN 2019019333| ISBN 9781250763006 (paperback) |
ISBN 9781250302892 (ebook) | ISBN 9781250248183 (audio book) |
ISBN 9781250248176 (audio download)
Subjects: | CYAC: Fantasy.
Classification: LCC PZ7.1.S51774 Thi 2020 | DDC [Fic]—dc23
LC record available at https://lccn.loc.gov/2019019333

Originally published in the United States by Henry Holt and Company
First Square Fish edition, 2021
Book designed by Katie Klimowicz
Square Fish logo designed by Filomena Tuosto

1 3 5 7 9 10 8 6 4 2

Myths are lies breathed through silver.

—C. S. Lewis

THIEVES *of* WEIRDWOOD

Kingsport, 1907

One light, rainy evening in April, eight-year-old Marie Wallace got the most pleasant surprise of her life—right before she got the worst one.

Marie was walking home from her aunt's house when she passed a dark alley and heard a tiny voice.

"Ma-ma."

Marie stopped and stared into the long shadows. The gas lamps had not been lit yet.

"Hello?" she said.

There was no answer.

She was certain it was a little girl's voice she'd heard, pinched and sugary. Marie was not one to leave a helpless child abandoned in an alley, so she carefully stepped around the puddles, venturing deeper between the damp and looming buildings.

"Hello-o?" she said again.

A small figure peeked out from behind a packing crate. The figure was no taller than Marie's knee. It had big blue eyes and shiny pink lips and blond ringlets that tumbled around the collar of its silk dress.

A chill ran up Marie's spine. It was a doll.

But her doll at home couldn't move like this. Sure, it blinked when she tipped it over and said "Mama" when she pulled the string on its back. But it certainly never walked around on its own buckled shoes.

The doll stared at Marie with its big blue eyes and then stiffly reached behind its back and pulled on the ring that dangled between its shoulders.

"*Ma-ma*," the doll said again in a warbled voice.

Marie took a step back, heart leaping in her chest. She squinted behind the packing crates to see if someone was pulling puppet strings to make the doll move. She checked the nearby windows for some sad little girl missing her dolly.

Marie was alone.

The doll's arms rotated upward like it wanted to be picked up. Marie blinked at it. This was everything she'd ever wanted. A walking, talking doll.

"You poor thing," she said, and forgetting her shoes, sloshed deeper into the alley. She scooped up the doll and held it to her chest. Its porcelain skin was cold through the silk of its dress. "Let's get you home. Mother will be excited to meet you."

As Marie stepped back into the street, she felt the doll's head rotate on her shoulder.

"There, there," Marie said as its porcelain lips placed a kiss on her neck.

* * *

The Oakers found Marie later that night.

She still had a pulse. Her breath steamed through clenched

teeth. But she couldn't move. Her skin was hard and shiny, and her mouth was frozen in a grin. She didn't so much as blink.

One of the Oakers shivered. "In all my years on the force, this is the strangest thing I've seen. That smile's gonna haunt me for months."

The other Oaker bent and lifted one of the girl's frozen shoulders. "Gor, she's cold. *Stiff* too. Almost like *porcelain*. Good thing she landed on this packing straw. Elsewise she might've shattered to pieces. Just like a . . . well, y'know."

The first Oaker hefted Marie's other shoulder. "I've half a mind to bring her home to my Leah. She's been begging for a doll, and them things is expensive."

The second Oaker chuckled. "Quiet, you. This girl might still be able to hear us. Let's get her to the hospital."

It wasn't until they pushed Marie upright like a plank that she finally blinked, and a faint "*Ma-ma*" whimpered through her smiling teeth. The Oakers glanced at each other uneasily.

Down the alley they heard the pitter-patter of porcelain shoes. And giggling, pinched and sugary.

1
WALLY

Comfortable?" the doctor asked.

Wally Cooper adjusted himself on the hard, leather chair. The office shone dully under the new electrics. A chill seeped from the marble hallway, and the occasional scream echoed from the cells. How could anyone feel *comfortable* in Greyridge Mental Hospital?

"Um, yes, sir," he said.

"Good," the doctor said. He flipped open a file bearing the name of Wally's older brother. "Let's see here . . . *Graham Cooper*. Ah, yes. Our resident artist." He gave Wally a flat smile. "Though I prefer paintings of flowers myself. Or a bowl of fruit. None of your brother's *outlandish landscapes*. How about you?"

"Yes, sir."

Ever since Wally could remember, his brother had drawn pictures. There had been no cause for concern until Graham had started sketching his otherworldly works on the sides of public buildings, catching the attention of the Oakers, who promptly arrested him. Before the Pox had taken Graham and

Wally's parents, their mom had asked Graham why he couldn't use paper like everyone else. Graham had answered that paper wasn't big enough.

I'm practicing my portals, he'd said.

The doctor shut the file and adjusted his glasses at Wally. "Your brother's condition is worsening, I'm afraid. He's having grand delusions about his role in a citywide conspiracy. Something about *Rifts* and *Fae-born*. When I asked what sort of evidence he has to back up these claims, he told me that he can see into the *future*." The doctor sighed. "If you aren't able to pay your brother's bill within the next week, the board will be forced to nominate him for some of our more *experimental* treatments."

Wally crossed his arms to keep them from shaking. "W-what are you gonna do to him?"

"Oh, nothing to be concerned about," the doctor said, avoiding Wally's eyes. "Some electrical shocks. Administering medication that hasn't made it to market yet. Perhaps a tiny hole in the back of the skull to release pressure on the brain."

Wally nodded. Or thought he did. His whole body had gone numb. This was it. The doctors were going to hurt Graham. Just as their mom had feared.

"Any questions?" the doctor asked.

Wally wanted to ask how his brother's condition was worsening. Graham seemed like the same old Graham. Sure, he had his delusions, but he wasn't hurting anyone. He was just drawing his landscapes on the walls of his cell, using dirt and cobwebs as naturally as if they were ink.

The doctor cleared his throat. "If you'll excuse me, I have other patients to see." He tapped another file that read *LUCAS*,

VALERIE. "We've got a woman here who believes her daydreams are trying to murder her." The doctor chuckled and, when Wally didn't crack a smile, scribbled something on his notepad. "Have the back payment by Friday. Otherwise we'll take care of your brother the way the hospital sees fit."

He tore the paper free and handed it to Wally. It was a list of the hospital's expenses. The number at the bottom made Wally's stomach flip. He'd never seen that much money in his life, let alone in three measly days.

He continued to stare at the paper as the guard led him out of the hospital's portcullis entrance. Wally's lock-pick set hung heavy in his pocket. Come nightfall, he could sneak back to the hospital and pick the lock to Graham's cell as easily as untying a pair of shoelaces. But then what would Wally do with him? The last time Graham had been loose in the city, he'd stolen a lady's feather boa and wiggled it through the air, claiming it was a *Serpent of the Heavens*—before getting cracked in the head by an Oaker's nightstick.

As much as Wally hated to admit it, his brother was better off in the hospital. So long as Wally could find the money before those experimental treatments began.

* * *

Wally walked down the craggy cliffs of the coastline and back into port. The horizon was shifting from blazing orange to sleepy purple, and the air was growing cool. The smell of ocean salt blended with that of coal from the steamships. The cries of seagulls were drowned out by the rattle of carts and merchants hocking their wares.

"Apples! Fresh apples! The mushiness brings out the flavor, marm!"

"Fresh fish! Still with the wiggle in their tails! Oops! Watch out, sir! It might slap ya!"

"And then the doll *kissed* him! I swear it! A peck on the ankle before skittering into the sewer. Now look at him! His skin's hard as a rock!"

"He just had one too many at the pub, ma'am."

"My husband's never drunk a drop in his life!"

Wally had no clue what the argument was about, but the man lying on the cobbles did have a big, dumb grin on his face. And his eyes did look glassy.

Wally continued toward the Wretch—the poorest quarter of the city. How was he supposed to come up with the money? He could try to multiply the few coins he had at the gambling houses. But Wally never did have any luck at cards. And those games were fixed. He could break into one of the fancy houses in the Gilded Quarter, but Oakers patrolled those streets. Besides, neither of those options had ever earned him a fraction of what the hospital was asking for. And if he was caught thieving, he'd get locked up just like Graham.

Wally did know someone who might be able to help. So long as this someone behaved himself, that is.

He entered the Wretched Quarter, heading down gloomy Paradise Lane and past the Ghastly Courtyard where the Oakers hanged members of the Black Feathers, Kingsport's most notorious gang of thieves. He continued beyond the dance houses and the gambling dens, past the boxing ring and the rickety tenements where Wally had spent most sleepless nights since the Pox had taken his parents.

From a high window, a young member of the Black Feathers hailed him with the sign of the Rook's claw. "Oy, Cooper!"

"Oy, Alek!" Wally shouted, hailing back.

Alek was looking as skeletal as ever. The Rook, the Black Feathers' leader, allowed young Black Feathers to keep just enough money to feed themselves so they could keep thieving without keeling over. Wally's own stomach had been grumbling for weeks.

He ducked behind a spice cart and down a narrow alley. He scaled broken crates, leapt a fence, and using the windowsills of the tenements, climbed past the laundry lines—careful not to look down—before scrambling onto the shingles of the roof.

He found Arthur Benton right where he'd expected—tucked between two chimney pots and reading a frayed book by evening light. The book had been thumbed through and rescued from puddles so many times that it resembled an old sponge. The tattered cover read *The Adventures of Garnett Lacroix* by Alfred Moore. Or it would have, had most of the lettering not peeled away.

"Evening, Arthur," Wally said, dusting soot from his shirt.

Arthur held up his pointer finger and turned a page.

"Oh, come *on*," Wally said. "You've read that story a hundred times now."

"Hush, Cooper," Arthur said, eyes fixed on the book. "I'm just getting to the part where the Gentleman Thief frees the children of the orphanage and tells the madam, 'That'll be enough of your *gruelty*!'"

Wally leaned against the chimney and stared at the ravens perched on the laundry lines. It was said that the Rook, the coldhearted boss of the Black Feathers, was always watching through the black birds' onyx eyes. Wally didn't believe stuff like that, but it was hard not to feel superstitious when he was weeks behind on his tribute.

If the Rook knew that the money meant for the Black Feathers' coffers was going to Greyridge, Graham's hospital bill would become the least of Wally's worries. Thieves who came up short on their tribute exited the Stormcrow Pub missing a finger or even a hand. And that was if they left the pub at all.

"Ha!" A laugh burst out of Arthur, and he snapped his book shut. "Gets me every time!" He rolled out from between the chimney pots and held up *The Adventures of Garnett Lacroix* like it was a holy text. "Did you know, Cooper, that Alfred Moore, author of these fine tales, is one of Kingsport's very own? And that all of the adventures take place on the streets of our fair city?"

Wally sighed. "Yes."

"And did I tell you," Arthur continued, "that Moore up and retired without so much as an announcement, leaving us with a cliffhanger so steep it would make a mountain goat cry?"

"At least a dozen times."

"Or that his adoring fans, myself included, have spent *years* trying to figure out where he lives so we can beat down his door and *demand* that he continue the story?"

Wally stopped responding. It didn't seem to make a difference anyway.

Arthur placed his hands on his hips and beamed over Kingsport. "What I wouldn't do for one last Garnett story. It would give me the clues I need to make this city bow before the grandeur of a *real* Gentleman Thief."

Wally rolled his eyes. With Arthur's soot-stained cheeks, oversized hat, and vest fraying at the seam, he was a far cry from a gentleman.

"So, um, Arthur," Wally said. "Do you still need people for that secret job you were working on?"

Arthur narrowed his eyes. "Who told you about that?"

"Priscilla. She was, um, talking about it in the Storm-crow." Wally didn't mention that she'd been making fun of Arthur at the time. Instead, he pulled out his pick set. "She said you were looking for someone who could open a tricky lock."

"I might be," Arthur said, folding his arms. "Why are *you* interested?"

Wally glanced away. He never breathed a word about his brother outside the hospital. It scared him to think that Graham's madness might be catching—that someday Wally too would start vandalizing city buildings and believing that feather boas were mystical flying serpents.

"Just need a new belt, is all," Wally said, adjusting the rope that held up his pants. "Who's the mark?"

Arthur plopped down between the chimney pots and started reading again. "I can't share that information with just anybody. I only need the best for this job."

"I can pick locks," Wally said. "And I can make a pocket-book vanish like a breeze."

"If you were that good, you would have risen higher in the Black Feathers by now," Arthur said.

Wally bit his lip. Nearly all of his money went to Graham's bills, which left Wally in poor standing with the gang.

Arthur turned a page. "I don't need an amateur slowing me down."

Wally knew that the real reason Arthur hadn't pulled the job yet was that no one wanted to work with him. Arthur was loud, brash, and paid himself too much credit. His grandiose plans tended to be disasters. Like the infamous narwhal blubber job, to name just one.

Still, Arthur could charm the pink out of a sunrise. And when his harebrained schemes actually worked, he brought in more money than most of the young Black Feathers combined. If Wally continued picking pockets for a handful of measly coins, he'd be lucky to pay off Graham's bill by 1910—long after the hospital had begun its experimental treatments.

Wally peeked over Arthur's shoulder at the book. "Doesn't Garnett Lacroix command his own gang of thieves?"

"They're called the *Merry Rogues*," Arthur said, still reading.

"Hmm." Wally searched the rooftop. "Where are *your* Merry Rogues?"

Arthur turned another page. "The other Black Feathers are intimidated by daring adventures. They've got cold feet. Er, *claws*, I guess."

"That's too bad."

"Too bad for *them*," Arthur said.

Wally scraped soot out from beneath his fingernails. "Seems to me that if there was a promising heist to pull, then

Garnett would jump right on it. He wouldn't wait for help."

Arthur snapped the book shut, stood, and slipped it in his back pocket. "Apparently I'm going to have to find a new reading spot."

Wally stepped behind Arthur. "Has Garnett Lacroix ever been so down on his luck that he had to wear a hand-me-down hat?" he asked, tapping the back of Arthur's head, drawing his attention away from his pocket.

"Of course not!" Arthur cried, pulling a loose thread from his ragged cap. "But he *would* if it helped feed the orphans!"

Wally circled Arthur. "Does Garnett Lacroix sit around reading books all day instead of stealing from the rich?"

"Probably!" Arthur said, spinning around to keep up. "He just reads *between* adventures. Where else would he get his smarts? Like in chapter six where he . . ."

He reached for his back pocket and found it empty. He turned and saw Wally leaning against the chimney, reading his book.

"Looks to me like the Gentleman Thief just starts the adventure," Wally said.

Arthur's frown thawed into a smile. "You say you can pick locks?"

Wally handed the book back. "Like Charlie picks his nose."

"All right, Cooper. You're in." Arthur placed his fingers on Wally's hat, rotating him toward the Gilded Quarter. "There," he said, pointing at a charred roof on Mulberry Lane. "*That's* the mark."

Wally stared at the burnt remains of the once stately house. The windows were shattered, the shingles were shedding, and the brickwork was charred black. It looked less like a house and more like an ashen skull.

"*Hazelrigg?*" Wally said. "There's nothing in there but burnt furniture."

Arthur tapped his temple. "That's just what it *wants* you to think."

Wally was about to ask how a house could *want* anything, but Arthur started pacing. "We'll steal everything that isn't bolted down and redistribute the wealth to lowly street urchins!"

"I hate to break it to you, Arthur, but *we're* lowly street urchins."

Arthur grinned. "Not for long, Cooper." He threw his arm around Wally's shoulders. "I'll be just like Garnett Lacroix, and you'll be my Merry Rogues! Or the start of them, at least."

Wally remembered the astronomical number on the hospital bill, and he swallowed another argument.

Arthur gave charred Hazelrigg a valiant look. "With the money we steal tonight, we'll build a secret hideout in the sewers and carve a daffodil above the entrance to let people know that's where they go for *chivalry*."

"I thought you said the money would go to street urchins."

"We'll steal enough for both!" Arthur said.

With a flourish, he leapt to another roof, heading toward the Gilded Quarter.

Wally clenched his fists. *"Don't follow him."*

But then he looked to the distant cliffs and saw Greyridge Mental Hospital, glimmering in the setting sun. And he followed Arthur Benton.

* * *

Wally tried to keep up as Arthur traversed the slanted rooftops with reckless confidence.

"Yesterday," Arthur said, "I saw a girl enter Hazelrigg in finery so fine she could only be the child of nobles. She carried two swords and wore golden robes embroidered with forests of black thread." He wiggled a hand over his shoulder. "Had rubies and lapis lazuli on her fingers too."

Wally sat and carefully slipped down the shingles. He'd never understood why anyone willingly climbed to a height where gravity was trying to pull their body down to a splattery death.

"Nobles?" he called after Arthur. "In a burnt-down house? That makes no sense."

"It makes *perfect* sense, Cooper! You just have to use your imagination." Arthur leapt to another rooftop. "Perhaps these nobles are the wealthy cousins of some foreign king, but they were discovered in a dastardly plot to steal his throne. The king loved them dearly, so instead of executing them, he exiled them from the kingdom. Now they live in a burnt-out estate to protect their valuables!"

"Arthur," Wally said, "you sound like an adventure story."

"Thanks!"

They descended a fire escape ladder to Fir Street.

"Robbing a burnt house is a waste of time," Wally said, relieved to be on solid ground again.

"You'd think locking a burnt house would be too," Arthur said. He pulled an onyx key ring from his pocket. "I nicked this from the girl in the fancy robes. Distracted her with the *Lacroix eyebrow*."

Arthur did his best flirtatious expression, and Wally did his best not to gag.

"Who makes a key ring out of *stone*?" Wally asked.

Arthur shrugged. "Why do rich people do anything they do?" He gave the key ring a twirl. "Strangely enough, none of these keys actually work on the front door. Must be for the rooms inside or something."

"Wait, if the keys don't work on Hazelrigg, then why aren't we looking for the house where they—"

"*Shh!*" Arthur said. "Time to be invisible."

Wally pursed his lips as they entered the crowds of bustling Market Square. He tried to ignore the clinking pockets that passed his fingertips. By trusting Arthur, Wally wondered if he was dooming Graham to a lifetime of experimental treatments.

* * *

By the time they reached Mulberry Lane, the lamplighters had ignited the streetlamps, bringing a gloomy warmth to the evening. Flames flickered across Hazelrigg's charred brickwork. A moan emanated from the chimney. On the front door, the face of an onyx demon scowled its fanged mouth, as if in warning: *Do not enter this place.*

"You sure about this?" Wally whispered.

"What, Cooper?" Arthur said. "Afraid of this little demon here? He's not snarling. He's smiling. See?" He patted its stone horn. "He's friendly."

"I *meant* that this burnt house isn't inspiring much confidence."

"Really? I'm getting more confident by the second." Arthur squinted through a smoky window. "When I tracked that girl in the robes here, I got a peek inside. You can't see it now because the windows are so dirty, but the whole foyer is done up as pretty as a music box. There's gold curtains and cranberry carpets and wallpaper that would make the dresses on Lacey Lane turn green with envy."

Wally wanted to ask how dresses could be envious, but he knew it wouldn't do any good.

Arthur gestured to the front door. "Sir?"

Wally took out his lock-pick set, glancing around the empty street. The people of the Gilded Quarter avoided Hazelrigg like they avoided sewage carts. The family had died in the fire, and some claimed they'd heard voices inside—like whispers mixed with crackling flames. But Wally didn't believe in ghosts.

Just then, a large black bird alighted on Hazelrigg's roof and cawed.

Wally stared at it. "What if the Rook finds out we're outside of our thieving zone?"

Arthur smiled. "The Rook will forgive anything if you pay him enough. With the riches we find inside, he'll probably promote us to Talons!"

"Arthur. We're *twelve*."

"I know," Arthur said, disappointed. "I was really hoping to get there when I was still in my single digits. Now, can you open this or not?"

Wally huffed and set to work. It didn't take much fiddling to discover that the door had no lock. It had a keyhole. But no tumbler. No mechanism.

"Weird," Wally said.

"What's the matter, Cooper? Lock got the best of ya?"

Wally offered him the picks. "You wanna try?"

Arthur stuck his hands in his armpits. "I need my hands clean to steal the precious silks."

Wally rolled his eyes, went to the side window, and bent his wire. He wriggled it between the glass and the frame, curving it upward and jiggering open the clasp. The window popped open.

"Some security for nobles," Wally said.

A whistle screeched through the night. "*Oy!* You there!"

Wally's blood ran cold as an Oaker came tromping down the street, brandishing his nightstick. Wally tried to make a break for it, but Arthur hooked an arm through his, spinning him around.

"Evening, officer!" Arthur said, hailing the Oaker.

"What're you urchins doing in the Gilded Quarter?" the Oaker demanded, tapping his nightstick against his palm. "Clear out before I crack ya both unconscious."

Wally clenched his fists, ready to fight. The Oaker would probably seize every cent they had, claiming it as stolen property, before hauling them to jail.

"Why, we're collecting ash for paints, sir," Arthur said, as easily as if it were the truth. "Apprentices for the great artist Herman Mahler, we is." He pointed a thumb at Hazelrigg. "Someone's gotta put this burnt monstrosity to use."

The Oaker lowered his nightstick. "Paint, eh? I do a little painting myself every now and then."

In the flickering gaslight, Wally saw blue flecks of paint on the Oaker's fingers—something Arthur must have noticed the moment the man approached.

Arthur squeezed Wally's shoulder. "See, Wilberforce? Wasn't I just saying that this fine specimen of an Oaker was an artist in disguise? Got a painter's poise, he does!" He smiled at the Oaker. "Finest black paint you've ever seen, sir. *Perfect* for capturing starry nights."

The Oaker scratched the back of his neck, thinking. "I'll be in a world of trouble if the chief finds out I let the likes of you waltz into Hazelrigg."

"We'll be in and out, quick as ferrets," Arthur said. "Once we've mixed up our world-class paint, we'll drop some off at the station."

The Oaker almost smiled, then caught himself. "Just make sure you're out by eleven bells. That's when the next watchman comes by." He tipped his cap. "I'll look forward to that paint of yours."

He whistled down the street, and Arthur stepped through the window.

Wally shook his head. "I'll never know how you do it, Arthur."

"It's easy," Arthur said. "Everyone's a book. I just happen to be very good at reading."

Wally followed him inside. The front room of Hazelrigg was lit by ash-smeared light. The walls were gray with soot, and the floor was a wreckage of charred furniture. The singed carpet curled around the edges, and a smoky chandelier dangled by a few broken links of chain.

"So much for cranberry carpets," Wally said.

Arthur removed his cap. "It was here. I *swear* it."

Wally sighed. "Let's head to Market Square and pick some pockets before we miss the dinner rush."

Arthur ignored this and searched the room, peeking behind disintegrating curtains and under blackened couch cushions.

"What are you doing?" Wally asked, foot propped on the windowsill.

Arthur tested the knobs on a dresser one by one. "I'm looking for the secret entrance."

Wally gritted his teeth as he stormed to the bookshelf and tilted the burnt books, pretending to search for a loaded spring. "Well, what do you know? No secret entrance."

"We have to find the thing that's *out of place*." Arthur eyed a charred sconce on the wall. "Aha! A secret lever!"

Before Wally could stop him, Arthur grabbed hold of the sconce and yanked. The wall cracked and then came crashing down on top of him.

Wally, in a panic, pulled the plaster chunks off Arthur. Only after he saw that Arthur was unharmed did he say, "Happy?"

Arthur spit out ash. "You're going to feel quite the fool once I figure this out."

Wally bent to pick up the onyx key ring that had spilled from Arthur's pocket and froze. It was the same color as the demon adorning the front door. He decided to try something, and when it didn't work, he would drag Arthur to Market Square by his suspenders.

Wally snagged the key ring and crawled out of the window while Arthur tried to reassemble a burnt footstool, as if the pattern on the upholstery would reveal some secret map.

Wally went to the front door and set the onyx ring in the stone demon's snarling mouth. It fit. He jumped back when the demon's teeth seemed to close around the ring, ending in a grin.

Impossible, he thought to himself. The shadows must be playing tricks.

"Hey, uh, Arthur?"

Arthur struggled inside. "Hold on. I've almost got—" There was a splintering sound.

"*Arthur*," Wally said. "Stop fooling around and come look at this."

Arthur climbed out of the window, rubbing soot from his hands. He saw the onyx demon and laughed. "Of course! It wasn't a key ring, but a knocker! I *knew* there was a secret!" As an afterthought, he patted Wally on the shoulder. "Oh, um, nice work, Cooper."

"Yeah, thanks."

Arthur wiggled his fingers. "Here goes."

He turned the door handle, pushed it open . . . and both boys gasped.

The burnt-out foyer of Hazelrigg was gone. It was replaced by another room, bright and polished and glowing into the gray of the street. Strangely, Hazelrigg's windows were still dark with smoke.

Arthur, eyes wide, tried stepping through the door, but Wally caught his arm. "If their security's this tight, who knows what else is in there?"

"Has anyone ever told you, Cooper, that you're too cautious?"

"I'm not cautious. I'm smart."

"Suit yourself," Arthur said. "I can take it from here. Of course, I can only carry enough gold and jewels for one person, so I'm afraid your cut will be relatively . . . *nonexistent*."

With that, he stepped into the golden light of the room. Wally hesitated.

A haunted voice echoed down the street. "Please, sir? Spare a few coins? I need to eat."

Wally followed Arthur into the glow.

2
THE MANOR

The new foyer was more richly decorated than any room Wally had ever seen—or even dreamt of. The burnt chandelier was replaced with another that blazed with golden branches and shone on a grand staircase. The walls were no longer ashen but wallpapered with what looked like golden fish scales. In the corners stood statues of a goat-legged man and a mermaid and vases painted with unfamiliar creatures: an underwater bird and a frog with antlers.

"Bet you feel pretty silly now, eh, Cooper?" Arthur said.

Wally touched his lips, numb with shock. "I don't know what I'm feeling."

Arthur sat in an ornate armchair and kicked up his feet. "See? I was born to be rich."

This broke the spell over Wally a bit. "Someone needs to tell your shirt."

Arthur leapt up and brushed soot from the fancy upholstery.

A creak in the staircase made Wally's eye twitch. They needed to grab as much as they could and get out of there before someone saw them. He grabbed a golden candelabra from the bannister, but Arthur snatched it away and replaced it.

"Don't waste our time with trifling objects, Cooper," Arthur said. "The real treasure will be farther in. As Garnett Lacroix says, we have to scrape off the crusty gruel to get to the good stuff."

"Alfred Moore sure seems to use the word *gruel* in his books a lot," Wally said, annoyed.

Arthur ignored him and studied the room. "Let's see . . ." Three doors led out of the foyer. A double door at the top of the stairs and one on either side of the staircase. Each was carved with a different image: a moon, a tree, and what looked like a fang. Arthur shrugged, stepped right of the staircase, and opened the door with the tree.

Wally's jaw dropped. The room was dark and overgrown, as if a forest had burst through the floorboards and grown right to the ceiling. The air smelled of wet soil and was silvery with cricket song.

Arthur swept into the forest room, giggling. "The things rich people come up with, eh? Flushing toilets. Gold teeth. Now *this*." He pinched a leaf. "Amazing."

Wally took a tentative step inside. The walls were twined with ivy, which wrapped around branchy armchairs that seemed to grow right out of the ground. The carpet was mossy and dotted with lilies, and a brook trickled through its center. Willow branches hung from a ceiling painted with twinkling stars. How someone got paint to twinkle, Wally had no idea.

"If these nobles can build an indoor greenhouse," Arthur whispered, "just imagine what treasures lie beyond!"

The boys moved as quiet as shadows through the forest room, around a giant willow tree and under its arching roots. The space stretched both wider and deeper than Hazelrigg's walls could possibly hold. Wally tried not to think about that.

On the far end of the room was an ivy-hidden doorway carved with a twisted ribbon. Arthur was about to open it when they heard voices on the other side of the willow. The boys ducked under a giant fern just as two robed figures entered the room.

"I can't even *count* the number of paper birds I've folded in the last two days," a girl said. She sounded young, but her voice smoldered with confidence. "I'll be the girl who died of a thousand paper cuts."

"You're preaching to the choir, Sekhmet," a man said. "I received my fair share of grunt work in my days as a Novitiate. Lady Weirdwood once had me groom a griffin's tail to make paintbrushes. She didn't realize the griffin was rabid."

"If I'm going to bleed, I at least want it to be in *battle*," Sekhmet said. "Let me come with you and Mom! I won't even bring my swords! I'll just watch."

"Do I need to remind you what happened last time?" her father said.

Sekhmet fell quiet.

"Besides," he continued, "those paper cranes you're folding are vital to the Wardens' mission. Ludwig's birds are flapping away the poisonous clouds and guiding us through the ever-shifting battlefield of the Mercury Mines."

"I'd *happily* get lost in a poisonous cloud if it meant avoiding more boring work."

"Since you're already upset," her father said, "I may as well tell you that you've been assigned to take Huamei on a tour of the Manor. Get him acquainted with our work here."

Sekhmet huffed, and it sounded like water sizzling on hot coals. "I'm surprised his *majesty* would stoop so low as to follow a human around."

Their shadows passed over the fern under which Arthur and Wally were hiding. Wally dared a peek between the leaves. The man was tall with white hair and matching eyebrows. His daughter, Sekhmet, had curly black hair that hung past her waist. Her skin was a shade darker than Wally's, which made the emerald of her eyes stand out. She wore two curved swords at her hips.

"Can you at least tell me *why* you're fighting in the Mercury Mines?" Sekhmet said.

"Lady Weirdwood believes the Order of Eldar is trying to tunnel into this Manor's Abyssment," her father answered. "They're hoping to overthrow the Wardens and replace us on the border. There's money to be made when you control the line between the Real and the Imaginary. If the Order gets their way, they'll tear more Rifts in the Veil—building tourist lodges in the centaur forest or selling unicorns as pets in the Real cities. Too many Rifts would tear the fabric of reality so that not even your mother could sew it up again. The Veil would fall, ushering in the apocalypse. The end of the world."

Sekhmet snorted. "*Jerks.*"

The man chuckled. "On that we couldn't agree more."

Their voices faded down a cave mouth into which the little brook trickled, and they disappeared from sight.

"Let's go," Wally whispered, making a break for the exit.

Arthur caught him by the rope belt. "Let's go *deeper*? Excellent idea."

"You heard those people," Wally said as Arthur dragged him back to the ribbon door. "They were talking nonsense. This might be some sort of, I dunno, *cult*. They could sacrifice us to their demon god or something!"

"Let them try!" Arthur said. "After we steal the treasure, we'll report them to the Oakers, and those robed people will be locked up with the rest of the dirty, raving lunatics in Greyridge. Now are you coming? Or do I have to go back to the Stormcrow and fetch a better lock pick?"

Wally balled his fists. He considered abandoning Arthur right then and there for implying that his brother was dirty and raving. But Arthur didn't know Graham existed. And Wally needed this money so the doctors would keep his brother safe and clean.

Arthur opened the ribbon-carved door onto a corridor. But this wasn't just any corridor. It spiraled like a licorice whip. From their shoes, the floor swirled up and around, the walls contorting with it. The corridor completed its spiral at another door, which was upside down on the ceiling.

Wally steadied himself on a nearby lampstand. "Oh no. No no no."

Arthur only smiled and shook his head. "Rich people."

He took Wally's arm and led him down the hallway. Wally shut his eyes so he wouldn't throw up.

"This, dear Cooper," Arthur said, "is nothing more than an *optical illusion*. It's a trick of perspective, executed with interestingly angled mirrors."

Wally cracked open an eyelid and then shut it again. He and Arthur were standing on the wall. Somehow, their shoes remained fixed to the rug, while the hallway spiraled around them. Even their hats remained in place.

A few steps later, Arthur patted him on the back. "Safe."

Wally opened his eyes to find they'd reached the far end of the corridor. The nearest door was now right side up while the one to the forest room was upside down.

They entered the next room, which led to even more doorways. Arthur tested the handles until he found one that was locked—a sure sign something valuable was kept behind it. The door was carved with a fairy.

Wally slipped his picks into the keyhole while Arthur kept a lookout. The lock was stubborn—almost as if something inside was wrestling with his picks. He swore he heard snickering, like a tiny creature was mocking his efforts. Not for the first time that night, Wally pushed away the thought that Graham's madness was setting in. He tinkered and twisted until he could've sworn he heard a tiny voice huff in the keyhole, and the door clicked open.

The room was full of treasure. Rows of casks overflowed with coins of copper and silver, jade and ruby.

"Jackpot!" Arthur said, sweeping into the room.

He plunged both hands into one of the vats while Wally eyed the exits. There was one other door with a carving of a sun. No sound came from behind it.

Wally plucked a green coin from a nearby vat. He'd seen dozens of currencies flow through Kingsport, but nothing like this. The coin had a strange blossom on one side while the other showed a coiled leviathan. This room was like a bank of the world. Or many worlds.

Arthur took off his pants.

"*What* are you doing?" Wally said, dropping the coin.

Arthur grinned as he tied the ends of his pant legs into knots, making a sort of two-sided sack. "Pockets aren't deep enough for riches like these!"

He was stuffing coins into his pant bag when the sound of keys jangled behind the sun door.

"Ludwig and Weston will require different funds for the Real and the Mirror," Sekhmet's father said, unlocking the door. "I'll show you how to distinguish between them."

"Great," Sekhmet said. "The *groundskeepers* can hunt the Fae-born, but I can't?"

Arthur managed to stuff one last handful of coins into his makeshift bag before Wally seized him by the arm and dragged him out the door from which they'd entered.

They'd just made it into the spiral corridor when the man said, "Did you see that?"

Wally slammed the door, grabbed a nearby lampstand, and wedged it under the handle just as it started to jiggle. Arthur had already slung the coins over his shoulder and was running up and around the spiraled rug. Wally tried to follow, but the corridor swirled in his vision, making him collapse to his hands and knees. He squeezed his eyes shut and managed to crawl a couple of inches before a blast struck the door behind him. Sparks spit through the keyhole as bright as fireworks, but the door held strong.

Wally froze. "Arthur, wait!"

Arthur spun around, continuing to run backward along the ceiling. "You'll be fine! Just *run!*"

He spun again, and his pant bag struck the curved wall. One of the cuffs came untied, sending dozens of coins rolling up and over the spiraled rug. Some of them hung in the air, spinning and gleaming. The sight flipped Wally's stomach. He couldn't move.

The door behind him started to smolder.

"Arthur, *please!*" he called.

But Arthur was too busy plucking spinning coins out of the air to hear him.

The door burst open just as Wally leapt back against the wall. He caught the handle and held tight, hiding himself behind the door.

"*You!*" Sekhmet said.

Arthur cleared his throat. "Hello again."

Wally peeked through the keyhole as Sekhmet's father bent and picked something up.

"So much for imp locks," the man said, inspecting Wally's lock picks.

Wally tensed. They must have fallen out of his pocket when he fell to his knees.

Sekhmet held up a hand to block Arthur's bare legs. "Why are you in your underwear?"

Arthur blushed. "Funny story. After my bag broke, I was forced to carry my tools with my pants." He jingled his trousers and then nodded toward the lock picks. "I'm a locksmith's apprentice."

Sekhmet smirked. "He's trying to use Wordcraft on us. Clearly an amateur. Using the first lie that comes to mind."

Wally stared through the keyhole, nerves buzzing. For the first time since he'd met him, Arthur's charms had fallen flat. Then again, it would be hard for anyone to be charming without pants.

Sekhmet's father took a step toward Arthur. "Why don't you hand over whatever it is you've stolen?" he said, his voice as steely as the blade he drew from its scabbard.

"Stolen?" Arthur said. "Why, sir, I resent the implication. This was merely a *demonstration*. We wanted to prove how easily we could break into this Manor so that you'd hire us to replace your locks."

"We?" the girl asked.

Wally held his breath. Arthur had just given him away.

"Oh, um, the *royal* we," Arthur said, covering his tracks. "You know, me, myself and . . . I should be going now."

He grabbed the handle of the door leading to the forest room. But in one swift motion, Sekhmet's father threw his sword down the spiraled hall. The sword struck the door, pinning it to the frame.

Arthur released the handle and turned, grinning. "Actually, I'm glad I ran into you." He nodded to Sekhmet. "You dropped something in the street. Your, um, key ring. I wanted to return it. And replace your locks, of course. None of those keys actually work, you know."

Sekhmet patted the pockets of her cloak while her father gave her a look.

"Don't look at *me*!" She pointed at Arthur. "*He* stole it!"

Sekhmet's father walked slowly down the corridor. "Drop the bag, son."

Arthur pressed his back against the door. Then he pointed directly at Wally. "*Now, Wilberforce, now!*"

Sekhmet and her father whirled, expecting someone to grab them from behind. Wally's heart leapt into his throat. What was he supposed to do? They had swords, and he was unarmed.

Just then, Arthur crouched and seized the edge of the spiraled rug, whipping it upward. Because of the hallway's tipsy gravity, the rug fell to the ceiling, blocking Arthur from view.

"The pants-less one is trying to get away!" Sekhmet shouted.

"Well?" her father said. "Isn't this the fight you've been waiting for?"

Sekhmet leapt down and around the hallway, drawing her swords and slicing through the dangling rug. Wally heard Arthur grunt as he tugged the man's sword free from the door. The sword clattered to the floor, the door flew open, and then it slammed shut.

It was only then that Wally realized that Arthur hadn't expected him to act—only distract the robed people so Arthur could escape with the loot.

The door Wally was hiding behind creaked open. The man arched a white eyebrow.

"It seems your partner has abandoned you, *Wilberforce*."

3
ARTHUR

Arthur hauled his pant bag through the crowded streets, heading toward the Wretched Quarter. He tried to stifle the telltale clink of coins as newsboys, street sweepers, and cinder collectors turned to stare at his underwear.

He needed to get back to the Stormcrow and mount a rescue for Wally. Arthur's eyes stung when he thought of his friend, upside down and helpless, in the spiral hallway. In the moment, Arthur had done what was necessary to get the coins and himself out of there. But Garnett Lacroix would never leave a fellow thief behind. Even in the face of swords and fireworks.

Arthur made it to Paradise Lane and through the swinging doors of the Stormcrow without incident. The air of the pub swam with smoke and the rank breath of its patrons. The walls echoed with garbled voices and the occasional shattered glass.

"Hey! Gimme back my leg!"

"Come on, ya lazy biter! Git 'im! I've got rent money on your sorry hide!"

"Oy! Liza! Carve another notch above the bar! Andrew's dead!"

Someone coughed awake.

"Never mind! Little more life in him yet!"

While most guests were welcomed to the Stormcrow with a warning knife to the throat, Arthur was greeted with smiles and claps on the shoulder.

"Oy! It's Arthur!"

"*Hic!* Lend us some timber for this cigar, eh, Arthur?"

"Why aren't your pants on your legs, boy?"

Clinging tight to the treasure, Arthur wove around the swaying customers to a table by the dead fireplace. He sat next to a man who was upright but fast asleep.

Arthur lightly slapped the man's cheek. "Oy! Harry! Wake up! It's an emergency!"

Harry snorted but did not wake. A line of drool trickled down his unshaven chin and onto his sweat-stained shirt. His belly rose and fell, tilting the table up, then down, then up again, sliding three empty steins back and forth with every breath.

Now that Arthur was safe from danger, he needed a moment to collect his thoughts while the color came back to his cheeks. The last hour felt like a fever dream. The strange Manor, the forest room, the spiral hallway. A part of him wondered if it had happened at all. He peeked inside his pant bag at the faint gleam of coins. The treasure was real enough.

"Getcha a sparkling cider, Arthur?"

Arthur quickly shut his pants. "Oh," he said, blushing and hiding his bare legs under the table. "Hullo, Liza."

Even though she was only a few years older than Arthur,

Liza managed the chaotic Stormcrow Pub, handling the dastardly patrons with her biting wit and the looming fear of her father, the Rook. Like Arthur, Liza had lost her mother at a young age. But neither Arthur nor Liza ever talked about their moms. In this city, it was better to forget about the past and focus on surviving.

Arthur smiled. There was no use causing a stir until he'd formed a rescue plan for Wally. "Tell me, Liza, how do you remain so radiant in such a miserable place?"

Liza smirked and collected Harry's empty steins. "I wonder if you'd say such flattering things if I weren't my father's daughter."

Arthur winked. "The moon may shine because of the sun's light, but its beauty is all its own."

Liza mopped off the table. "And is that cloying quote *your own?*"

Arthur's ears grew hot. He'd stolen the line from Garnett Lacroix, and Liza knew it. She was the only person Arthur knew who read more than he did.

"One cider, please," Arthur said, "spilling over the brim."

"You know the price," Liza said.

Arthur's throat was parched from running halfway across the city and the fear of nearly being impaled by a sword. He considered using a few of the Manor's strange coins to pay, but if any of the Stormcrow's customers discovered the treasure he held, it could spell trouble.

Arthur nodded to Harry, who was still asleep. "Put it on the old man's slate?"

Liza quirked an eyebrow. "Think he'll actually pay for it?"

Arthur sighed. "Give me five minutes. Then you can bring me a dozen ciders, and a round for everyone in the pub."

Liza snorted. "That'll be the day."

Today *was* that day, Arthur realized, and a warmth washed over him. He glanced around the Stormcrow at the Black Feathers, who spent their measly earnings to drink and forget their horrible deeds. Arthur would be different. Now that he was rich, he would act the perfect gentleman. He'd show the rest of these lowlifes how it was done.

"Just know I don't serve anyone in their underwear," Liza said, peeking under the table at Arthur's bare legs. She wiggled his ear. "Not even the handsome ones."

Arthur tried to keep his face from catching fire with embarrassment while Liza stepped behind the bar and picked up her book.

Arthur's smile deflated. Here he was, living it up while Wally was probably being sacrificed to a demon god. Why was it that whenever Arthur tried to act like the Gentleman Thief, something always got in the way? The Rook. Harry. A kidnapped friend. Life never seemed to work the way it did in Alfred Moore's books.

"HCK! KOFF! KOFF! KOFF!"

Harry choked on a bit of phlegm and coughed himself awake. He blinked at Arthur and then frowned at the stein-less table before him.

"*Harry*," Arthur said, scooting his chair close. "We need to mount a rescue."

Harry massaged his forehead and squinted at the window. "What time is it?"

"I dunno," Arthur said. "Eleven bells maybe. Listen—"

"Morning or night?"

Arthur blinked at the dark windows. "Night, of course."

Harry kicked Arthur's chair away. "Leave me be." His eyes drifted shut again as he tilted back in his chair. "Wake me when Liza starts cooking eggs."

Arthur smirked. "It may be night, but there's still a golden sunrise."

He reached into his pants and took out a coin. Harry's eyes slit open then went wide. He snatched the coin and turned it over, making it flicker in the pub's sickly light. Arthur had been so busy escaping, he hadn't had time to get a good look at the coins. One side showed a leafless tree that grew into the heavens. The other side showed the same tree, upside down, growing underground.

Harry hid the coin under the table. "Where'd ya get this?"

"Stole it," Arthur said.

"I didn't think ya *earned* it, son. Where?"

"Nobles," Arthur said. "On Mulberry Street. But listen, we've got bigger problems."

Arthur told Harry the story of the Manor while Harry stared at the coin, eyes swimming in their sockets.

"So," Arthur said, "how do we get Wally back?"

Harry shook his head and grumbled. "Shoulda never read you those cursed Garnett Lacrotch books when you was little. Packed your head with nothing but nonsense."

"It's *Lacroix*," Arthur corrected.

Harry peeked under the table. "You got more?"

"Well, yeah, but—"

Harry pulled the pant bag into his lap, and his face lit up. "Used your pants to carry the lot, did ya?"

"Yes, but—"

"*Attaboy!*" Harry said, ruffling Arthur's hair.

Arthur swiped his hand away. "What do we do about Wally?"

Harry sniffed, counting coins. "If he was thief enough to escape, you'd both be safe in the pub now. You were forced to do the only thing that would get the cash out of that place. No, Arthur, you done right by the Black Feathers." He gave the coins a jingle and chuckled. "This'll pay our debts, it will."

"You mean *your* debts."

Harry banged his fist down on the table, his face suddenly red with fury. "Who fed you when you were just a whelp, boy?"

"Dad . . ." Arthur said.

"Oh, so it's *Dad* now, is it?"

Arthur's mom had died of the Pox when he was eight. His dad's job at the factory couldn't feed them both, so Harry had set out to find better work. Once money started rolling in again, Arthur followed his dad to the Stormcrow and discovered that he'd joined a gang. After that, Arthur had done everything in his power to be enlisted into the Black Feathers. He hoped to become just like the Gentleman Thief in the book his mom had given to him from her hospital bed on their last Christmas.

But the Black Feathers didn't see fathers and sons. They only saw thieves of different rank. So when Arthur showed up at the Stormcrow, he started referring to his dad as Harry. And that had been their relationship ever since.

"Who will join our rescue mission?" Arthur asked. "Murderous Maggie? Dishonest Desmond? Pancake Jack would have to put his leg on . . . Whoever it is, we'll knock down the door, nab Cooper, and—"

"That ain't how the world works, Arthur," Harry interrupted. "There's not a soul in this pub what would stick his neck out for some kid who got himself caught. Black Feathers look out for themselves."

Arthur wanted to argue. Garnett Lacroix always protected his Merry Rogues and split the earnings even. But then again, the Gentleman Thief never had to put up with insubordinates. The Rogues always followed orders with smiles and swagger and a song on their lips.

Wally, on the other hand, had argued with Arthur every step of the heist. Sure, the kid picked a couple of locks and figured out the secret about the door knocker moments before Arthur probably would have. But he'd made everything else more difficult. If Wally hadn't frozen at the first sight of the spiral hallway, they never would have been caught.

"Okay, Harry," Arthur said, swallowing his guilt as best he could.

Harry stood and swayed toward the back of the pub. Arthur followed him to a door painted with a giant rook—wings spread, beak shrieking, talons poised for the attack.

Arthur licked his fingers and smoothed his eyebrows. He'd never met the Rook before, but everything he'd heard about the Black Feathers' leader was intimidating. The Rook had arrived in Kingsport a mere five years ago as a weapons dealer. He managed to gain the trust of every gang in the city.

And then he'd turned the gangs against one another. Through rumor and coercion alone, the Rook was able to spark the Battle of the Barrows, forcing the gangs to face off until their power dwindled to nothing.

Once the dust was settled, the weapons dealer collected the surviving members beneath his wing and dubbed them the Black Feathers. The Rook had conquered Kingsport without lifting so much as a brickbat. It was said his tongue was made of sharpened steel.

Harry knocked, and the door opened, revealing a guard who was nearly as big as the frame. Charlie crossed his thick arms over his chest, making the chain mail beneath his shirt clink. "We're not giving out no more loans, Harry."

"Not asking for none." Harry gave Arthur's coins a shake. "Got something shiny for the Rook."

Charlie's expression remained stony and his arms remained folded. "Say it."

Harry rolled his eyes. "The Rook is my king, his feathers my nest, et cetera, et cetera, blah blah blah."

Charlie sneered at this lack of respect. But the sneer quickly faded in the glow of the coin Harry handed him.

Charlie narrowed his eyes. "Where'd *you* get something like this?"

"Nobles—" Arthur began, but Harry shoved him back.

"Stole it meself off a traveler," Harry said. "A duke I think he was."

Arthur was too shocked to speak.

Charlie gestured Harry into the back room. "Kid stays here."

Harry nodded. "You heard the man, Arthur. Go flirt with Liza."

Arthur puffed out his chest. "I belong in there too. I'm the one who—"

Harry clamped a hand over Arthur's mouth and chuckled. "Kids and their fancies, eh?" He gave Arthur's head a shove. "Go on now, Arthur. Git."

Harry turned to enter the office, but Arthur wasn't about to let his dad steal all the credit. He rolled up his sleeves and marched forward, forcing himself between Harry and Charlie.

Something struck him hard in the face.

Arthur stumbled back, catching the blood that gushed from his lip. He looked up and realized Harry had backhanded him. His dad looked as surprised as he was.

Stools scooted as every eye in the Stormcrow fixed on Arthur. Even Liza's. Heat flooded his cheeks. This wasn't a fight between Black Feathers, but a father slapping his disobedient son.

Harry cleared his throat and, avoiding Arthur's eyes, thrust a coin in the air. "Next round's on me!"

The pub erupted in cheers while Arthur licked the blood from his lip.

Charlie snatched the coin from Harry's fingers. "Rook counts it first. Probably need it for your interest anyway."

The door slammed in Arthur's face. He considered pounding as hard as he could, demanding to be seen. But things did not end well for those who interrupted the Rook's business.

A cloth dabbed at Arthur's lip. "He got you good," Liza said.

Arthur turned away before she could see the tears in his eyes and stormed out of the pub. He sat on the stoop and held his split lip. The sky was the color of dirty water. A light rain hissed on the cobbles.

Was Harry about to be promoted to Talon—one of the Rook's four leaders who reigned over the quarters of Kingsport? The position Arthur *earned* by stealing those coins and leaving Wally behind? He spit blood into the gutter.

"I'm tellin' ya!" someone shouted inside the pub. "It happened right outside! The thing had blue eyes that shined like the devil's teeth! It kissed my grandmother, and now she's bedridden! Poor old bird can't even move!"

Another man laughed. "Hear that? Trevor's afraid of a harmless *witto dolly*! Ha ha ha!"

A thought tickled the back of Arthur's mind. Strange. This conversation reminded him of the story where the Gentleman Thief stole a priceless doll with sapphires for eyes . . .

The door to the Stormcrow smacked open, giving Arthur a start. He expected to see the man who was afraid of little dollies calling out his accuser to fight him. But instead he found the Rook's guards dragging Harry into the street.

"Get yer filthy hands offa me!" Harry screamed.

Arthur leapt to his feet as one of the guards wrenched Harry's arm behind his back while the other gagged him with a rope. They marched him toward a horse and cart.

"Where are you taking him?" Arthur demanded.

The guards ignored him.

Desperate, Arthur stepped in front of their horses, heart thudding. "Where are you taking my dad?"

One of the guards laughed. "Kid's gonna get himself trampled."

"We're hauling him to our friends up at Greyridge," the other said. "You're lucky the boss didn't choose the cellar."

Arthur winced. The Stormcrow's cellar was where the Rook tortured information out of his gang members. It was said to be full of fingers and skeletons.

"You can't take him to Greyridge!" Arthur said. "My dad's not insane!"

The other guard chuckled. "Wait till he spends a coupla nights in a cell. Or gets one of them *experimental treatments*."

An icy feeling rushed through Arthur's chest. He'd heard that the Rook disposed of useless gang members by committing them to Greyridge—volunteering them for experimental treatments and being paid handsomely for it. Arthur had hoped it was just a rumor.

The guards loaded Harry onto the cart and then climbed atop the driver's bench.

"*Move*, kid," one of the guards said to Arthur. "I don't want to have to spray your remains off the cobbles when I get back."

He whipped the reins, and Arthur had no choice but to step aside as the horses clopped past. He stood in the hissing rain and watched the cart carry his dad up Paradise Lane.

Behind him, the Stormcrow door creaked open. Arthur turned. His heart skipped a beat.

A man stood hunched under the pub's awning. He wore a feather-lined cloak and scorpion rings on his fingers. His head was entirely hairless. The moment Arthur realized who this man was, he quickly wiped the tears from his cheeks and the blood from his lip.

The Rook held out Arthur's pants. "I believe these belong to you?"

Arthur jerked forward, took his pants, and slipped them on. "Thank you . . . um, sir." He tried not to stare, but he couldn't help but glance at the Rook's lips, hoping to catch a glimpse of his steel tongue.

The Rook folded his tattooed hands into his sleeves and considered the falling rain. "It must be odd, having your own father take credit for your efforts."

"H-how did you know?" Arthur said.

The Rook arched an eyebrow.

"Sorry," Arthur said. He wasn't used to his voice shaking.

From his sleeve, the Rook took out one of the Manor's coins and turned it over, showing tree, upside-down tree, tree. "It is a strange sight, isn't it? Tell me where you found it."

Arthur searched for the right words. He barely believed the story himself.

When he didn't answer, the Rook grinned. "Fair enough. I didn't get to my position by spilling information about every little pocket of treasure I knew."

Arthur stayed quiet, pretending like that's what he'd intended. The Rook had such a smooth way of speaking it left him almost speechless. Almost.

"Why did you have Harry committed?" Arthur asked.

The Rook sighed and slipped the coin back in his feathered sleeve. "I do have sympathy for your father, you know. I'm a single father myself."

Arthur glanced through the pub's window at Liza, still reading behind the bar. It was strange to think that the man who ruthlessly conquered every gang in Kingsport had someone he cared about.

The Rook gestured to the street. "I run the entirety of Kingsport, from the casinos in the Gilded Quarter to the sewers of the Wretch. Do you know how many would like to see me dead? If I show so much as an ounce of weakness, I put both myself and my daughter in danger."

Arthur nodded. That made sense.

"It's difficult being honorable in this world," the Rook continued. He stared at Arthur with his yellow eyes. "Perhaps, unlike your father, you can prove that it's possible to be both a gentleman *and* a thief."

Arthur tried not to let his surprise show. It was like the Rook was reading his mind.

Arthur looked toward the Gilded Quarter, grayed out by rain. What would the Gentleman Thief do if his father were locked away in a fortress—even if his father was a good-for-nothing lout?

"I can get more coins," Arthur said.

"That will do for your father's debt," the Rook said. "But for his freedom, I want *information*. I'm familiar with every type of currency that flows through Kingsport. But this coin you stole is foreign to me. What did these people wear? What is their business in my city? I want to know everything you can tell me about these . . . *nobles*."

"I can do that."

The Rook flashed his teeth, and Arthur finally saw his

tongue. It wasn't made of steel but tattooed with swirling black shapes. Like spiderwebs. Arthur looked away and gazed up Paradise Lane. The wagon carrying Harry had shrunk to a speck in the night.

"Don't worry, Arthur," the Rook said. "I'll make sure Harry is comfortable in Greyridge. Though I would hurry if I were you. The doctors are always eager for more subjects for their experiments."

Arthur's stomach dropped into his shoes.

The Rook held out his ringed hand. "Say it."

Arthur swallowed and knelt. "The Rook is my king, his feathers my nest. I am encompassed in the black of his eye and protected in the claws of his talons. I will serve him as the earth serves the sun, as the worm serves the rook."

4
THE GIRL WITHOUT SHAPE

Wally lay in a tower room, wrists bound to his ankles, cursing himself for trusting Arthur Benton. Arthur may have thought of himself as a Gentleman Thief, but Wally had never met anyone less gentlemanly. And Arthur wasn't even a good thief, always relying on others to help him get to the treasure. Wally was determined to tell him so when he managed to escape this creepy old Manor.

But first, Wally had to find a way to escape his own rope belt.

The wind blew and the tower swayed, masking Wally's grunts as he loosened the rope. When he was younger, Graham had made a habit of tying him up whenever their parents were at work, promising Wally that he'd be grateful someday. Wally had spent hours escaping all kinds of binds—rope, fishing line, potato sacks—learning to flex his muscles when his brother tied the knot so that the binds fell slack when he relaxed. After that, it was just a matter of removing his shoes and wriggling free.

Wally had despised his brother for every excruciating second. But now . . .

"Thank you, *Graham*," he said to himself as his hands slid out of the rope.

He studied the room while untying his ankles. Curtains of moss swayed over two windows that each looked out over a different moon.

Wally's heart skipped a beat.

No. Not two moons. Across from the window was a self-standing mirror *reflecting* the moon.

The high tower room was dark so Wally grabbed hold of the mirror and tilted it, beaming moonlight onto the walls. There was no door.

"What the—?"

The door had been there when the robed man had dumped him inside. But it seemed to have vanished the moment it slammed shut.

"That's impossible."

Wally abandoned the mirror and peered out the window. The night was bright and misty. From this high vantage point, he could see the entire layout of the Manor. Its four wings made an X shape, a bulbous roof crowning the center. How all of this could possibly fit inside Hazelrigg was something he could think about after he'd escaped.

He scanned the Manor's layout, just as he'd done whenever robbing the homes in the Gilded Quarter. It wouldn't be too difficult to find the exit—so long as he could escape this tower first.

Wally turned away from the window and froze when he saw the door.

He rubbed his eyes, wondering how he hadn't seen it

before. Then he realized he was looking at the mirror, this time from a different angle. It reflected a door that didn't appear on the wall. By shifting his position, Wally had discovered a hidden exit.

"Just an optical illusion," Wally muttered, trying to comfort himself with Arthur's words.

Keeping an eye on the reflection, he felt along the wall until he clasped the handle of the invisible door. It was locked, and the robed man had taken his pick set. But in the reflection, Wally noticed the door's hinges were located on the *inside*. He removed his shoe and, watching the mirror, carefully knocked out the pins holding the hinges together.

The door fell inward, and Wally set it aside.

"Amateurs," he said.

Even though he was free, he didn't feel much safer. He had told Arthur he hadn't wanted to travel deeper into the creepy Manor, but that was exactly where the robed man had brought him: through a room wallpapered with leaves, down a hallway made of bark, up the twisted staircase of a hollow tree, and finally here, to this tower room.

Now Wally just had to retrace the man's steps without getting caught. He quietly worked his way down the staircase. At the bottom, he opened a door onto a hallway flickering with candlelight. The walls were made of green sandalwood and smelled of rose oil. The floor was a bed of roots. Several more hallways opened on either side, and Wally was uncertain which way led back to the spiral passage.

A creak made Wally spin around. There was no one there. He had the eerie sensation that the walls were watching him.

But walls couldn't watch. He'd just spent too much time around Arthur, who talked about thinking houses and envious dresses.

Halfway down the hall, Wally found a passage that looked different from the others. Its walls were a verdant green and curved sharply to the right. Hugging one side, he walked around it . . . and ended up right back where he'd begun.

"Why would they build a hall that doesn't go anywhere?"

Unless, he thought, *they're hiding treasure.*

If Wally made it out of this place alive, he'd want this disastrous heist to have been worth something. He didn't trust Arthur to divvy up the coins they'd stolen together.

Again, Wally ventured down the coiled hallway, feeling along the wall for hidden compartments that might hold treasure or a secret doorway. Halfway around, he tripped on a root and stepped out into the middle of the rug. The walls made a stretching sound as the floor seemed to shift beneath his feet, sliding toward the spot where he'd stepped.

Instead of leaping back to the wall, Wally decided to try something.

He tried the hall again, this time crossing to the other side. The moment he did, the floor began to straighten. Once it curled to the right, he strayed left to bend it back the other way. On his first two trips around, he'd kept to one side, so the hallway had remained coiled in that direction. But by wobbling back and forth, he was able to make it unfurl into a straight line. Like a sprout in spring.

"Ha!" Wally opened the door at the end in triumph. "Whoa."

He was in a small garden. Only instead of green leaves and colorful flowers, the plants sparkled silver. Wally plucked the largest rose he could find and twirled it. It was more awkward than carrying coins, but if the silver was real, it could pay off part of the hospital bill and Wally's Black Feathers tribute. Wally could keep his fingers, and Graham could keep his head.

Wally would celebrate once he found his way out of this place.

He returned to the sandalwood hallway and found another passage. This one had walls of scarlet and was hung with hundreds of portraits: an aristocratic goblin, an owl with glasses reading an upside-down book, a slug wearing a suit of armor. Wally might have laughed if it wasn't all so strange.

This hallway was as crooked as a winter branch and stretched on and on, ending at a door in the distance. He walked down it quickly, stealing glances over his shoulder. He couldn't shake the sense that he was being followed. Maybe it was the creaky wooden floors. Maybe it was the eyes of the paintings. Or maybe . . .

"Just break the news to mother.
She knows how dear I love her.
And tell her not to wait for me
for I'm not coming home."

Wally's breath stopped short. He slowly turned around. The hall was empty. He wiggled a finger in his ear, certain he'd heard singing. He took careful backward steps as the singing continued.

"Just say there is no other
can take the place of mother.
Then kiss her dear, sweet lips for me,
and break the news to her."

Wally stopped. The voice sounded like a young girl.
Only . . . shinier.

"Hello?" he whispered.

The singing stopped. The hall stretched, silent and scarlet. The portraits stared.

"Who's there?" he whispered. "Who's singing?"

The voice gasped as bright as a coin striking concrete.
"Can you . . . *hear me?*"

Wally frantically searched the hallway.

"*Well?*" the girl asked with building excitement. "Can
you?"

He was having difficulty catching his breath. "Of course I
can hear you."

"That's *amazing!*" The girl's voice shined so brightly,
Wally had to plug his ears. "No one's been able to hear me
in—months? Years? *Augh!*" She screamed and it turned into
a giggle. "Time gets kinda slippery when you have no one to
talk to."

Wally searched the hallway, eyes wide. "Where are you?"

"In your pocket!"

Wally slowly took out the silver rose. A face reflected in one
of its petals. The girl's skin glowed like winter light through a
frosted pane.

"Hi!" she said. "I'm Breeth!"

Wally threw the rose. It tumbled along the floor, coming

to a stop against one of the baseboards. He stared at it, trying to assure his pounding heart that he was just tired and hallucinating.

"*Ahem.*"

Wally leapt away from the wall, which seemed to have just cleared its throat.

The painting of the aristocratic goblin scowled at him. "You shouldn't throw people, you know," it said with the girl's voice. "It's very *rude.*"

Wally might have screamed if his breath hadn't been stolen.

The ghost, or whatever she was, could *move* between objects. He sprinted down the hallway.

"Wait!" the girl said, her voice now a creak in the wall. "Don't run! I'm nice!"

Wally reached the door and threw it open, only to find two robed people—a redheaded woman with an eye patch and a small man in a military getup, as hairy as he was thin—hunched over a map of tunnels.

"We'll send Ludwig's birds through here," the woman said, tapping the map.

The hairy man saw Wally and nudged the woman. "Isn't that the thief Linus caught?"

The woman looked at Wally, narrowing her one eye. "How did you escape?"

Wally slammed the door and sprinted back past the portraits. The door flew open behind him, and the robed people were on his heels.

"Stop him!" the woman cried.

The hairy man drew out a garden sprayer and pumped mist into the hall. The roots on the floor writhed to life. Wally was able to leap over them and make it to the sandalwood hallway, but then he was trapped. The roots grew into the exits, sealing them shut.

Wally turned around, backing away as the robed people came around the corner.

"There, there now," the man grumbled. "That's a good street urchin. We're not gonna hurt ya."

"For heaven's sakes, Weston," the woman said. "He's a *child*, not a dog." She looked at Wally. "Surrender now and we'll lead you safely back to your cell. I promise we'll be kinder than the Manor. There are rooms here that will swallow you whole."

Wally raised his fists, ready to fight. But then he noticed something slithering on the floor. The roots coiled around the man's and woman's ankles, and with a yank, pulled their legs out from under them.

"Stand down!" the man bellowed at the roots as they dragged him and the woman through the hallway. "I wanted you to block the *exits*, not *us*!"

The woman snagged a pair of shears from Weston's belt and started slashing. Wally stared a moment, dumbfounded at his luck, then tried to loosen the roots blocking an exit. It was like trying to claw through solid wood.

"Um, you're welcome?" a voice said above him.

Wally looked up at a wooden chandelier, which swung with the ghost girl's voice.

"I tripped them for you!" she said, her face smiling in the intricate leaf carvings. "You should say thank you."

"Thank you?" Wally said numbly.

"You're *welcome*!"

The chandelier stopped swaying, and Wally watched the ghost girl creak through the ceiling and then inhabit the roots of one of the blocked passages. The roots untangled, creating an opening.

"This way!" she said.

Wally stared. Was this how it started? If he followed the ghost, would that be the first step into madness that would land him in Greyridge with his brother?

"Trust me!" she said.

The robed people were almost free of the roots. Wally would have to take his chances with the ghost. He ran down the passage.

"Turn right!" the girl cried, a groan in the floor.

Wally went right. Then left. Then left again. Then zigzag. Then straight ahead. The girl's creaky voice led him through the twisted forest passageways—moss and leaves and crumbled earth—until he came to what looked like a garden of suits and dresses.

"In here!" she said as an armoire opened with a gust of pollen.

Wally slipped inside, and the armoire shut behind him. He held his breath and hugged his knees as footsteps entered the room.

"How did he manage to navigate the forest wing?" the red-headed woman asked. "I've been here fourteen years, and I still get lost."

The hairy man grunted. "Better question is how he got my roots to ignore a direct order."

"It seems we have a mage loose in the Manor," the woman said.

"That kid? Unlikely. Did you see the look on his face?"

Once their voices faded, the armoire's woodwork sighed.

"*Phew!*" the ghost girl said. "That was close."

In the faint keyhole light, Wally could make out a face in the wood grain. He'd seen human-looking patterns like this before, but they'd never actually spoken to him. The girl's voice was like the squeak a drawer makes.

"What's your name?" the girl asked.

Wally stared at his knees, hoping if he ignored her, he would stop hallucinating.

"I'm not going to hurt you." She giggled. "Unless I accidentally close your fingers in a door or something."

This wasn't very reassuring. He kept his lips shut.

"Oh no." The girl gasped. "Can you not hear me anymore?"

She sounded so disappointed that Wally felt a twinge of guilt. If this ghost was real, she had saved him from being caught. And she hadn't done any of the things ghosts usually do in stories. Her eyes didn't drip blood. Her hair didn't rage like dark fire. Her teeth and fingernails didn't grow to monstrous lengths as she flew shrieking at him. She just talked like a normal kid. If that kid had wooden vocal cords.

"CAN. YOU. HEAR. ME!" she shouted, her voice rising from a creak to a groan.

Wally plugged his ears and finally looked into her knotted eyes. "What are—How can—Why did—?"

"So you *can* hear me!" The girl smiled, making the wood squeak. "That's good. For a second there, I was worried I broke your brain! What's your name?"

Wally swallowed, trying to keep his mind from unspooling. "Wally."

"I'm Breeth. Not sure if you caught that before you threw me down the hallway."

"Oh, um, sorry about that," Wally said, fully aware that he was apologizing to an armoire.

"As for your question," Breeth said, "or *three* questions—I don't know how I'm doing this! I just know I can possess anything so long as it was alive at one point. Wood. Old bones. Roots. Silvered flowers. It's like I'm taking over for a soul that's no longer there!"

Wally nodded slowly, trying to wrap his head around too many things. "What about the painting?" he said, remembering the angry goblin face.

"That paint's made of mashed-up lilac petals!" Breeth said.

He nodded like that made sense. "What were you . . . ?"

"What was I doing in that rose?"

"Uh, yeah," Wally said, even though he wasn't sure what he was going to ask.

The armoire made a creak, and a flurry of moths fluttered out of an old fur coat. They flapped their desiccated wings, arranging themselves in the shape of a face.

"I was hoping you'd help me with something!" Breeth said, her voice dusty and fluttery. "I was watching you walk around the Manor, and I thought, *huh*, I've never seen *him* before. And then I thought, *wait a second*, he must be a thief! And then I thought some not-so-nice things about you that I won't repeat. But *then* I watched you some more, saw you were harmless, and realized, *This boy can help me!* I've been stuck in this boring old Manor ever since I died. So I kept my splinters crossed that you would steal something I could possess. And then I was like, *Duh*, Breeth. You can just move the hallways around to get him to steal a silver rose and then hide inside it. So that's what I did!" The moths made a swirl of delight. "I never thought you'd be able to talk to me!"

Wally frowned. Had he not solved that coiled hallway? He'd felt so smart for a second.

Breeth put a moth-winged finger to her lips. "How can you see me, by the way? No one else in the Manor even knows I exist."

Wally shrugged. But then he remembered something Graham once told him—that people only saw what they wanted to see.

"Take the color blue, for instance," Graham had said. *"People went thousands of years without having a word for it. They called the sky green and the oceans gray as slate. Then one day someone held up a cornflower and said, 'This is blue,' and suddenly everyone saw it. There are all sorts of interesting things that people can't see just because they don't have the words, or their minds aren't ready to accept them."*

Wally had decided, right then and there, that if his mom was a ghost, he would want to see her, no matter the consequences. He never did, of course.

"I don't know how I'm doing it," he told Breeth.

"Well, we're just a couple of perplexed peas in a pod then, aren't we?" she said.

The dead moths fell to the floor and the armoire flew open. Wally flinched, expecting one of the robed people to seize him.

"Oops," Breeth said, snorting. "Sorry. That was me. Should have warned you. I'm still getting used to the whole people seeing and hearing me thing." She creaked out of the armoire and into an old rocking chair. "It's safe to come out. I can feel Weston's and Amelia's footsteps a few halls from here."

Wally stepped out, brushing pollen from his pants. "Can you get me out of this place?"

"Sure!" Breeth said, rocking the chair. "I know this Manor

like the back of my hand!" She held up the chair's armrest. "Literally! Ha!" She creaked out of the chair and up a wall so that she was knot-to-nose with him. "But if I help you, you have to do me a favor."

Wally steadied himself. "What's that?"

"Help me find my killer."

His heart started to race again. "You were murdered?"

"Yeah." Breeth made a sad sound, like a house settling in winter. "I've given it a lot of thought, and I think that's what's keeping me in the land of the living. I have to bring my killer to justice. Then I can, y'know, *move on* and see my parents again."

"Are your parents . . . dead?"

The sad sound echoed through the wall again, and it sort of slumped. "Yeah. My kidnapper attacked them." For the first time since Wally had met her, Breeth went perfectly silent. A few seconds later, the wall straightened itself. "How about you? You got a family?"

"Um . . . no," he said. "They all died in the Pox."

"Oh," Breeth said. "Maybe they're haunting their own furniture somewhere."

Wally thought of Graham in the hospital and his heart squeezed. "How am I supposed to help you?"

"My killer isn't in this Manor anymore, I don't think. I want to go out and find him, but I've been too afraid to leave because the Manor moves around the world, flying off to a new location at least once a week. Every time I open an exit, I find myself in a place I've never seen before. Even if I spoke the language, I couldn't ask anyone where I am! 'Cause, y'know, I'm dead. So I creak right back into the Manor every time. But now you can help me find my way around and track down my killer!"

"Great," Wally said, feeling less than enthusiastic.

"All I know about him is that he's muscly and wears a mask made of steel and glass. Oh, *and* he smells like melting metal, if that makes sense."

Wally rubbed the back of his neck. He had enough to worry about *without* tackling a murder mystery. All he wanted was to be back in Kingsport so he could check on his brother. But he didn't think he could escape this Manor all by himself. And Wally sympathized with Breeth for wanting to see her parents again.

"Okay," he said. "I'll help you if you help me."

"Yay!" Breeth creaked across the wall and opened a door. "This way!"

Wally relaxed a little then. If he was losing his mind, at least it felt better than being alone in this place. Maybe that was why Graham always seemed so happy. People who saw things that weren't there were never lonely, at least.

Wally followed the ghost girl toward the Manor's exit.

Or, for all he knew, deeper in.

5
GREYRIDGE

Midnight struck stale and windless as Arthur scaled the craggy path up the sea cliffs to Greyridge Mental Hospital. Waves gnashed against the rocks. The wind moaned through the hospital's barred windows. Arthur slowed his steps. It seemed silly, but he felt more afraid of this place meant to keep people safe than he was of the Stormcrow filled with murderous thieves.

By the time he reached the front gate, the Rook's guards were riding out in their wagon. "Visiting hours are over, kid," one of them called. "Go home."

Arthur clasped the bars of the gate. The hospital was a fortress. Thorny hedges and a wrought iron fence wrapped around the border. The portcullis was sealed with chains. What he wouldn't give to have Wally and his lock picks there with him.

"What floor is he on?" Arthur called after the wagon.

One of the guards sneered. "Second. Won't do you any good anyway." He gave the horse a whip, and the wagon went rattling down the hill.

Arthur considered the fence. Fortunately, it ended just a few yards from where he was standing. Unfortunately, it ended at a rocky cliff that plummeted two hundred feet into the sea.

He followed the fence to its corner, slipped around the bars, and climbed the side rungs down to the jagged rock face. Waves exploded over the ocean's breakers as Arthur scaled the cliff to the hospital's seaside walls. His fingers strained between the stone slabs, but he managed to climb to the second floor. His toes perched on three inches of limestone as he slid from window to barred window.

Each cell looked the same—murky rooms lit by faint storm light—but each inhabitant was unique. The first cell held a young man drawing a city on the wall using only cobwebs and his fingertips. The second held a woman rocking and chanting herself to sleep. Arthur had to duck past the third cell to avoid two orderlies with a lantern.

"Whaddaya mean frozen?"

"Hasn't moved a muscle. That's why her family dumped her here. Listen."

The cell echoed with a hollow sound, like tapping on porcelain.

The first orderly shuddered. "That smile's giving me the creeps."

"You and me both."

Arthur fought the temptation to take a peek. This sounded a lot like the conversation he'd overheard at the Stormcrow about the doll with blue eyes. He dismissed the thought and slid to the corner cell where Harry lay on a stained mattress no thicker than a folded sheet.

"Evening, Harry."

Harry's head jerked up. "*Arthur*. What are you doing here?"

"I've come to rescue you, obviously."

Harry laid his head back down. "Don't bother. This ain't one of your adventure stories."

Arthur grinned. "You also have our apartment key."

Harry didn't respond, and Arthur's heart sank. He'd been trying to make his dad laugh.

Arthur gave the cell's bars a wiggle. They were solid in their stone, and his hands were numb with ocean cold— another frustrating reminder that life didn't work like it did in books. He took out the bundle Liza had given him at the Stormcrow and tossed it through the bars.

Harry picked up the meat pie and began scarfing it down. "How's the lip?"

Arthur touched the raw spot where his dad had struck him. "I think it makes me look distinguished. Better than a mustache, really."

Harry softened. "I didn't want you talking to the Rook, son. Don't want you getting tangled up like I did."

Arthur looked away. Harry always grew sentimental when he sobered up, and it made Arthur uncomfortable.

"Don't worry, Harry!" he said, bringing the adventure back in his voice. "I'll steal so much cash for the Rook, he'll free you from this hospital, and then we'll *buy* the place!"

Harry fixed his red-rimmed eyes on Arthur. "You didn't make a deal with him, did you?"

Arthur scratched under his hat. "Well . . ."

Harry shook his head. "I made that mistake when you was

younger. The Rook's talons will slide into you so slow-like, you'll bleed out before you realize what happened."

Arthur scraped rust from the bars. "It seemed square enough. He gave me my pants back."

Harry snorted without amusement as he crammed the last of the meat pie into his mouth. "I'm just glad your ma's not alive to see what a fool you've become."

"*I've* become? At least I don't drink away every cent I earn."

Harry wiped his mouth on the sheet. "You don't understand the world like I do."

And I hope I never do, Arthur thought.

He stared at Harry's measly bed, the slimy walls, the bowl of gruel veined with mold. "I can't just leave you in here."

"Yes, you can," Harry said. "You can't go saving every soul who gets themselves in trouble, Arthur. Not your friend. And not me."

"But, Dad—"

"Stop arguing and listen." Harry nodded out the window. "Go find yourself a job in the city. Keep your nose down and do the work. If you ever see a member of the Black Feathers, you hide. Hear me?" He pulled his hole-ridden sheet back over him. "Tell the landlady I'll be late on the rent again."

"I'll tell her you'll be back by tomorrow! With enough money to buy the tenements!"

Before Harry could respond, Arthur slid back along the limestone. He passed the cell with the frozen patient, then the cell with the chanting woman. He was about to pass the last cell when a hand shot between the bars.

Arthur's foot slipped on the limestone and he barely managed to catch himself. His hat wasn't so lucky. It twirled down a hundred feet and was swallowed by the waves.

As Arthur regained his footing and his heart rate, the hand turned its palm downward toward the sea. Then it pressed its thumb into the flat of its fingers, as if wearing a sock puppet. The hand looked left and then right and gasped when it seemed to actually *see* Arthur.

"Arthur Benton!" the hand said. "How lovely of you to visit!"

"Um . . . ," Arthur said, sliding back a few inches. He was afraid the cell's occupant would try and strangle him, or worse, shove him to the breakers below. How did this patient know his name?

The hand tilted, like the head of a curious dog. "How are you this fine rainy eve?"

It opened and closed its fingers in a mimicry of speaking while the patient in the cell provided the words. The young man's skin was dark, his lighter palm flashing each time the hand opened its "mouth" to talk.

"I'm all right," Arthur said. "How are you?"

"I'm splendid!" the voice said, the hand opening and closing. "Would you like to see my drawing?"

"Uh, sure?"

If there was one thing Arthur knew about unsettled people it was that you didn't argue with them. He got up on his tiptoes and peeked through the bars. The patient was eighteen maybe, and something about him looked familiar . . .

"You're not gonna grab me, are you?" Arthur asked.

"Not if you look at my drawing!" the hand said in a sing-song voice. "Ha ha!"

Arthur hesitated. The sea roiled below. One misstep and he'd plummet to the same fate as his hat. He inched a bit closer and peered through the bars. The cell's drawing was meticulously made from spit and cobwebs. It looked like a map of Kingsport, only everything was *backward*. The Gilded Quarter was to the west while the cliffs of Greyridge were to the east. Two robed figures walked the cobwebbed streets: a boy who looked a lot like Arthur and a girl holding two swords.

Arthur frowned. Was that the girl from that weird Manor's forest room? Sekhmet? It couldn't be . . .

"Who are you?" Arthur asked.

"My name is Graham," the hand said, bowing. "But it's my last name you'll find interesting."

"Okay," Arthur said. "What's your last name?"

The hand cleared its throat. *"I build the fort so it's wide and strong, and the ladies have somewhere to lay. And if the thieves and husbands keep out, then breakfast will be on my tray."*

"Huh?"

"The boy has never heard a riddle before?" the hand asked.

Arthur loved riddles. He'd solved dozens in Alfred Moore's books, refusing to flip to the answer before he'd figured out the solution himself. But he'd never solved a riddle while balancing on a lip of limestone, facing a mental hospital patient who could push him to his death.

"Let's see . . . ," Arthur said, heart quickening.

Riddles were designed to force your brain into a box that it couldn't think its way out of. You had to take a mental step back and consider every possible reading of the words.

"A *fort*?" Arthur considered. "I don't think it's an army barracks. That's too obvious."

The hand nodded encouragingly.

Arthur considered the phrases *somewhere to lay* and *breakfast will be on my tray*. So it was a fort that provided breakfast. When Arthur had first heard it, he'd thought the word *lay* had been grammatically incorrect. Ladies *lie* down. But if it wasn't, then the ladies were laying something . . .

"Are you a chicken coop?"

The hand's fingers puckered in disappointment. "No, I'm sorry. I have to push you to your death now."

Arthur slid away. "I don't know what it is!"

The hand threw back its head while the guy in the cell laughed. "I'm kidding! You must remain alive to face the wonderful and terrible things that await you."

Arthur relaxed. Kind of. He considered the riddle again and realized the wording suggested it wasn't about the chicken coop itself, but the person who built it.

"A coop builder . . . Coop . . . Coop maker . . . mak*er*." Arthur's heart lit up. "Cooper?"

"Yes!" the hand cried and did a little jig. "Graham Cooper! That's me!"

"I knew you looked familiar!" Arthur said, feeling a little relieved. "Are you related to Wally Cooper?"

The hand nodded fervently. "He's my brother!"

Arthur wondered why Wally had never mentioned Graham before. Harry was a little odd, but Arthur never pretended like his dad didn't exist.

"Wally's my friend," Arthur said, hoping Graham would let him pass.

The hand snaked closer, finger to nose with Arthur. "You, my fair *gentleman*, are a liar."

Arthur recalled the last moment he'd seen Wally—crawling on the ceiling of the spiral hallway—and he fought down the guilt. Graham must've been the reason Wally wanted to join Arthur's heist in the first place. So he could pay his brother's hospital bill.

"Your brother's getting the money," Arthur said. "He's going to get you out of here."

The hand shook its head. "Wally's a sweet child. But I'm

in here because I choose to be. I had myself committed on purpose."

"What? Why?"

"To meet *you*, of course! This is exactly where I'm needed to usher in the Great Slumbyr."

"What's the *Great Slumbyr*?" Arthur asked. The name made his heart tremble, though he wasn't sure why.

Graham's hand ignored him. It gazed toward the backward drawing of Kingsport and sighed. "My brother is doing his part. Wally's nearly through the Mirror now. Ready to be reversed." The hand looked back at Arthur. "Ready for another riddle?"

"Um, do I have a choice?"

"I rise with a gasp, and it begins, an evening of sorrow and tears. And though death and carnage may ensue, when I fall the night fills with cheers."

Arthur thought a moment. When would people ever cheer for sorrow and death?

"Oh," he said. "That's easy. You're a theater curtain."

The hand tilted its head. "Are you sure?"

A chill went through Arthur. "What else could it be?"

The hand gave him a reassuring smile. "Don't be afraid, Arthur. The end of the world won't be as painful as most people believe."

Arthur had flashbacks of the Pox: the streets filled with coughs and wailing, the creak of carts collecting the dead, his mom's skin turning papery yellow as the disease consumed her from the inside out.

Arthur swallowed. "The world isn't going to end."

The hand chuckled. "Oh, but it will. And *you're* going to make it happen."

"Me?"

"I refuse to tell you any more!" the hand said brightly. "It could spoil the surprise. Anyway, your solution to my riddle was close enough. You deserve a prize." It disappeared through the bars, and the cell fell silent.

"Hello?" Arthur said, voice echoing against the stones. "Graham?"

Had he left? That was impossible. The cell's door was almost certainly locked.

Arthur squinted into the darkness. He thought he saw the cobweb drawing ripple like waves on a dark pond. Then the hand came shooting through the bars with something clamped between its fingers. Arthur let out a little yelp of surprise, but then recovered when he saw the object. It was a Golden Scarab. A pendant shaped like an ornate beetle that gleamed in the faint storm light. Graham set it in Arthur's palm.

"This precious object comes from the Temple of Kosh," Graham said with quiet reverence. "I bought it from a Mirror merchant for a song. Literally." He chuckled, then grew serious again. "You must promise me you will not sell it. Or tell anyone who gave it to you."

Arthur closed his fingers around the Scarab. "Okay. I promise."

The hand bowed. "You may pass now, Arthur Benton. And don't be scared. The Veil will fall before the year is through. And you'll receive the cheers you've always craved."

Arthur slid past the window, ducking in case Graham made a grab for him.

Once Arthur was clear, the hand bid him farewell. "Don't get kissed by any dolls! Hee hee."

Arthur rubbed his hatless head. What was all this talk of dolls lately?

As he made his way down the hospital walls, across the cliff face, and back along the fence, he thought about this strange exchange—Wally's mad brother, the drawing of Arthur and Sekhmet, the strange riddles, the Veil, the Great Slumbyr. He also remembered the conversation between Sekhmet and her father. What had they said? The fall of the Veil would bring the end of the world?

Arthur reached the Port and paused. What would Garnett Lacroix do if his father was locked up and his friend was being held captive by evil robed people? Arthur reached into his pocket and pulled out the onyx knocker, which he'd managed to steal on his way out of Hazelrigg. At least the Gentleman Thief would be proud of him for one thing.

reeth talked a lot for a dead person.

"Every time someone walked by, I'd creak the rafters and rattle the floorboards and scream, '*Hello-o! Why are you ignoring me?*' If they walked past the piano, I'd play the loudest, silliest song I could: '*Oh, my name is Breeth, I've got keys for teeth, and I'll bite you if you don't answeeerrrrrr!*' No response. They didn't even blink. I think it's because they're used to this Manor moving all by itself. Also, that piano was the kind that plays itself."

Breeth opened a door for Wally and then shut it behind him.

"*Anyway,*" she said, continuing down the hallway. "I thought I was going to be stuck here *forever!* Just creaky old Breeth, haunting musty walls until the universe turned itself inside out. But then you came along, and now I can finally come out of the woodwork! *Get it?* Ha ha!"

At first the constant gabbing made Wally nervous. He kept glancing over his shoulder, worried the ghost girl's voice would draw unwanted attention. He had to constantly remind himself that he was the only one who could hear her.

"Through here!" Breeth said, creaking down another passage.

She may have been noisy, but having a ghost companion was as good as having a lock pick. Better really. No door went unopened, no corner unchecked. As they traversed the tangled hallways, Breeth said things like, "This wing's safe!" Or "Trust me, that way's boring," Or "*Yeeshk*. Definitely not down there."

"Why not?" Wally asked.

"That's where I was killed."

"Oh."

They found their way out of the forest wing and arrived at a new wing that seemed to be dedicated to time. Wally followed Breeth through a courtyard growing with pocket watch flowers and through a room with what could only be described as a moondial.

Breeth continued to talk. "One time I was inside a pencil, trying to write H-E-L-P when a fly landed on me. Suddenly, the whole world looked like a kaleidoscope, and I realized I'd accidentally slipped inside the fly's buzzy little body! I was stuck! I lived an entire life as a fly. I had a little fly wife and a pile of mouse droppings that we called home. Mouse droppings are *way* more delicious than you'd think, by the way. Oh, and we had maggot babies! They were so cute and pudgy. I died of old age the next day."

They arrived at a widely curving hallway lined with grandfather clocks that ticked in perfect sync—*tick tick tick*. The hall was dark, but Wally was able to follow Breeth's brassy voice, echoing through the clocks' chimes.

"Why haven't we reached the exit yet?" he asked.

"'Cause this Manor *refuses* to hold still."

"What do you mean?"

"Depending on which wing you're in, the hallways grow like branches or rotate like gears. One wing is *super* melty."

"What? Why?"

"It has to be like that in order to fit itself inside other buildings. Like the one you broke into."

"Okay, but *why*?"

"The Manor travels to different cities so it can fix stuff. And by that I mean so the people *inside* it can fix stuff."

"What kind of stuff?"

Breeth possessed a wooden clock face. "Okay, so this is really complicated and took me a while to figure out, but you seem smart, so I think you'll get it. Weirdwood Manor sits on the border between the real world and the imaginary one. All the doors on the *south* side of the Manor open onto places in the *Real*. Like coffee shops and toy stores and one time a bathhouse. That was gross. The doors on the *north* side lead to the Fae, or *imaginary* places. They're filled with things people in the Real dreamt up, like unicorn cobblers and cloud cuckoo land and one time a goblin screamatorium. That was scary."

Wally's mind wanted to reject these ridiculous ideas. Then again, he was talking to a ghost-possessed clock.

"Sometimes," Breeth continued, "a creature from the imaginary side manages to make a hole—or Rift—in this thing called the *Veil*, which separates the Real from the Fae. Then a creature Fae-born will slip into the Real side and cause a bunch of trouble. An imp might steal people's dentures, or a giant will sneeze lava all over a circus or something."

Wally hugged his elbows. "Did those things really happen?"

"Maybe! It's definitely possible. But that was just an example. Anyway, whenever Fae-born creatures escape into the Real, this Manor travels to that place and squeezes itself into an empty building, and I squeeze with it—kind of like putting on too-tight stockings. Then the Wardens of Weirdwood go in, catch the imp or giant or whatever, send it back to the Fae, sew up the Rift in the Veil, and then the Manor is off to the next problem."

Wally's thoughts felt more tangled than ever. But that didn't matter. He didn't need to know about this stuff. He just needed to get back to Kingsport and start pickpocketing. He had wasted an entire night in this Manor.

It dawned on him that if he brought Breeth to the gambling dens, she might be able to control the wooden roulette table so it always landed on black. She could even reshuffle the paper cards in the deck, stacking it in his favor. With Breeth fixing the fixed games, he'd be able to pay off Graham's hospital bill in a couple of days.

So long as he made it out of this Manor in one piece first.

The clock hallway curved on and on, refusing to end. Wally remembered the passage that had uncoiled like a sprout.

"I've seen a hall like this before," he said. "I'm not sure it's going to end."

Breeth paused in a clock, ticking with thought. "Huh. You might be right. I was talking so much I got distracted. I'll head up to the next floor and figure this out. Be right back. Don't get caught or eaten."

He frowned at the ceiling as she creaked away. Why did she have to say it like *that*?

Wally waited in the darkness. The grandfather clocks ticked. The air smelled of dust and gear oil. He hadn't realized how soothing Breeth's presence was until she was gone.

After a few moments of ticking nothingness, a light came bobbing around the bend. With it came the faint scent of sea salt. Wally took a step back.

"*Breeth?*" he whispered toward the ceiling.

The light cast a spindly shadow. It twined and slithered like a giant snake. Upon its head, two horns stuck out of a mane of hair. Wally's nerves went electric. Was this one of the Fae-born from the imaginary side of the Manor? Had it escaped?

"*Breeth!*" Wally whispered again with more urgency.

The shadow drew closer, its body coiling like wisps of smoke. The hallway curved behind Wally. If he ran back the way he'd come, he might loop right back around to the dragon and a quick, crisp death.

He opened one of the clock's glass doors and tried to hide himself inside. He didn't fit. The swinging pendulum kept striking his shoulder. He tried to pull himself out, but his pant cuff caught on one of the hinges.

"*Come on!*" he mumbled, frantically tugging at it.

He was just able to free himself as the light rounded the corner.

The shadow didn't belong to a monster, but a boy. The boy stopped and stared. He was about Wally's age but held himself with more poise. He was tall and muscular and wore simple, ocean-colored robes and a silken cap. He held a candle and a glass of milk.

Relief tingled through Wally. What had looked like a dragon tail must have been nothing more than the shadow of the black braid hanging out of the boy's cap.

"You're just a kid," Wally said.

"So it would appear," the boy said in a voice like royalty.

Wally studied the kid's face. He didn't have scales or fangs—only a smear of red at the corner of his lips, like he'd just eaten a jam sandwich.

"You're that thief the Wardens caught," the kid said.

"Uh . . . no," Wally said, taking a step back.

"Where I come from, we execute thieves on the spot." The boy's eyes sparkled like the sea at daybreak. "Drown them, actually."

"Good thing I'm not a thief then," Wally said, slowly backing away.

What he wouldn't give to have Arthur's charm right then.

The boy wiped his mouth with the sleeve of his robe, and the red smeared like blood. He set his glass of milk on the floor near a roman numeral VI set in the marble and drew out a calligraphy brush. He painted a strange symbol that hung in the air. The moment the symbol was complete, something whizzed over Wally's head, shaving off a bit of his hair.

CUCKOO!

It was a bird, sprung from one of the clocks. Another

darted from the clock opposite, and Wally ducked right before its razor-sharp beak took out his eye.

The boy picked up his milk. "Enjoy the rest of your stay, *thief*."

Wally ran. The boy and his candle vanished around the bend as more birds sprang out of the clocks, pecking at Wally's head.

CUCKOO! CUCKOO! CUCKOO!

Wally hadn't run far before he circled around the hallway and arrived back at the boy, who started to paint another strange symbol. Wally didn't wait to find out what this one did. He turned and ran back the way he'd come—only to find two people running toward him. One was Amelia, the redheaded woman with the eye patch. The other was huge, with blond hair, pink cheeks, and lederhosen—like someone had blown up a baby to the size of an ox.

"You'll only make it worse for yourself if you run!" the woman shouted.

"I'll take my chances!" Wally said and sprinted back the other way.

He skidded to a stop halfway between the kid with the calligraphy brush and the others. They had him surrounded. Wally looked around helplessly, trying to puzzle this place out like he had the sprout hallway. Or thought he had, anyway.

"Vorry not, fräulein," the baby-faced giant said in a thick accent. "Zat boy is going novhere. Ze exit is currently behind us."

The exit was *behind* the giant? Wally hadn't seen one. And what did the man mean by *currently*?

"Huamei!" the woman called. "Can you flood him to us?"

Flood me? Wally thought, heart racing even faster.

He needed to get out of that hallway. Searching for clues, Wally looked at the floor and found that he was standing between a III and a IV set in the marble. He remembered the VI beneath the dragon boy's feet. If the circular hallway was shaped like a clock face, then maybe the hands on the grandfather clocks pointed toward an exit.

A sound like ocean waves came rushing from the direction of the boy with the calligraphy brush. Wally had to act fast. All the clocks in the hall read 7:42. Wally was standing closer to the III, roughly at the 3:15 position. Was there a way to get the exit to come to him? He tried opening a clock face to spin the hands, but the glass was sealed shut.

A cuckoo bird sprang from the opposite side of the hall, missing Wally's ear by an inch.

"I told you not to get caught!" it sang with its wooden beak.

"Breeth!" Wally said. "Thank goodness. Can you change these clock hands?"

The cuckoo bird turned on its spring and pointed its beak at the clock. "Only if there are wooden parts in the gears."

"Well, try!" He double-checked the number at his feet. "Change it to three o'clock!"

The cuckoo bird hung limp on its spring.

"*Breeth?*" Wally said.

A four-foot wave of foaming water sloshed around the bend, crashing toward him. Wally braced for impact.

But then the clock hands started to spin. They struck

three, the bells chimed, and Wally felt a great rumbling. The clock in front of him clicked, and its pendulum folded back. Wally threw open the door to the main case just as the wave splashed over the spot where he'd been standing. He slammed the door behind him, heard the hands spin and the lock click, and then ran down the dark passage.

"Ze door is locked!" the giant cried. "Did zat urchin just make ze clocks to change?"

"Curse it!" Amelia said. "He *is* a mage."

"He von't get far," the giant said. "I vill change ze time."

The passage was dark. Wally found himself walking down a slim path that was growing slimmer by the second. It continued to narrow until he was forced to turn his feet sideways and shuffle along it, keeping balance.

"Breeth?" he whispered. "Are you here?"

The darkness was silent. There was nothing nearby for her to possess. He remembered the theme of this wing—time—and realized that he was balancing on the arm of a giant minute hand. It was the only thing between him and a pit of darkness. He would be fine so long as the minute hand didn't—

It started to jiggle back and forth beneath his feet.

"It von't allow me to turn it!" the man said behind the locked door. "Somesing is fighting me!"

"I'm trying to stop him, Wally!" Breeth shouted in the distance. "But it's like arm wrestling, and I was never good at arm wrestling!"

"Is it the boy's magic, Ludwig?" Amelia asked.

"I do not know," the giant said. "He should not be able to

do zis! Ze gear feels *stuck*, like it does not vant to turn ze ozer way. If I can just—" The giant grunted with effort. "*Zere!*"

BONG!

The hour hand ticked beneath Wally's feet. His arms wheeled as he wavered on his arches, trying to keep balance.

It didn't work.

He pitched forward, falling into nothingness.

* * *

Wally awoke on a large pillow. He was in a room with cinnamon-brown walls that were decorated with weapons and artistic instruments, like paintbrushes and pencils and type-writer keys. The ceiling was plastered with what looked like maps of other worlds.

The pillow's feathers rustled beneath him. "Um, Wally?"

Breeth. He remembered where he was. The Manor. The impossible corridors. The ticking hallway. The pit . . .

He sat up. Three figures stood in a half circle around him. Weston, the slight, hairy man was there. As was the baby-faced giant, Ludwig. Amelia, the woman with the eye patch was absent, but in her place was a pretty, smirking woman with short green hair. She was grinding something with a mortar and pestle.

"You're quite the slippery one," a voice said behind him.

Wally turned and found an elderly woman, her shoulders wrapped with a caramel-colored boa constrictor. She wore a decomposing wedding dress and sat in an ornate chair made of candle wax. Her hair was wild and weedy, and she resembled one of the many bag ladies in Kingsport—the kind you'd avoid when she asked you for change. But this woman held herself with dignity.

"I had to contort my Manor so the fall wouldn't kill you," the old woman said, a starry glint in her eye. "Its hallways will be healing for months."

Wally rubbed his head, remembering his great fall. He was still in one piece.

"How'd you pick my imp locks?" Weston asked in a gruff voice.

"And how did you escape ze spiral hallvay?" Ludwig asked.

"You use magic?" Weston asked. "Huh?"

The woman with the mortar and pestle only giggled.

"I . . ." Wally was at a loss for words.

That started a flood of questions.

"Are you a spy for the Order of Eldar?"

"How did you know to rotate ze clock hands? Unt *how* did you rotate zose clock hands?"

"Did you bribe my imps with nectar?"

"Vhat art did you use?"

"Wally?" The pillow beneath Wally bristled with Breeth's voice. "You won't tell them about me, will you?"

He gave his head a little shake, and the robed figures took this as a refusal to answer their questions.

"I don't think this boy works for the Order," the old woman said. "He has too much color in his eyes." She petted her snake. "In fact, I don't believe he has a magical bone in his body. He used . . . *other* methods."

Wally clamped his mouth shut as Breeth's pillow fell flat.

The door opened, and Amelia entered and bowed. "Sorry to interrupt, Lady Weirdwood. But we need to get back to work. The Wardens are struggling to fight the Order without our assistance."

Ludwig's hands startled as if he remembered something. He took small square pieces of paper out of his cloak and started folding them into little birds. The woman with the mortar and pestle continued to grind, giggling.

Lady Weirdwood sighed. "Well, we can't return to the Mercury Mines until we've neutralized the threat to Kingsport. What's our status with the Fae-born?"

"A sort of *contagious* porcelain doll has made its way into the city," Amelia said. "I haven't been able to track it or the Rift it escaped through yet. I've been too busy sending supplies to the Mines."

"Contagious doll, eh?" Weston said, scratching his scruff. "Wonder which degenerate dreamt that up."

"Could've been anyone," the old woman said. "The Veil grows as thin as webs in cities. Too many hungry people dreaming of a better world."

"Vhat do ve do wis ze boy?" Ludwig asked, nodding to Wally.

"I say we turn him loose in his city," Amelia said. "It isn't our place to interfere with their lives."

"He *broke* into the Manor," Weston said. "Who knows what kind of damage he could've done?"

The giant hugged himself. "Already did, really."

"Hee hee hee."

Wally gently nudged his pillow and whispered, "Can you get us out of here?"

"I'm trying!" Breeth said. "But this room's made of metal. All I can possess is this pillow's goose down. Oh! I could tickle them if you want?"

Wally frowned.

"We can't leave the Fae-born loose much longer," Amelia said. "We don't want another Daymare on our hands."

The giant shuddered. Wally did too. Daymare? Was another catastrophe headed to Kingsport? One that involved monsters from another realm?

"Perhaps it's best if we don't discuss such things in front of our guest," the old woman said, then smiled at Wally. "My name is Lady Weirdwood. I'm this Manor's architect." She gestured to the others. "This is my staff."

Only the giant waved.

"Before I decide what to do with you," Lady Weirdwood said, "I want to have the pleasure of knowing the name of the boy who bested my Manor's security."

"Um . . . ," Wally said.

Before he could respond, the door banged open again, and Weirdwood's staff spun around. Wally's heart leapt. Arthur Benton stood in the doorway, pants slung over his shoulder.

"Oops!" Arthur said. "Heh heh. Wrong turn. Could someone point me to the exit?"

The robed people only stared, clearly trying to puzzle out how this boy had managed to break into the Manor yet again, let alone find his way to this room. Arthur saw Wally and his eyes widened. But only for a split second.

"You see," Arthur said. "I have a pet ferret. Audrey's her name. She's the last thing my sweet mother gave me before she died, but she can be a *scoundrel*. The ferret, that is—not my mother. Audrey has a penchant for slithering into places she isn't wanted: restaurants, houses, even had to fish her out of a bank vault once. So when she scampered into this fine home of yours, my friend there volunteered to help me catch her. Hey there, Wilberforce."

Wally nodded numbly.

Arthur hefted his pants higher on his shoulder. "The one place I know Audrey feels most secure is bundled up in my very own dirty laundry. I had no choice but to remove my pants to catch my beloved pet." He gave the robed people a wary look. "But, um, don't ask to see her. She's a biter."

At the end of Arthur's speech, everyone sat in silence. Then the pretty woman giggled and Lady Weirdwood started to clap. A couple others followed, but it quickly died away.

"Now this one," Lady Weirdwood said, pointing at Arthur. "This one has something. Wordcraft, is it? And he doesn't even realize he's casting a spell. Not to mention the fact that the Manor's enchantments seem to have no effect on him."

Arthur beamed. Even in a situation like this, he couldn't reject a bit of praise.

"Still," Lady Weirdwood said, petting her snake, "we can't have this child compromising our security. Seize him."

Amelia drew out a whip, cracked it at Arthur, coiling it around his body, and yanked him into the circle.

"Unhand me, you slimy villain!" Arthur screamed. "I will not bow to your demon god!"

Amelia upended his pant bag, dumping coins and the onyx door knocker across the floor, before returning the pants to Arthur.

Arthur slipped them back on and sat next to Wally. "How you holding up, Cooper?"

"Oh, y'know," Wally said. "Just struggling to survive in an evil Manor where I was *abandoned*."

Arthur's smile twitched.

The door opened again, and Sekhmet and the boy with the calligraphy brush entered.

"Ah!" Lady Weirdwood said. "Our multitalented Novitiates. Excellent timing." She steepled her fingers. "The Manor is spread thin. Our Wardens in the field require so much assistance that we've had to enlist the help of our doctor, chef, and groundskeepers." She gestured to the Manor's staff members. "Amelia, Pyra, Ludwig, and Weston must remain here to send supplies to the Mines and protect the Manor." She looked at Sekhmet and the boy with the calligraphy brush. "I need you two to secure the Fae-born in Kingsport and sew up the Rift."

Sekhmet stood tall. The boy's face remained expressionless.

"Sekhmet," Lady Weirdwood said, "this is your chance to make up for old mistakes. If you complete this mission, I will advance you to full Wardenship."

Sekhmet bowed. "I'll do my best, Lady."

"Huamei," the lady said to the boy. "I'm hoping you can rise high enough in our ranks to help us mend the Manor's relations with the Court of Sky. Things have been tense ever since one of my Wardens stole a bone from the grave of your royal ancestor. I also know your relationship with your step-father has been less than ideal lately."

Huamei's jaw tightened, but he nodded.

"Kingsport is a large, confusing city," Lady Weirdwood said. "Locating the Fae-born in the Real and the Rift in Mirror Kingsport will be difficult. But I believe in you."

Wally gave Arthur a look. Did she just say *Mirror* Kingsport?

"I expect you to complete this mission by dawn," Lady Weirdwood said to Sekhmet and Huamei. "Then we can all return to the Mercury Mines and help our Wardens in need." She gave the Novitiates a surprised look. "Why are you still here?"

Huamei turned as Sekhmet bowed again. And with that, they left.

"Ludwig and Weston," Lady Weirdwood said to the baby-faced giant and the small hairy man, "I need you to figure out why your defenses didn't stop two street urchins from breaking into my Manor."

The two bowed and left.

"Pyra, see if you can mix up a concoction that will cure porcelain skin. A nice gazpacho, perhaps?"

The woman with the mortar and pestle giggled and departed.

Lady Weirdwood stood from her chair. "Amelia, lock these thieves in the first floor of the Abyssment." She quirked an eyebrow at Arthur and Wally. "I would send them back to Kingsport, but I wouldn't want their precious thieving fingers to turn into porcelain and shatter."

Arthur opened his mouth to protest, but Wally quickly

pinched his arm and gave him a look: *I can get us out of here*. Breeth would be able to possess the doors and help them escape.

As Amelia led Wally and Arthur out of the room, Lady Weirdwood cleared her throat. "Barring any magical ability, Wilberforce here seems to have found a way to get the wood of the Manor to cooperate. Make sure to lock them in the *iron* cells."

And with those words, all hope of escape was lost.

7
BREETH

Breeth had never creaked so wonderfully in her life—er, *death*.

During her time in the Manor—a year? three?—she'd grown used to the stuffy rooms and drafty hallways. But she could also feel herself growing old with it. Her bones were the groaning walls, her hair the shedding shingles, the floorboards her trembling knees. She'd started to forget what it felt like to be that ten-year-old girl in the periwinkle dress catching frogs on her family's estate.

But then she'd met Wally. He could see her face in the woodwork. He could respond to her creaks. And for the first time since that masked figure had taken her life, Breeth felt *alive*—or as alive as a dead girl could feel, anyway.

Unfortunately, Wally was currently being held in an iron cell, made of nonliving materials Breeth could not possess. She creaked down the wooden railing that ran along the basement steps until the railing ended. Then she peered down the tunnel to the first level of the Manor's Abyssment. It seemed Wally was locked up with a boy who was quite full of himself.

"Could be worse," the boy named Arthur said. "At least they didn't sacrifice us to their demon god."

Wally grunted, trying to force open the bars.

"Oh, come on," Arthur said. "You can at least *laugh*."

No response.

"I find," Arthur continued, "that remaining lighthearted in intense situations keeps you clearheaded. Panic and anger cloud the mind, leaving you as helpful as a wolverine in a sewing class. Clear thoughts bring clear solutions."

"Oh yeah?" Wally said. "Is keeping a clear head how you got us into this Manor? Is it how you got us both out of that spiral hallway? Oh, wait. *I* solved the door knocker thing, and you *abandoned* me."

"It was all part of the *plan*, Cooper," Arthur said. "You distracted those weird robey people, and I escaped with the treasure, only to triumphantly return and rescue you! Now we just have to find our way out of this cell, score another pantload of coins, and then we'll be on our way home to fame and *glory*!"

Breeth's railing groaned in irritation for Wally.

Arthur stroked his chin. "Maybe if I make a rope out of my shirt and pants, I could create a lasso and toss it around that loose bar on the floor. Then you could use the bar to pick the cell's lock!"

Wally huffed. "Removing your pants doesn't solve every problem, Arthur. Besides, that bar clearly won't fit in the lock. I need something small and spindly."

Arthur's eyes went wide as he patted his vest and pulled out a Golden Scarab. "Will this work?"

"Where did you get this?" Wally asked, taking it.

"I, um, stole it from upstairs," Arthur said.

Wally stuck one of the Scarab's thin legs into the lock and wiggled it up and down. There was a small metallic *click*, and Wally triumphantly pulled the Scarab out. Then he grimaced. Its leg had snapped off.

Arthur shook his head. "I knew I should've found a better lock pick."

Wally suddenly jerked, dropping the Scarab, which pinged across the stone floor.

"That thing just *moved*," he said.

The boys stared at the golden insect, lying on its back, its five remaining legs sticking into the air. The Scarab twitched again, and their eyes went wide. It started to struggle, spinning in shrieking circles, its metal wings grinding against the stone. Finally, it was able to flip itself over. The Scarab buzzed once and then marched like a mechanical toy toward a crack in the wall where it disappeared and did not come out again.

"Let's maybe be careful about what we steal from here," Wally said.

Arthur gulped and nodded.

Breeth sighed. It didn't look like either boy was going to come up with a way to escape. She would have to take matters into her own splintered hands. She took a long creaking breath—or something like a breath—and made a big decision.

She creaked back up the wooden railing to the Manor's main floor, and then groaned toward the west wing. Breeth had spent her time in Weirdwood Manor studying the Wardens and their staff. She wanted to learn to distinguish good people from those who were rotten to the core. She'd trusted too easily when she was alive, and it had gotten her kidnapped.

Since Breeth had died, Wally was the first person she had seen who seemed to be made of good stuff right to his bone marrow . . . even if he was a thief. Sure, he was a little shy, but most of the good ones were. If Wally swore he would help track down her killer when she got him out of this place, she believed him. That's why she was willing to do what she was about to do.

By the time she reached the west wing, Breeth's boards were trembling so badly, she accidentally broke a vase. She stretched her senses through the rooms, feeling for the vibration of two particular sets of footsteps—heavy and soft. She felt them in the feasting hall and entered through the high vaulted ceiling, creaking down the cedar walls and thumping into the grand table, heavy with platters of roasted yams and plum stew.

"It's your fault and no two ways about it," Weston grumbled, pointing a spoon at his considerably larger brother. "Your spiral hallway's meant to stop non-magical types, but those thieves waltzed through like it was a pleasant promenade."

"I—I don't understand how zey did zis!" Ludwig said, tears trembling in his baby blue eyes. "One peek at ze twisted corridor should have sent ze urchins running in ze opposite direction!"

The twins, Ludwig and Weston, were always arguing about something. You wouldn't know they were twins by the looks of them. One was small and hairy, the other large and soft. They even had different accents, which was *really* confusing.

Weston oversaw the living elements of Weirdwood—like gardening and pests—carpeting the floors with vines and populating the locks with imps. Ludwig, meanwhile, was in charge of the *non*living elements—designing beautiful woodwork and manipulating the corridors. Together they controlled the growth of Weirdwood Manor like a bonsai tree, trimming and wrangling its many rooms and hallways. Breeth loved traveling through their work.

Ludwig stared at the table. "And vhat about your imp locks? Perhaps if you did not spoil zem vith so much nectar—"

"Don't you question how I run my platoon!" Weston said, shaking his spoon and spattering the top of Breeth's table with soup.

Breeth softly creaked through each of their benches, searching for a cold weight against her top. She found it and sighed. Of course, it was Weston who held the keys to the Abyssment's cell. It had to be the twin who was in charge of exterminating pests.

"'Sides," Weston said, "my soldiers are on their last legs. We haven't been granted leave in months, and I haven't been able to head to the imp forest for fresh recruits."

Ludwig scooped up a yam and let it thud to his plate. "Little chance of a vacation after zose urchins broke in."

Weston grunted. On that much, at least, the twins could agree.

Breeth creaked through the floorboards into Pyra's kitchen, which was mercifully empty. She seeped into the prep table where she found a lone crumb of cheese. By wobbling the table, she was able to knock the crumb to the floor where she creaked next, and then waited. It wasn't long until a strange creature came hopping out of a hole in the wall.

Breeth would have called it a mouse, but this creature was slightly bigger. Its back was striped purple and black, and its tail curved like a curlicue. Still, with its big dewy eyes, oversized ears, and needle whiskers, it was just as adorable.

The mouse thing plucked up the cheese crumb and began to nibble. Breeth's nerves trembled the floorboards. This was it. She may have been able to creak from dead thing to dead thing, but she still hadn't figured out how to escape *living* things—not until they died, at least. Hence her life as a housefly.

If she were to possess this mouse, she could be stuck for years. And then she would have to experience death yet again. The fly had been easy enough—just a single day before her wings stopped buzzing, her legs curled to her abdomen, and her dusty heart beat its last.

But this death could be far more unpleasant. People hated rodents. Her life could end in one of Weston's mousetraps in a stomach-squishing, backbreaking snap. She reminded herself that her parents were waiting for her in the afterlife and the only way to reach them was to free Wally so he could help her catch her killer.

"All right, little guy," Breeth whispered to the mouse thing. "I need you not to panic, okay?" If she had a stomach it would have flipped over then. "You either, Breeth."

With that, she seeped into the mouse thing's paws.

Breeth's whole being became a confusion of senses. First came the prickly feeling of fur all over her body, the cold of stone against her naked tail and paws, the brush of air against her whiskers. Next was the aromatic taste of cheese, gummy on her bucked teeth.

But then the mouse thing's tiny heart started to race. Its body tensed, and its breath grew short. It knew something was terribly wrong.

"Hi!" Breeth thought into the mouse's mind. "My name's Breeth. There's no need to pan—"

The mouse thing shrieked. It scampered across the kitchen, frantically trying to escape the voice that had entered its thoughts. Breeth was dragged along, her entire being jounced in frantic hops.

"You're okay!" she thought as sweetly as she could. "I'm not going to hurt you!"

This only made the creature shriek even more wildly as it continued to tear around the kitchen. If the sound drew Weston's attention, he would come stomping in to end this creature's life, and Breeth would feel every second of it.

She tried not to panic as she held on to the mouse thing's mind like a bucking bronco. How had this worked with the housefly? The answer was it hadn't. The fly didn't put up a fight. It just let her take over. Breeth guessed that the simpler a creature's thoughts, the easier it was to possess.

As the mouse thing continued to shriek and scamper, Breeth tried to imagine what would relax her if she were a mouse. She thought of cheese. Of calm, rooted burrows. Of slow, cherry pit–sized heartbeats. The mouse thing's shrieking began to settle as its paws stopped galloping and it came to a standstill, breath still short and quick.

"There you go," Breeth whispered inside the mouse thing's mind. "I'll take care of you. I'll keep you safe. I promise."

A shudder ran down the creature's hunched spine. It got low on its haunches until its stomach touched the floorboards. Its long lashes fluttered closed.

"That's it," Breeth cooed in thought. "You're safe."

The mouse thing released control, and Breeth blinked open her oil drop eyes. She stretched her legs and swirled her tail. She flexed her sharp claws against the floorboard she'd possessed just moments before. Then her whiskers twitched upward.

The kitchen was overwhelming. The ceiling rose as high as the sky. The counters loomed like giant cliffs. But the *smells*. Breeth pushed up on her hind paws and sniffed the air. There were sweet things on those cliffs. Ripe plums. A bowl of sugar. And *bread*. A boulder-sized loaf with scrumptious rock crumbs tumbling off it. Her tiny stomach gurgled, but she shook her whiskers. She couldn't let herself get lost in this mouse thing's senses.

She hopped across the vast floor and stuck her whiskered nose under the kitchen door.

"If we can't stop a couple of street urchins," Weston said, "then how are we going to stop the Order of Eldar when they show up to destroy us?"

"*If* zey show up," Ludwig said.

"*When*." Weston pushed away his bowl and dabbed a napkin at his lips.

They glared at each other and then simultaneously scooted back in their stools, finished with their meal and their argument.

Oh no, Breeth thought. The keys had been so easy to reach when Weston was sitting.

As the twins exited the feasting hall, she scrambled along the baseboard, keeping like a shadow on Weston's heels as he marched to his workshop.

"Formation!" he shouted as he entered.

Several doorknobs hopped from out of the shadows and formed straight lines on the floor.

Weston saluted them, then crossed his hands behind his back. "I want a full report, you lousy bunch of lowlifes! You embarrassed me in front of Ludwig." He pointed at a brass doorknob. "You! Marsden! What happened?"

The doorknob responded in a squeaky voice. To Breeth's mouse ears it sounded like gibberish.

"A master lock picker, eh?" Weston said, taking out a pick of his own. "We'll see about that."

As he ran the imps through several drills, Breeth crept to the bottom of his giant chair and gazed up at the keys dangling from his belt, high as an apple on a tree. How was she supposed to reach them? On her hind paws, she was barely three inches tall. She scampered to the other end of the workshop and scaled a rope onto a table of miniature tools. With a swipe of her tail, she knocked a tiny screwdriver to the floor.

"Hmm?" Weston stood and about-faced as Breeth scurried behind a lamp. "Mortimer? That had better not be you."

He searched the area for what Breeth guessed was a deserter imp. When he didn't find it, he bent to retrieve the screwdriver from the floor.

Breeth had mere moments to act. She scrambled to the edge of the table and reached out her tiny claw, trying to snag the keys. Her fingernail was a mere whisker's length away. But for Breeth's tiny mouse paw, it might as well have been a meter.

Weston marched back to his imp formation, and Breeth decided to knock down another tool. Hopefully this time Weston would bend a little closer to the desk. But the moment she brought her tail back to swat the tiny hammer, Weston spun on his heels.

"Aha!" he said. "So *you're* the culprit."

Breeth leapt from the desk and made a break for the door, but in two giant steps Weston slammed it shut. The space beneath the door was too small, even for a mouse body, so she skittered under the shadow of the desk.

"Imps dismissed!" Weston shouted, and the doorknobs rolled away, loud as thunder. He opened a drawer and fished out an object. Breeth could see the shadow of the thing as he tossed it up and down in his hand. It looked like a stone, ready to smash her. With a floor-quaking tremble, the desk scooted away from the wall, leaving Breeth out in the open.

She was trapped. She couldn't get her paws to scamper left or right, certain one of Weston's military boots would come crashing down, big as a house, spewing her mouse guts across the floor. She'd promised she'd take care of this mouse. She'd promised Wally she'd get him out of the Manor. She—

"Hello there, little fella," Weston whispered, breaking up the bread roll and scattering crumbs in front of her. "A little energy for your journey through the great, tangled Manor."

Breeth could only stare at the crumbs with her big black eyes.

Weston smiled. "Just don't tell anyone what a softy I am."

He marched off to his quarters, leaving the cell's key on his work desk.

Breeth blinked. Maybe she needed to work on her character analysis.

* * *

"Why don't you just *charm* the bars open, Arthur?" Wally said.

"If they had a beating pulse, I would!"

The boys were so busy arguing neither of them noticed the mouse that slipped through the bars, dragging a key by its tail. Breeth sat up on her hind paws trying to get the attention of the giant boys towering above her.

"Besides," Arthur said, "*you're* supposed to be the master lock picker."

"I know. But *someone* got me caught and my picks taken away."

"I got you temporarily imprisoned so I could heroically return and—"

Breeth let out a squeak.

Arthur saw her and screeched. He hefted a wagon-sized shoe and brought it hurtling down. Breeth tried to run, but her tail was still coiled around the key. Before Arthur could squish her, Wally seized him by the arm and threw him back.

"Look!" Wally said. "It brought us the key!"

"And maybe the Pox!" Arthur said, scrambling to the far side of the cell and covering his nose and mouth.

Heart pounding, Breeth managed to unwind her tail from the key, and Wally picked it up. He stared into her eyes.

"Breeth?" he whispered.

Breeth nodded and squeaked. But with her mouse tongue and bucked teeth, it came out as nonsense.

Blocking Arthur with his back, Wally held out his hand and Breeth hopped onto it. His palm was warm beneath her bare paws. Wally rubbed his finger down her snout and along her back, relieving the pain in her spine from hauling the key across the Manor.

"What's it like in there?" Wally asked.

Breeth could only wriggle her nose.

"You can't talk?"

She shook her head.

"Hmm. It would be hard to speak English with a mouse tongue, I guess. Can you get out?"

Breeth hung her head in disappointment. Wally frowned. At first, Breeth thought it was because he was upset she could no longer help them navigate the Manor. But then . . .

"Thank you for doing this," he whispered, scratching between her ears. "We'll figure out who killed you. In the meantime, I'll keep you safe. I promise."

Breeth's oil drop eyes filled with tears. Wally had used the same words she had to calm the mouse thing.

8
THE PORTAL

The moment they unlocked the cell door, the rodent scampered up the staircase. Wally ran after it, while Arthur tried to keep up.

"Um, why are we following a rat?" Arthur asked.

"It's a mouse," Wally said. "Or something like that. And it brought us the key. Maybe it will lead us to an exit."

"But rodents like being *inside*!" Arthur said. "It's where all the food is!"

Wally ignored him and continued to follow the mouse—or whatever it was.

Arthur hadn't trusted rodents since they'd spread the Pox through Kingsport. He used to bring sacks full of dead rats to the Oakers for a small reward. He still saw rodents as valuable little carriers of disease. And he wouldn't hesitate to kill this one if it came near him.

The rodent led them down several stone passageways.

"How can you be sure that thing's headed in the right direction?" Arthur asked.

"It's proven to be a lot more helpful than you are," Wally said. "And I've had practice figuring this place out since someone left me here."

"If I really left you, would I be able to do *this*?"

Arthur gathered Wally into a bear hug, but Wally shoved him away and kept moving.

"Okay," Arthur said, catching up. "I'll admit things didn't go exactly to plan. And that you may have taken the fall for a, um, brief lack of preparation on my behalf. For that I'm, well—what I'm trying to say is . . ."

Wally peered over his shoulder. "You're sorry?"

Arthur nodded. "I'm sorry you were the victim of uncontrollable circumstances."

Wally rolled his eyes and followed the rodent down a dirt tunnel.

How could Arthur get his friend to recognize that he was a bona fide Gentleman Thief? He remembered Wally's brother Graham locked in Greyridge. That would tug at his heartstrings.

"Say, Cooper," Arthur said. "You've never told me about your family."

"You never asked."

Arthur cleared the embarrassment from his throat. "I know your parents died in the Pox. But do you have any brothers or sisters or anything?"

"Nope," Wally said.

That stung. Arthur figured he and Wally had been through enough together that Wally would at least open up a little.

"The Rook locked my dad in Greyridge," Arthur said.

Wally stopped. He turned and stared at Arthur, as if trying to determine whether or not he was lying.

Arthur started to feel uncomfortable in his skin. "My old man has his problems," he said, scratching his hatless head. "But I wouldn't wish that mental hospital on my worst enemy."

Wally stared at him a second. "Good luck with that, Arthur."

He continued on, and Arthur felt even worse than before. He'd given Wally the perfect chance to talk about Graham, but Wally had refused it.

The rodent bounded through a side cavern and into an underground office. It hopped up to an oval window and then wiggled its nose at them. The window looked onto a ghostly field of blue reeds swaying in a soft wind.

"*Whoa,*" Arthur said, peering behind the window at the dark space between it and the wall. It wasn't a window at all. "Um, Cooper? I'm starting to think this is no ordinary manor."

"No kidding."

Arthur stuck his hand through the window and felt a warm breeze.

"I don't think we should go in there," Wally said.

"Why not?"

"From what I've learned about this place, that might not even be the real world."

The rodent hopped to the side of the window and pointed its whiskers at an ornate lectern. It was made of copper tubing that twined with newfangled electrics, which connected to the window. It also held an open book.

Arthur closed the book to read the title, and the blue reeds vanished like a snuffed candle. Instead of an exit, a mirror stood before them, reflecting Wally's and Arthur's confused expressions. Arthur opened the book again, and the field flickered back into view.

Arthur removed the old book from the lectern and replaced it with another from a nearby shelf. The moment he opened it, the mirror filled with a new, leafy light. Now it looked onto a purple jungle.

"It's a *portal*," Arthur said, dumbfounded. "A portal into . . . *books*."

Wally just stared.

The leaves rustled and then parted. And out stepped a tiger. Or something like a tiger. It had black and green stripes, and its eyes smoldered like volcanos. The tiger sniffed at its surroundings and then saw the boys. It gave a steaming snarl, full of heat and magma, crouched low, wiggled its hips, and then pounced.

Wally slammed the book shut just as a wave of hot air from the tiger's claws slashed across the boys' shirts. The rodent scrambled up Wally's pants and hopped into his pocket.

Arthur started giggling. "That was amazing!"

"I don't think you and I have the same definition of amazing," Wally said, feeling his chest to make sure he was still in one piece.

Arthur scanned the books.

"What are you doing?" Wally said.

"Looking for a book with treasure in it."

"And what if that treasure is guarded by another tiger? Or something *worse*?"

Arthur kept searching. "Worth the risk."

Wally seized his arm and spun him around. "Enough playing around, Arthur! That's what got us into this mess in the first place! We need to go *home*. Now."

Arthur remained calm. "*Home is where the hero goes once the journey's said and done.* Know who said that?"

"If it's Garnett Lacroix, I'm going to scream," Wally said. "He's a *fictional* character with an author who can write him out of sticky situations. You don't have an Alfred Moore protecting you everywhere you go. That's why copying the Gentleman Thief always lands you in trouble."

Arthur tried not to let the hurt show on his face. Instead, he stared deep into Wally's eyes. "There's nothing you need money for? Nothing at all?"

Wally looked away. "I just want to go back to Kingsport. You heard that old lady with the snake. The city's in trouble. The people are under attack by some *Fae-born* or something." He studied the bookshelf. "If only they had a book about Kingsport . . ." His eyes went wide. He went to a nearby desk, grabbed a quill, a loose page, and an inkpot. "If this portal opens onto whatever's written in the book," Wally said, slapping the page on the lectern, "maybe we can *write* our way home."

"Cooper, that's *brilliant!*" Arthur said. He plucked the quill from Wally's hand. "Better leave this to the storyteller."

He placed the tip of the quill on the page, then hesitated. He had no problem making things up on the spot, but when the words were on paper, there was a permanence to them.

Wally tapped the page. "Try '*Wally and Arthur blinked, and there was an exit to Kingsport waiting for them.*'"

"*Please*, Cooper," Arthur said. "If we're going to do this, we're going to do it with *style*." He thought a moment and then began to write. "*Arthur Benton may have begun his career as a humble thief, but he quickly rose in the ranks of the Black Feathers using charm, wit, and a seemingly endless well of—*"

"Bull crap," Wally finished for him. "Hurry up and get to the part where we go *home*."

"You can't rush art," Arthur said.

"No," Wally said, "but I can rush *Arthur*. Now write us an exit."

Arthur tickled his chin with the quill's feather, thinking. He started a new line and read aloud. *"With a slight blip, the portal opened like a popped soap bubble. And Arthur and Wally looked with adoration upon their very own magical Kingsport."* He dropped the quill. "There. Happy? I am."

They stared at the mirror. Their reflection started to flicker. Then it popped—much like a soap bubble—revealing a familiar brick wall.

"That's Lacey Lane!" Wally said.

"Sure is!" Arthur clapped him on the shoulder. "I'd recognize it anywhere! This is where I steal necklaces for my many gentlewomen callers. Er, Liza, at least."

They stepped through the portal, and it flickered and vanished behind them, leaving nothing but bricks.

A chill ran up Arthur's spine when he realized he hadn't grabbed a single coin or collected any information from the Manor. The Rook was going to sink his talons deep.

"Um, Arthur?"

"Yeah, Cooper?"

"Does something seem . . . *off* to you?"

Arthur gazed up and down the street, all silver and shadows. It was late. The stars shined darkly. They were definitely in the Gilded Quarter, but something did feel different. Staring down Lacey Lane gave him the same kind of vertigo Wally must have felt in the spiral hallway.

Then it hit him.

"Everything's . . . *backward*," Arthur said.

Instead of the street curving up and to the right like it did back home, this street curved up and to the *left*. The shops were warped and gleamed silvery.

"I think I know where we are," Wally whispered, fear in his voice. "That woman with the snake mentioned a place called *Mirror* Kingsport . . ."

Arthur gulped as he recalled the conversation he'd had with Graham.

Wally's nearly through the Mirror now. Ready to be reversed . . .

MONSTER
GREYRIDGE

THE
PEARLED
QUARTER

COBBLER'S ROW

BANNED
THEATER

DROWNED TOWN
BOOKSTORE

FORTUNE SMELLER'S ALLEY

FOOL DREAMER
GREENHOUSE

GHOSTLY
COURTYARD

9
THE MAGE AND THE PALADIN

Things only grew stranger as Wally and Arthur walked through Mirror Kingsport's silvery streets. The buildings were not only backward but like exaggerated versions of themselves. Some stretched as long and skinny as upside-down icicles while others blobbed stoutly like failed cakes. Lampposts grew spindly against the sky, and chimney stacks belched clouds of ash across the black stars.

"You just *had* to add style to that sentence, didn't you?" Wally said. "You just had to say *magical* Kingsport? You couldn't just write *Kingsport*. You couldn't write *home*."

"It was a first draft!" Arthur said.

The tension left Wally's shoulders, like he couldn't really blame Arthur. Not for this part anyway. "I can't believe I'm about to say this, but I wish we were back in the Manor."

Arthur nodded. "Should we head to Hazelrigg and try to find another portal home?"

"I'm afraid of what we'd find there," Wally said. "But I don't have any better ideas."

A door opened in the night. The boys slowly turned as a

figure in a yellow trench coat and top hat exited a building as crooked as a lightning bolt. The figure's hands had three fingers each, and they held a scythe. Arthur and Wally hustled away, hoping to keep their necks intact.

Soon they arrived at a dress shop. A line of shadows stared with moony eyes through the large, glistening windows. The dresses on display didn't look like the ones in Kingsport, but what those dresses aspired to be. The shoulders swept up like great thorns around the collar while the trains stretched impossibly long into the dark shops. The street sign read not *Lacey* Lane but *Licey* Lane.

Arthur reflexively scratched under his vest. "Let's keep moving."

They'd almost made it to Port when something large roared at the end of the street. It sounded like boulders getting into an argument.

Wally's eyes went wide. "That's coming from the Oaker pub."

"Yep," Arthur said and gulped.

Black Feathers avoided the officers' watering hole like it was a lit stick of dynamite. How the pub would manifest in the Mirror sent Arthur's imagination spiraling.

The sounds grew louder, like a mountain splitting in two. Then a vast shadow stretched across the moonlit buildings. The figure came grunting around the corner, dragging something heavy across the cobbles.

"Back the way we came?" Wally asked.

"Uh-huh," Arthur said, already hustling away.

They hadn't made it a half block before they heard a snort

of confusion behind them. Arthur dared a peek over his shoulder and immediately regretted it. From around the corner swayed an ogre the size of a small house—a great mass of muscle and fat. One of its eyes was bruised, and blood trickled from its tusked mouth.

It had spotted them.

The ogre came bellowing down the street. Arthur and Wally ran as fast as they could, but the ogre's legs were thick and long, and its great sloshing belly only added to its momentum. When the ogre's shadow passed over them, it hefted its tree-sized club overhead and—

An alley opened in the wall beside them. "*Psst!*" a voice said. "In here!"

Arthur and Wally leapt into the alleyway just as the club came crashing down, making the ogre belly flop on the cobbles.

Arthur blinked in the darkness. It was Sekhmet, the girl with the swords, and Huamei, the boy with the braid and calligraphy brush. They wore cloaks, hoods obscuring their faces.

"What are you doing here?" Sekhmet said. "How did you escape the Abyssment?"

Arthur glanced at Wally. Where did they begin?

The ogre grunted as it pushed itself up off the cobbles.

"Wait here," Sekhmet told the boys with venom in her voice.

She stepped out of the alley, drawing her swords. Arthur couldn't see what happened next, but it sounded windy and sizzling, and the ogre's grunts were quickly replaced with peaceful snores.

Huamei smirked at Wally. "Hello, thief."

"You know this guy?" Arthur asked.

"He tried to murder me with cuckoo clocks," Wally said.

"Ah," Arthur said.

Sekhmet stepped back into the alley, holstering her swords.

"We can't stay here," she said. "The other Ogre Oakers will come to investigate."

Ogre Oakers? As if regular Oakers weren't bad enough. Arthur searched the alley, tracing a path up packing crates, ivy, and broken fire escapes to the top of the impossibly tall building. At least some things were the same in Mirror Kingsport.

"This way," he said.

Sekhmet looked like she wanted to argue, but then a herd of grunts echoed down the street. Arthur climbed the spindly building while the others followed. The climb was thrice as high as it would've been back home, but they made it panting onto the slanted roof. Wally collapsed and covered his face.

He was missing out on an unsettlingly beautiful sight. The four quarters of Mirror Kingsport looked more like an exaggerated sketch of the city than their Real counterparts. The Gilded Quarter shined like a jeweled casino. The Bliss was filled with ivory spires, and the Wretch resembled an exploded sewer main. The Port sat on a sea as black as ink, and Greyridge Mental Hospital towered as ominous as a vampire's castle, drinking up all the moon's light.

Sekhmet threw back her hood. "How did you escape the Manor?"

"Someone left our cell unlocked," Arthur said. "If I were you, I'd fire that woman with the eye patch because—"

Sekhmet patted down Arthur's pockets and was about to pat down Wally's when Wally voluntarily handed her the cell key. He seemed to be protecting that rodent in his pocket.

"Looks like Amelia keeps her job," Sekhmet said and drew her swords.

"Whoa, whoa, whoa," Arthur said. "What are you—?"

She slashed just as he squeezed his eyes shut. When he felt nothing but a warm gust, he cracked open an eye and raised his wrists to find they were bound in glowing red shackles.

Sekhmet holstered her swords. "Those magma manacles should hold until we get back to the Manor."

Arthur frowned. "Where are Cooper's *magma manacles*?"

"He hasn't lied to me yet." Sekhmet stepped to the roof's edge. "Come with me."

"Here's a better idea," Arthur said, feeling less than charming with his wrists bound. "You turn us loose in our own city after paying us handsomely for leading you to safety from those ogres."

"You're kidding, right?" Sekhmet said. "*You* were the ones who blew our cover. And we don't need two thieves to help us avoid danger."

"We could pretend we never saw them," Huamei said. "I tire of this mission and don't want it to drag on any longer."

"Okay, *your highness*," Sekhmet said. "Do you want to be the one to tell Lady Weirdwood that we left two kids from the Real in the Mirror? They could compromise the stories of this city and maybe even open up another Rift."

"Two *handsome* kids," Arthur added. "Young men, really."

"Dawn will break soon," Huamei said, gazing over the

inky sea. "We still don't know where the Rift is." He glanced at Sekhmet. "Your precious Wardenship is slipping away."

She hesitated a moment, then gave her head a shake. "I'll get these boys back to the Manor. You find the Rift. I'd check the bookstore next."

She pointed, and Arthur's eyebrows leapt. Sekhmet had pointed in the wrong direction, and Huamei hadn't corrected her. When it came to Kingsport, these two didn't know the Wretch from the Bliss.

"We can help you," Arthur said.

"Oh yeah?" Sekhmet said with disbelief.

She may have been able to see through his lies, but that didn't mean she didn't need something. And she'd just shown him how badly she wanted to complete her mission.

Arthur nodded at Wally. "Cooper here and I are celebrated members of the Black Feathers gang. We know the streets of Kingsport like the stains on our shirts." He gestured to the Mirror horizon. "Even if those shirts are turned inside out."

Wally said nothing. He was no help in situations like these.

"Lady Weirdwood wants this mission completed by dawn?" Arthur continued. "We can make that happen. Cooper and I know what it's like to disappoint a superior. Ours is a lot scarier than yours. He collects fingers, and he doesn't wear a wedding dress."

Sekhmet didn't crack a smile, but Arthur didn't waver. "We'll help you out for, say, a few choice items from that treasure room of yours. Once we find the Rift and this Fae-born thing, you can release us, and we'll all be better off for it. Whaddayasay?"

Sekhmet sighed. "I say you broke into our Manor, stole our money, and then breached the Fae, compromising the Veil's security. I don't trust you any more than I trust those ogres."

Arthur was tempted to lie to try and clinch the deal, but lies never seemed to work on Sekhmet.

"We have a personal stake in helping you too," he said. "We don't want to see any harm come to our fair city. And with the funds you give us, I'll be able to save my dad, who's being held hostage in a mental hospital."

Sekhmet looked at Wally. "Is he telling the truth?"

"I doubt it," Wally said, not meeting Arthur's eyes.

Huamei cleared his throat. "I am not opposed to accepting the thieves' assistance. I'm unaccustomed to traveling without a servant anyway."

Sekhmet looked skeptical, and Arthur felt a glimmer of hope.

"We could divide our efforts," Huamei said. "One of them could guide me through Real Kingsport while the other guides you through the Mirror. We'll finish in half the time, and you'll be awarded your little Wardenship."

"We're Kishar and Anshar," Sekhmet said. "We're supposed to stay together."

Arthur cleared his throat. "I don't know what Keester and Anchor is, but I have to disagree with Huamei here." He awkwardly threw his manacled hands around Wally's shoulders. "Cooper and I are a team. We work together or we don't work at all."

"Actually," Wally said, ducking away from Arthur, "we have plenty of experience going our separate ways."

Even though he should have seen that coming, Arthur still felt like he'd been punched in the heart.

"Fine," Sekhmet said. "We'll let you help us." She addressed Huamei. "But if we're caught, I'm telling Lady Weirdwood you transformed into your true form and forced me to let two thieves help us."

Huamei smirked and bowed his head.

"And our payment?" Arthur asked.

Sekhmet considered this. "*If* we find any treasure in the Mirror, it's yours for the keeping."

Huamei snorted and averted his gaze.

"What?" Arthur said. "Why is that funny?"

"No reason." Sekhmet pointed at Wally. "You. Quiet one. You're going to the Real to track down the Fae-born with Huamei."

Wally nodded nervously.

"And *you*." Sekhmet lifted her sword so Arthur could feel the cold metal under his chin. "You're going to stay here and help me find the Rift so I can keep an eye on you."

Arthur gulped, and the blade's sharp edge grazed his Adam's apple. He smiled. "I'm just happy to be on the team with the swords."

She dissolved his magma manacles, holstered her blade, and descended a wobbly fire escape. Arthur rubbed his wrists and stepped to the ladder, pausing to take one look back.

Huamei painted a doorway on the side of a chimney. The

brickwork opened with a goblin's mouth, revealing a bright and shining day in Real Kingsport.

Wally stepped through. He didn't bother looking back at Arthur.

MAIN STREET

Wally led Huamei through Kingsport. The sky was starting to brighten, and Wally's skin tingled to be back in his city. The damp stone of Greyridge glistened on the cliffs. The sight usually filled his heart with dread, but just seeing it in the pre-dawn light gave him hope that he might be able to save his brother.

VEIN STREET

Arthur led Sekhmet through Mirror Kingsport. The sky swirled darkly, and Arthur's skin tingled to be in this strange place. The slimy stone of Greyridge glimmered on the cliffs. The sight had always filled his heart with dread, but seeing it in the Mirror light emptied him of hope that he would ever be able to save Harry.

MISTLETOE WAY

"So you can just paint stuff into being?" Wally asked as they stepped onto the bustling street. Maybe Graham didn't belong in a mental hospital after all.

"It's not that simple," Huamei answered. "My art requires years of training and is impossible for those without royal blood. Where's the bookstore?"

Wally sighed and pointed.

GRISTLETOE WAY

"Can I carry one of your swords?" Arthur whispered as they stepped into the empty street. "I promise I'll be awesome with it."

"I wouldn't trust you with a safety pin," Sekhmet said, keeping both hands fixed firmly on her sword hilts. "Where's the bookstore?"

Arthur sighed and pointed.

CANAL STREET

They walked across the black and white cobbles, footsteps lost in the bustle of shoppers. Huamei crouched low, eyes searching the drains and underneath the carts.

"What are we looking for?" Wally asked.

"A doll," Huamei said.

Wally arched an eyebrow. "A *doll*?"

"This particular doll is not to be trifled with," Huamei said. "One touch of its lips will turn your skin to porcelain."

CARNAL STREET

They walked across the white and black cobbles, footsteps echoing against the shop fronts. Sekhmet searched the rooftops and the windows.

"What are we looking for?" Arthur whispered.

"A Rift," Sekhmet said. "Like a tear in fabric, only in the air."

Arthur snorted. "A hole?"

"It isn't the hole you should fear," Sekhmet said. "But whoever created it. And whatever crawled through it."

FIR STREET

A scream tore through the streets. It was coming from Market Square.

"That's bad, right?" Wally said.

"No," Huamei said, heading toward the scream. "That's good."

FEAR STREET

A shriek tore through the darkness. It was coming from Maggot Square.

"That's bad, isn't it?" Arthur said.

"Yeah," Sekhmet said, heading in the opposite direction. "That's bad."

Wally and Huamei ran through the streets of the Wretched Quarter, tracking the scream they'd heard. Huamei tried turning down Paradise Lane, but Wally caught him by the silken sleeve.

"Trust me," Wally said. "You don't want to go down there unless you want those fancy robes stolen off your back."

Huamei stared at Wally's hand. "Where I come from, we use our words to guide each other."

Wally released his sleeve. Funny that people were so polite in a place where they drown thieves, he thought.

They continued the long way around.

It was true that Paradise Lane was no place for a person who wanted to keep their fancy belongings. But Wally was also trying to avoid running into the Black Feathers. He was so behind on his tribute, the Rook would probably make a whole necklace out of his fingers.

Wally led Huamei up Center Street. Now that Wally was free of the Manor, his internal compass was fully operational again. The moment someone had screamed, he knew it had come from Market Square.

"How do you catch a doll you can't even touch?" he asked as they crossed crowded First Avenue.

"By an act of creativity," Huamei said, as if speaking to a child. "The doll is Fae-born. That means—"

"That someone in this city dreamt it up, right?" Wally said, remembering what Breeth had told him back in the Manor.

He slipped his hand in his pocket to make sure mousey Breeth was secure. Her fuzzy ears and pinprick breath tickled his fingertips.

"That's correct," Huamei said, clearly wondering how a mere thief could know about the Fae-born. "I'll use magic to add to its story, changing its nature and making it easier to contain. Then I'll open a portal, and we'll scare it back into the Fae."

"How do you *add to its story*?" Wally asked.

Huamei drew out his calligraphy brush. "For this particular Fae-born, I believe I'll use strings."

"Strings?"

"You'll see."

They arrived at the port, and Wally considered making a break up the cliffs to Greyridge to check on his brother. But there was no use returning to the hospital without money for the hospital bill.

Another scream rang out and Wally and Huamei ran faster, finally arriving in Market Square. It was early Wednesday morning, so the Square was packed with eager customers trying to buy the freshest fish. On the far side of the Square, panic spread like wildfire—more and more screams blooming to life every moment. The crowd cleared around a small form.

The doll.

"How's it walking?" someone shouted.

"How is it *smooching*?"

"It must be possessed!"

"Get it away from me!"

The doll looked just like the ones Wally had seen in shop windows—pink dress, blond curls, white buckled shoes—only instead of holding still and looking pretty for the customers, it toddled across the stones, arms outstretched, giving the market shoppers sweet porcelain kisses. Everywhere it toddled, another porcelain body fell. The crowd stared, not sure whether to laugh or scream, and too fascinated to run away.

"I'll weave the strings," Huamei said. "You calm these humans down."

Wally's heart skipped a beat. "*Me?* I thought I was just a guide."

"You've been promoted. Sekhmet is usually crowd control, and I have to focus on my calligraphy."

"But, but—How do I calm them down?"

Huamei sneered at the people. "Humans are gullible creatures. I will paint strings that appear to be connected to the doll, making the crowd think it's a mere puppet. You will convince them this is all a performance. And quickly. If these humans keep screaming, the Fae-born will grow more confident in its current story, and it won't adopt the new story I weave for it."

Wally suddenly felt exposed. He never did anything that

drew attention to himself. It was against his every instinct as a thief.

Another of the doll's victims fell to the cobbles.

"The sooner you act," Huamei said, "the more humans you'll save."

Before Wally could second-guess himself, he leapt on top of a crate. "Um, excuse me? Everyone?"

No one looked. They stared at the doll.

Wally cleared his throat and yelled, "LADIES AND GENTLEMEN!"

A few people glanced his way, terrified expressions on their faces. Wally's words evaporated under their gazes. But then Huamei swept his brush overhead, and strings shimmered to life above the market.

"Uh, don't be scared," he told the crowd. He thrust his hands in the air and wriggled his fingers as if they were connected to the strings. "I'm the one controlling that doll!"

The people looked from his fingers to the strings to the doll, walking by itself.

"See?" Wally called. "Just a puppet show!"

"What about them?" someone asked, pointing to the porcelain shoppers.

"They . . ." Wally said, sweat pouring down his face, "are *actors*! Yeah, actors. They're part of my troupe. And wearing the best makeup you've ever seen."

A few people chuckled. Others broke into applause. The doll continued to reach out to the crowd, making kissy faces. Sweat trickled down Huamei's brow as he continued to paint spells.

"That's right, folks!" Wally said, feeling a bit more confident. He continued to wiggle his fingers in the air. "All part of the show! Now if you'd give my puppet some space—"

"Hey!" a man said next to a poor porcelain woman. "My wife's never acted in her life!"

"Uh . . ." Wally said. "Your wife's secretly been taking acting classes, sir!"

"No, she hasn't! She hates the theater!"

"It's okay," Huamei whispered, still painting. "You don't have to get everyone to believe. There's always a skeptic."

One person chuckled. Then another. And another. And laughter blossomed through the crowd, extinguishing the screams. The people clapped and cheered and tossed coins at Wally's feet. He bowed and scooped up the coins, pouring them into the pocket opposite Breeth.

"Good work, thief," Huamei said.

Wally blushed. The word *thief* hadn't sounded as degrading this time.

"So what happens now?" he asked.

"Any moment, the strings I painted should become solid and slow the doll down," Huamei said. "The more the crowd treats it like a puppet, the more harmless its kisses will become. The people's active imaginations will outweigh that of whoever created it. Once we can safely approach the doll, I'll open a portal, and we'll drag it back to the Mirror."

Wally smiled. The few coins he'd collected wouldn't pay a fraction of Graham's hospital bill, but at least he helped save his city from another Pox-like disaster.

Clink! Clank!

The warmth left Wally's cheeks the moment he heard the distinct sound of porcelain bodies falling to the ground.

"Hold on a minute!" someone cried. "How many actors you got in your troupe?"

More and more people collapsed like dominoes. Now that the crowd saw the doll as harmless entertainment, they had drawn closer, giving it a chance to plant kisses on their ankles.

The puppet strings Huamei had painted unraveled into the sky. The doll toddled free.

Huamei leapt onto the crate, his royal air melting into shock. "It didn't work. Those strings and the crowd's imagination should have turned it into a puppet."

Wally's stomach kept tumbling. Magic was bad enough. But magic that even a magician didn't understand?

"What do we do?" he asked.

Huamei shook his head. "I would be able stop it in a heartbeat if I weren't bound."

"Bound?"

"There are *rules* that prevent me from taking on my true form," Huamei said, flexing his hand. "Human minds are fragile and could splinter if they saw it."

Wally didn't have to ask what that true form was. He'd seen Huamei's shadow in the clock hallway, the blood smeared on his lips.

"This is no ordinary Fae-born," Huamei said. "We'll have to bring the doll back to the Manor. See what Lady Weirdwood thinks."

"*Catch it?*" Wally said, heart racing even faster. "With our *hands?*"

One slip and porcelain would spread across his skin faster than the Pox.

"Do you want to get paid, thief?" Huamei asked.

Wally bit his lip, then dropped from the crate and pulled one of its boards loose, hoping to smash the doll. He pushed through the panicking crowd, but it was like trying to swim upriver.

From the other side of the Square came a gruff voice. "Quit yer panicking! Help is here!"

Wally watched as two Oakers forced their way through the crowd with their nightsticks. One of the Oakers, a hefty man who'd clearly had his nose broken a few times, patted his nightstick into his open palm.

"Fear not, folks!" he said, squinting at the doll. "That thing's made of nothin' but fragility!"

He tromped after the doll, hefted his nightstick, and brought it swooping down, cracking the doll on the side of its pretty blond head. The doll went flying, curls over shoes, doing several cartwheels through the screaming crowd until it fell, facedown, in a puddle.

There was a breath of silence, and then the crowd broke into applause. The Oaker doffed his cap and gave a deep bow. "Happy to be of service! All in a day's work, it is!"

Relief flooded through Wally.

"This isn't over," Huamei said, keeping a wary eye on the doll.

"But the doll's dead," Wally said. "The Oaker crushed it."

A woman screamed, and the Oaker jerked up from his bow. The doll pushed itself up and out of the puddle, sticking its lace-covered bum in the air and then working its pudgy porcelain hands back until it was upright on its buckled shoes. Its head rotated around its mud-spattered shoulders until it was staring over its own back. The club had shattered half the doll's face, leaving it with one eye and half a smile. It fixed its remaining blue eye on the Oaker.

"Hoo boy," the Oaker said, color draining from his cheeks.

The doll went after him, quick as a spider. The man was so startled he stumbled backward, swinging his club erratically. The other Oaker, who had stepped forward to help, was struck in the forehead and collapsed across the cobbles.

The first Oaker stumbled over his unconscious partner and sprawled flat on his back. The doll crawled up his leg and over the swell of his belly. The Oaker blubbered as the doll bent at the waist and gently planted a kiss on his big broken nose. His blubbers died away as the spreading porcelain forced his lips into a grin.

The crowd screamed and made a break for the alleys, shoving and clawing to the edges of the Square. Huamei tried pushing through the crowd, but they swept him back. Only Wally was small enough to weave his way through. He dropped the board with a clatter—it wouldn't do him any good—and removed his jacket to grab the doll.

He was about to take mousey Breeth out of his pocket when a man knocked Wally over, tearing the jacket from his hands. "*NO!*" Wally screamed, hitting the cobbles. "Breeth!"

He watched in horror as the fleeing crowd trampled his jacket.

Once the people were clear, he snatched it up and checked the pocket, fearing he'd find nothing but fur and guts inside. But the pocket was empty. He searched the Square for a tiny fuzzy shape. Breeth was nowhere to be seen.

The crowd poured down the alleys, back to their homes, where they slammed their doors. Once the last person had fled, Huamei painted a symbol that made the abandoned carts roll to the Square's exits where they tipped over, blocking him and Wally in with the doll.

Everything was quiet.

Until the doll spotted them.

"*Ma-ma!*"

Wally stepped beside Huamei, keeping an eye on the doll's movements. Its head spun like a top around its shoulders as it playfully marched toward them. With a pained look on his face, Huamei painted symbol after symbol, wrenching up stones around the doll's feet and trying to catch it with loose ropes. But the doll eluded the spells with ease, dodging left and right at an unnatural speed, as it continued to march toward them, its one blue eye gleaming.

Huamei let his brush hang by his side.

"We should split up," Wally said, as if they were about to pickpocket a mark. "One of us will keep it distracted. The other will grab it from behind."

Huamei nodded.

Wally prepped his jacket while Huamei snagged a loose potato sack. Huamei broke right while Wally ran left. Relief flooded through Wally when the doll chased after Huamei. The magician had dealt with this kind of stuff, after all.

Wally pivoted and was about to sneak up behind the doll when it plucked its head from its neck with a small *pop!* and threw it at Huamei. The blond ringlets sailed through the air, and the Novitiate barely had time to turn before the doll's severed head planted a kiss right on his forehead. Huamei's mouth stretched into a smile, and he fell over flat.

Wally skidded to a stop. The doll collected its head, popped it back on its shoulders, and then flashed him its broken smile. Wally's skin ran cold.

"*Ma-ma!*" the doll's voice echoed through the empty Square.

"I'm not your mama," Wally whispered.

The doll came at him like a blond bolt of lightning. Every inch of Wally wanted to flee and never look back. Instead, he took a deep breath and ran *toward* the doll. In the center of the Square, he threw his jacket . . . and missed.

He leapt over the doll as it reached up for him, its porcelain fingers brushing the bottoms of his shoes. Wally tumbled in a somersault on the other side, landing on his stomach. He felt the doll scramble up his pants and along his back. Wally rolled, trying to throw the doll off, but its tiny shoes ran around his torso like a spinning log, then continued to march up his stomach.

This was it. Wally would spend the rest of his days made of porcelain. Maybe the Oakers would stick his frozen body in Graham's cell.

The doll had reached his chest when a fuzzy form leapt in front of its face.

"*Ma-ma?*" the doll said, head rotating toward the mouse.
Breeth.

The doll seemed as curious about adorable animals as her youthful looks implied. It hopped off Wally's chest and chased after the mouse. The doll was fast, but on four paws, Breeth was faster.

Wally leapt to his feet. "This way, Breeth!"

The mouse bounded back toward Wally, and the doll followed. Wally crouched low, preparing to throw his jacket more accurately this time. But before Breeth could reach him, the doll popped off one of its arms and hurled it into her path. The tiny arm clinked and clattered across the stones and then came to a stop, creating a barrier before the mouse. Breeth tried to leap over it, but the porcelain hand closed its pudgy fingers around her tail.

"No!" Wally screamed, running toward them.

Breeth's paws scrambled to escape, but the porcelain fist held tight. The one-armed doll caught up to the mouse and crouched over it just as Wally tossed his jacket over them both. He scooped his jacket up as the doll struggled inside. "*Ma-ma, Ma-ma, Ma-ma!*"

Wally crouched and gently turned the bundle around, hoping Breeth had escaped from the doll's grip before getting kissed. After a couple of turns, several fuzzy shards tumbled out of the jacket's sleeve, clinking across the cobblestones.

The mouse had turned to porcelain. And it had shattered.

"Oh no," he said. "*Breeth.*"

He heard a shudder behind him. One of the overturned apple carts was crying.

Wally ran to the cart. "Breeth? Is that you?"

"Wally! It was *awful!* My ears grew stiff. And then my neck and my body and my tail! And I was inside its thoughts when it . . . when it—"

Wally leaned against the cart's handle, relieved to hear Breeth's voice again.

"I never want to do that again," she whispered, her cart shivering.

"You won't have to, Breeth," he said. "Never again."

Wally stared in shock around the Square—at the unconscious Oakers, at the porcelain shoppers, at Huamei grinning his frozen grin—all while trying to keep the doll from escaping his jacket and patting Breeth's wooden side as she sniffled.

Now what was he supposed to do?

11
MIRROR KINGSPORT

Arthur and Sekhmet crouched in an alley, eyes wide and fixed on the street. One of her hands was clamped firmly over his mouth, while the other pointed a sword toward the alley's end.

Arthur held his breath as the *thing* rolled past. It was as yellow as a sickly moon, and its body was made of feelers, like withered elephant trunks. They suctioned along the cobblestones, snorfling and oozing as the creature rolled its great mass through the twilight.

The thing paused at the alley's end. Sekhmet squeezed Arthur's mouth tighter. One of the feelers sniffed toward them, and Arthur and Sekhmet held still as stone. When the feeler didn't find anything, it retreated, and the creature continued down the street, like some deep-sea anemone searching for prey.

It was only when the sniffing faded completely that Sekhmet released Arthur's mouth.

"That was unnecessary," he said, stretching his jaw. "I wouldn't make a sound around something like *that*."

Sekhmet sheathed her sword. "Have control over that mouth of yours, do you?"

"I don't talk that much," Arthur said.

"Oh good." She stepped into the street. "I'll look forward to complete silence for the rest of this mission then."

Arthur bit his lip.

"Where's the bookstore?" she asked.

Arthur led her up Meadow Street—that is, *Mildew* Street—through First (Thirst) and Second (Fecund) Avenues. They climbed toward the black, sparkling stars, keeping behind trash cans and scaling fire escapes to avoid being spotted. The path was familiar to Arthur, yet not—like something in a dream.

They passed a bank that resembled a hunched and looming giant, glaring at the city with its dark, windowed eyes. The corners where street musicians often performed spouted with fountains of light, filling the sky with images of hope and heartbreak. And Arthur could have sworn he spotted a flock of black, feathered shadows, perched on the laundry lines and leering at them with their all too human eyes.

He was proud of himself for keeping silent when there were so many wonders to discuss. In fact, he managed to not say a single word . . . for half a block.

"So how do I become a Novitiate?"

"*You* don't," said Sekhmet.

"Aw, come on. I'd be *great* at this stuff. I'll be . . . What did you call 'em? Caviar and Antsy?"

"Kishar and Anshar."

"Yeah! Those! What are those?"

"Mage and paladin," she said. "Huamei uses painting for his art. I use swords. He casts spells. I fight things. That's why we're supposed to stick together."

"Great. So how do I become the Kisser to your Asher?"

"First, you pronounce them correctly." Sekhmet was distracted, searching the oddly sloping rooftops for something. "After a child is selected by Lady Weirdwood, they study the delicate Balance between the Real and the Fae until they understand it as well as something so complicated can be understood. Then the true work begins. Novitiates train in their art for as many years as it takes for them to pass a test given by Lady Weirdwood."

A great sloshing sound made her go flat against a building, pulling Arthur with her. They peeked around the corner and spotted the bookshop where, in Real Kingsport, Arthur had stolen every new installment of Garnett Lacroix's adventures . . . or had before the owner threatened to drown him in ink. Strangely, the Mirror bookstore was flooded with black liquid, sloshing in the windows but remaining perfectly flat against the open door. In the murk, a cuttlefish handed out books to swimming customers, rainbows rippling along its many tentacles.

"Wait here," Sekhmet said. "And do not move. Don't even look around. Unless you don't mind dying. Painfully."

She dove into the bookstore and vanished in the inky darkness. Arthur held his breath and waited. A few moments later, she exited, gasping for breath and dripping black. With a single swipe of her glowing sword, she cleaned herself of ink.

"Not here either," she said, disappointed.

"That was *amazing*!" Arthur said. "You just dove in, like—"

"Where's your theater?" she interrupted.

Arthur gestured. "Right this way, madam captor." He led her up Center (Centaur) Street. "So what does this Rift look like?"

"Imagine a hole in fabric."

Arthur stuck his finger through a hole in his shirt. "Don't need to."

"A Rift is like that, only hanging in the air. When one opens in the Mirror, the Real bleeds through it, turning everything near the Rift back to normal. The buildings straighten their backs, the Mirror citizens look human again, and the bookshops won't be flooded with ink."

"Got it," Arthur said, scanning the street. "We need to find the patch of normal in this garden of oddities."

They reached the Grand (Banned) Theater, whose giant façade was composed of two giant, hideous masks that laughed and wept into the street. Sekhmet made Arthur wait outside again while she bought a ticket and went inside. She exited a few moments later, looking a little disturbed but shaking her head.

"Where next?" Arthur asked.

"That's the question of the hour," she said. "Rifts usually materialize because a mage from the Order of Eldar tears a hole in the Veil between the Real and the Fae. They tend to target areas where the Veil is thinnest because it's easier to break there. Wardens are trained to search places where people use the most imagination. Theaters and bookshops. Orphanages and operas. But I've checked all of them, and they're as solid and strange as ever." She huffed. "My parents would have had this Rift sewn up in less than an hour."

"Imagination, eh?" Arthur said. "Why didn't you say so? Fortune-Teller's Alley is this way!"

They climbed to the top of a roof and gazed out over River (Reaper) Road. Beastly lovers exited the Fortune-Smeller's, holding hands and smooching—far too wetly and noisily for Arthur's taste. There was no Rift.

"I'd pass that Novitiate test of yours in a heartbeat, you know," Arthur said, leading Sekhmet across the rooftops and brainstorming where to look next.

"Think so, huh?" Sekhmet said.

"Yeah! I mean, this is all standard fairy-tale stuff, right? A world in peril. Fantastical creatures run amok. I've read a hundred books like that! Here, I'll prove it."

He examined the strange landscape, trying to solve the riddle of this world so Sekhmet might see him as something more than a glorified tour guide.

"It seems to me," he said loftily, "that this *Mirror* is a reflection of the citizens of Kingsport's hopes and fears. These are not the buildings of my fair city, but how the people *imagine* them. It's like Kingsport as seen in a distorted photograph. Or a fun house mirror."

Sekhmet's face remained neutral as they gazed over Willow (Wallow) Street. The gambling dens were pasted with posters showing animals swimming in gold. But the sounds behind the doors were more like the noise of animals going to slaughter. Arthur and Sekhmet departed quickly, descending the opposite side of the building.

Arthur continued his theory. "An important building like the bank hulks toward the stars while the poorhouse droops toward the ground. The people of Kingsport are afraid of Oakers, so in Mirror Kingsport, the officers grow to ogre-ish proportions."

He led her down the knotted twists and turns of the back alleys, like holes through cheese, taking a shortcut past the orphanage where a tarantula fed soup to a line of little birds, its fangs drooling as it watched them with its eight black eyes.

"Meanwhile," Arthur continued, "the casinos appear to be paradise but are actually slaughterhouses, Fortune-Smeller's Alley is filled with empty promises of love, and the dresses on Lacey—er, *Licey* Lane grow as ridiculous as bird feathers. You call it a *Mirror* because it reflects not only the city but all of the dreams and nightmares the citizens hold in their hearts."

They passed the green glass walls of the city's greenhouse, the Emerald Roof, which twined with vines that slithered like serpents with thorns and pulsed with red poisonous bulbs. A manhole cover burst open, and a bloodthirsty plant lunged at Arthur. Sekhmet decapitated it easily.

"Thanks," Arthur said, trying to pretend like he hadn't almost had a heart attack. He took a breath and regained his train of thought. "*Finally*, that unsettling ball of elephant trunks we saw earlier must've been some great fear shared by the people in Kingsport. Let's see . . ." He thought a moment, then snapped his fingers. "Aha! Debt! All of the unpaid bills and overdue rent are constantly rolling through the city, searching for delinquents."

Sekhmet nodded. "Not bad, kid."

Arthur wasn't sure whether to feel flattered for the compliment or insulted because she called him *kid*.

"Just one little correction," she said. "You used words like *imagination* and *fun house* and *photograph*. But those are harmless. That would be like me referring to a knife in your heart as an insult. We're walking through the *literal* hopes and fears of Kingsport—be it a mountain of gold or a ghost in your attic. Not to mention its legends and stories."

She pointed to a black cloud spewing from a factory. The cloud was made of tiny fanged mouths, which descended onto the city, hoping to chew up whatever lungs breathed them in.

"If people have a nightmare or write a tall tale in the Real," Sekhmet said, "it comes to life *here* and could murder us."

"Jeez." Arthur rubbed his throat. "And I thought I'd read killer poetry before."

"And that ball of feelers?" Sekhmet said. "That wasn't debt. Debt manifests as quicksand in the cobblestones and will swallow you as fast as falling. The city will chew you up and spit your bones into the sewer."

"Oh," Arthur said, his pockets suddenly feeling light. "What was that thing then?"

"That was a disease of some sort."

A coldness spread through Arthur's chest. *The Pox.* That monster had slipped one of its many dripping snouts down his mom's throat and stolen her life.

"But—the Pox was wiped out four years ago. We have a vaccine for it and everything."

"I'm sure you do," Sekhmet said. "But there is no vaccination for *fear*."

Arthur walked in silence, imagining what would have happened had that thing's feeler caught them.

"Don't beat yourself up for not figuring all this stuff out," Sekhmet said. "After we sew up this Rift, wherever it is, you'll return to your life as a thief, and it won't make any difference whether you understood the Mirror or not."

This pulled Arthur out of his dark thoughts. "I can't just go back to my old life." He stared at the stars, which had lines connecting the constellations. The crab was scratching the bear's back. "Not after I've walked through an actual fairy tale. Kingsport will be so . . . depressing."

"You should be grateful to have a normal childhood," Sekhmet said.

Arthur was about to argue that his childhood was anything but normal, but she wasn't finished.

"Life in Weirdwood Manor is demanding. We're constantly leaping from city to city, catching Fae-born, securing Rifts, and fighting the Order of Eldar, who want to poke holes in the Veil for their own personal gain. I didn't have the luxuries that most kids did. No hobbies. No friendships besides my fellow Wardens. People close to me have died defending the Manor."

"Then why do it?"

"My family has dedicated their lives to Weirdwood for sixteen generations. It's been my honor to serve the Wardens since I was five."

Arthur quirked an eyebrow. "If I'd joined the Black Feathers that young, I definitely would have made Talon by now. Why are you still a Novitiate?"

Sekhmet whirled on him. "For your information, I was the youngest person Lady Weirdwood ever granted full Wardenship."

"Jeez, sorry," Arthur said. "Then what happened?"

Her gaze fell to the ground. "I . . . proved I wasn't worthy." She took a deep breath. "Don't ask me any more questions. I need to concentrate."

She quickened her pace, and Arthur followed at a distance.

Surely, all this information he'd gleaned from Sekhmet would be enough for the Rook to release Harry. So long as Arthur could scrape up enough money in the Mirror City to pay Harry's debt. But Arthur was starting to feel hesitant about sharing treasure or information with the leader of the Black Feathers. Arthur would keep it all to himself if he thought he could save Harry *and* become a Novitiate like Sekhmet, replacing a life of thieving and desperation with magic and adventure.

"Well, it will be my honor to serve the Wardens as well," Arthur said. "And to eventually rise to the lofty position of Lady Weirdwood—minus the wedding dress, of course. All we have to do is wipe out this Order of Eldar, right? They don't sound too tough. More like a bunch of old people with canes and wooden teeth."

Sekhmet snorted.

"Did I just make you laugh?"

"I'm just imagining what the Order would do to you if you ever met them."

That shut Arthur up for a while.

They arrived at the Ghastly Courtyard, where the dreams

of hundreds of condemned Black Feathers took wing into the sky instead of being hanged. Sekhmet made Arthur stay put while she walked the perimeter. She returned a minute later, shaking her head.

"Why do you keep making me wait outside?" Arthur asked. "Why can't I join you?"

"You're not cloaked like I am. You stand out. If some of the more dangerous Mirror citizens realize you're Real, they'll eat you. Or worse, turn you into a pet."

Arthur's eyes widened, but Sekhmet didn't notice.

"Where's your Shopping District?" she asked. "If we're going to search the more populated areas, we need to get you a cloak and me a Turkish delight cappuccino."

* * *

The Shopping District—er, *Slopping District*—was overrun with beastly shoppers—tusked and fanged, scaled and feathered, squawking and roaring as loud as a zoo fire.

"Quick," Sekhmet whispered. "Pretend you're grieving."

Arthur hid his face in his hands as she threw a cloaked arm around his shoulders, hiding him from view. From that point forward, the Slopping District was nothing but sounds and scents. The clink of coins blended with snarls and purrs and the wet slop of unsettling wares. Through his fingers, Arthur could smell wafts of desert incense, sweaty jungle air, and something cold and heavy hauled from the ocean's depths.

"Here's the shop," Sekhmet said. "Hide behind this trash can. And remember. No moving. No looking. Unless you want a painful death."

Arthur slumped into the shadow behind the trash, feeling like a disobedient child. Sekhmet entered the shop, which was called Peevish Peter's Cloaks & Masks. It was run by a giant creature with an elongated snout and overlapping golden scales covering its body from head to foot. "*Hhhow can I hhhelp you, mithhh,*" the pangolin asked, tongue slipping in and out of its snout.

Arthur remembered Sekhmet's warning and looked away. He was trying his best to keep his eyes on the cobblestones when he heard a voice—a familiar voice, comically high-pitched.

"Ladies and gentlemen, boys and girls! Gather round for a tale so true it will leave you breathless!"

Arthur peered around the trash can and saw a puppet theater, just like the ones in Market Square. But instead of a fantastical backdrop of dragons and castles, the theater showed a plain city street. And instead of puppets performing, it was just a hand.

Graham? Arthur thought. Impossible. Wally's brother was still locked up in Greyridge. And yet, how many people mimicked a naked puppet when they spoke?

An audience gathered around the smaller theater.

"This story takes place in a different world," Graham's hand said in a quiet, urgent voice. "In a world where your socks don't slither away like snakes every time you try to put them on."

"Ooooohhhhhh," the children in his audience said.

Arthur blinked. Not children. But a duckling, a piglet, and an egg with two scaly legs and a tail poking through the shell.

Graham's hand continued. "A world in which humans locked up an innocent boy because they knew his drawings showed the *truth*."

The piglet snorted. "They locked him up for *art*? Is that really *real*?"

The hand looked down, insulted. "As real as you or me."

Wally would want to know how his brother had escaped Greyridge and made it all the way to the Mirror City. It might even place Arthur back in Wally's good graces. So Arthur slipped out from behind the trash can and crept toward the theater.

But the moment he was in the open, the hand snapped up and looked right at him.

"Arthur!" Graham cried. "You made it!"

The critter kids turned and stared. So did their beastly parents, whose lips curled into snarls. But before they could come after him, a cloak swept around his shoulders.

"Did I forget to warn you that you could be *killed* in this place?" Sekhmet asked, hustling him away from the theater.

"I know, I know," Arthur said. "But—"

"Don't argue. Just come on. We need to find the Rift. It's almost morning, and I should have located it by now." She stared across the sketch of an ocean to the horizon, beginning to glow with the eraser of dawn. "This doesn't make sense."

Arthur stared back toward Graham's puppet theater. "Tell me about it."

* * *

Arthur led Sekhmet through the Golden and Pearled Quarters, searching for the Rift in less obvious places, like the spice and bicycle shops. But everywhere they went, the sky was as solid as a well-woven shirt.

The animal constellations started to die in the predawn light. Sekhmet was becoming more visibly frustrated.

"Cheer up!" Arthur said. "Enjoy this beautiful morning! And how handsome I look in this cloak you bought me!"

It was made from golden scales, shed from the pangolin shopkeep.

"Apologies for my *mood*," she said sarcastically. "I'm just trying to protect your entire city from being turned to porcelain by an infectious *doll*."

Arthur stopped walking. "The doll with the sapphire eyes."

"Have you seen it?" Sekhmet asked.

"No. But I heard a conversation about a doll in the Stormcrow Pub back in the Real. Is *that* the Fae-born?"

"Of course! Why didn't you mention this before?"

"I thought the guy was off his rocker!" Arthur said, quickening his pace. "Don't worry. The Stormcrow isn't far."

***

Mirror Stormcrow was the most twisted building Arthur had seen in the Mirror. Its windows stretched like giant smiling teeth. Purple flames threw maniac shadows against the fogged panes. The shadows laughed and screamed and plunged knives into one another's backs.

Arthur crouched behind a dribbling fire hydrant, fearing one of the monstrous customers might spot him, even in his cloak. The pub's clapboard sign creaked in the night. It read *Stormcrow*.

"Why didn't the name change?" Arthur asked.

But Sekhmet didn't hear him. She was already approaching the entrance.

"*What are you doing?*" he hissed after her.

"My job," she said, glancing over her shoulder. "I thought you said you were an expert on this stuff."

Arthur couldn't get his legs to move. Why was he so much more afraid of the Stormcrow than he was of the rest of the Mirror City? Probably because he knew what horrors thieves dreamt up at night.

"Hmm," Sekhmet said as she stepped inside. "Guess you aren't Novitiate material after all."

Outrage brought Arthur to his feet. He tried to summon bravery as he approached Mirror Stormcrow. He had his charm. And good looks. And maybe a Mirror version of Liza would be inside to give him cider.

He pushed open the door and froze. The pub was in chaos. It looked like every predator and scavenger had escaped the zoo and were wreaking havoc. Giant carrion beetles dueled one another with serrated legs. Three squealing warthogs broke open a cask with their tusks and drank their fill of smoky liquid. A circle of hyenas feasted on a zebra in a green suit. The hyenas' whooping laughter made Arthur's heart shake.

"No Rift," he said. "Let's go."

"Wait," Sekhmet said, catching his arm. "The Rift could be small. Just big enough for a doll to fit through. We need to check under the tables." She tugged his hood lower on his face. "Stay calm. The Fae-born can smell panic."

"Knowing that makes it *worse*!" he mumbled as they headed in.

Arthur tried to avoid the hungry eyes in the pub by gazing downward and just managed not to trip over the Venus flytraps growing through the floorboards. Shuddering, he looked up and found buzzard-headed men glaring down from the chandelier. Nowhere was safe to look.

Sekhmet made her way toward the back of the pub. Arthur was about to join her when a squawk spun him around. A raven-headed girl held a pencil and pad between the feathers of her wing, waiting to take his order.

"*Liza?*" he whispered. "Is that you?"

The bird girl quirked her head. A group of wolves snarled, and she waddled over to their table where she regurgitated a steaming pile of worms. The wolves began to feast, and Arthur looked away before he regurgitated something himself.

He joined Sekhmet at the bar where a blond-haired lizard cleaned mugs.

"Find that Rift yet?" Arthur whispered.

"No." Sekhmet looked distracted. "Do you smell that?"

Arthur glanced back at the bird waitress. "All I smell is bird puke."

"It smells like a forge," Sekhmet said. "Weirdwood's blacksmith smelled like that. Her name was Rose. She created my swords and taught me everything she knew about fighting before—before she died."

"Oh," Arthur said. "But if she died, that can't be her smell, right?"

Sekhmet shook her head. "Smells last longer in the Mirror

because they're closely connected to memory. What would Rose have been doing here?"

BOOM!

The Mirror pub shook as if struck by a cannonball. The scavengers stopped fighting and feasting and turned their eyes toward the back door. The pub grew as silent as a cemetery.

BOOM!

The back door was painted just like the one in the Real Stormcrow: a black bird, beak shrieking, wings spread, claws poised for the attack.

BOOM!

With each deafening blow, the door splintered outward, threatening to release whatever was inside. The wolves whimpered. The carrion beetles curled into their shells. Even the buzzards shivered in the rafters.

The booming ceased, and the scavengers slowly returned to their revelry. But a molten fear had crept through Arthur's veins. If the human Rook cast a feathered shadow over every heart in Real Kingsport, then what was the Mirror Rook like? Arthur imagined a giant bill, as black as night and as sharp as a scythe, snipping off his appendages one by one before piercing Harry straight through the heart.

A caiman customer dropped coins onto the bar, scaring

Arthur so badly he nearly jumped out of his skin. The blond-haired lizard barkeep handed the caiman a smoky stein, but before she could collect the coins, she grew distracted by two hyenas getting into a snarling argument over the zebra carcass.

The coins gleamed in the purple firelight. Arthur bit his lip. There was only one thing that would satisfy the Rook. One thing that would convince the gang leader to release Harry and let Arthur keep all of his appendages. Arthur slid his hand across the bar, curled his fingers around the coins, and brought them into his lap.

But then Arthur felt something strange. The coins seemed to turn papery in his hand. He looked down and found he was holding a book. A Garnett adventure he'd never seen before: *Garnett Lacroix and the Infinite Heist*. When Arthur tried to open it, the book turned inside out into a fancy new cap. Then the hat filled with golden liquid as it reshaped itself into a frothing mug of cider . . .

Arthur glanced around the rest of the pub. None of the creatures' money was transforming. He looked back at his hands as the cider twined into a pet ferret and then a dagger and then a fake mustache and then a dozen other things in quick succession before bursting into a cloud of silver that drifted to the ground.

Arthur held his silver-dusted fingers out to Sekhmet, who was still lost in thought.

"You promised I could keep any treasure we found here," he said.

"Right," she said, glancing at his fingers. "About that. Mirror money can't hold its shape when someone from the

Real touches it. Your imagination transforms it into all of the things you dream of buying. After several transformations, it grows overwhelmed and self-destructs."

Arthur shook the remaining silver dust onto the floor. Invisible claws tightened around his heart. "You ripped me off! I showed you around the city. Now I need my pay."

"No. I told you that you could keep any money you found here. I just neglected to tell you that you couldn't bring it back to your world."

"I thought we were partners," Arthur said.

Sekhmet scoffed. "Where in the world did you get that idea?"

Arthur felt stupid. This was why Harry told him to only look out for himself. Arthur had let his guard down, and he had wasted time helping a liar who had no interest in helping him.

He needed to get away from Sekhmet. But how? He could try to instigate a fight between the warthogs and those hyenas . . . But no. He didn't speak their language. Maybe he could pull back Sekhmet's hood so the beastly customers chased after her, giving him a chance to escape . . . But no. The Gentleman Thief would never do something so cruel.

Even if he could come up with an escape, then what? Where would he go?

And then he saw something that didn't exist in the Real Stormcrow . . . though it was certainly joked about. A big jar sat on the corner of the counter. But instead of being filled with pickled eggs, the jar was floating with pickled *toes*. Dishonest Desmond had made up a story about how he'd found a toe in the pickle jar once, and now there they were, just waiting for someone daring enough to try one.

Of course. Why hadn't Arthur thought of it before? If this was the imaginary version of Kingsport, then . . .

The fear in his muscles melted. He knew just where to go. He just needed to find a way out of this cursed pub first. If his theory was right, and the Mirror contained what he thought it did, then he could pull off heroic feats of bravery here. Arthur's brain was an encyclopedia of heroic tricks. He looked up at the old rusty chandelier and grinned.

"Good luck finding that Rift on your own," he said to Sekhmet.

"What?" Sekhmet said. "What are you talking about?"

Arthur leapt onto the bar. "Ladies and gentlemen! Warthogs and buzzards! May I please have your attention?"

"What are you *doing*?" Sekhmet whispered, trying to tug him down by his cloak.

Arthur threw back his hood, revealing his face. Snarls and hisses erupted around the pub. "Who wants their very own pet?"

"Congratulations, idiot," Sekhmet said, drawing her swords and hopping onto the bar beside him. "You just got us killed."

The scavengers lunged as Arthur leapt from the bar and grabbed onto the rusted chandelier, swinging across the pub and over the heads of the snarling creatures toward the exit. He was almost home free when a buzzard in the rafters pecked at the rusted chain, snapping it.

"Oh no," Arthur said before he fell screaming right into the writhing mass of beasts.

He was nearly overcome with fangs and claws and drool when a fiery wind swept the creatures away. Arthur leapt to his feet and kicked open the front door. He glanced back long enough to see Sekhmet slicing her swords, creating whirlwinds of flame before he fled into the street.

He sprinted downhill, through Centaur and Thirst, searching the gutters as he went. When he found what he was looking for, he skidded to a stop. It was nothing more than a sewer drain, collecting the runoff from the hill. And yet, that drain didn't exist in Real Kingsport.

Above the grate was a lamppost, carved with a daffodil. Just the sight of it made the Rook's invisible talons release Arthur's heart. Arthur had never actually seen that daffodil. But he had *read* about it hundreds of times.

Back in the pub, Sekhmet gave a war cry, swinging her swords and creating sizzling gusts that charred the door and shook the windows. The pub door burst open.

"Arthur!" Sekhmet screamed. "Come back! It's not safe!"

But Arthur was already crawling into the sewer, a smile spreading across his lips. If the Mirror was where every imagined thing came to life, then naturally it would contain the hideout of a certain Gentleman Thief.

"*Arthur!*" Sekhmet called. "You don't know what you're doing!"

Arthur didn't care. He was off to meet his hero.

12
THE MOUSE'S FUNERAL

Breeth wasn't used to dying. Even though she'd done it three times now.

This most recent death had brought back painful memories of her first. Of her *own* death. She recalled the moment when her life had seeped out of her ten-year-old body and into the wooden hilt of the sacrificial knife. Breeth hadn't known where she was. Everything had felt upside down and claustrophobic and violent, violent, *violent*. She'd leapt out of the knife, whirling and tumbling through the air, before landing in a floorboard, then creaking up a wall.

It was only when she blinked open the knotted whorls of the Manor's ceiling and saw her own body below that she realized what had happened. And that was how Breeth had come to possess the Manor. Light as a feather one moment. Heavy as a house the next.

But this newest death hadn't been hers. It had been the mouse thing's. Breeth had promised to take care of the poor little creature. But now it was dead. Lying on the cobbles of Market Square. All in pieces.

Breeth stifled a sob and tucked herself inside an apple that had spilled from an overturned cart. She tried to find comfort in its round shape, in the seeds of her core, in the chubby worm happily munching away at her sweet insides. It didn't work.

Wally seemed to be in as much shock as she was. He sat on the cobbles, staring at porcelain Huamei as the doll struggled to escape his jacket.

A whistle screeched up Center Street, making Wally jump to his feet.

"*Oakers*," he whispered. "Breeth! I need your help."

She shrank into the seeds of the apple.

"Can you get one of these carts back on its wheels? Huamei used them to block the exits, and they're too heavy for me to lift."

Breeth peeked through the shine on the skin of the apple. If Wally got caught, then he wouldn't be able to help find her killer. Besides, he was too nice to be locked up. She gathered courage from the happy worm and then exited the apple, seeped along a vein of moss between the cobbles, and entered a tipped-over cart, jostling it until it flipped upright.

Wally stuffed his jacket and the doll into one of the cart's compartments. The doll banged against the wood, but its tiny fists weren't nearly as powerful as its kisses. Next, Wally hefted porcelain Huamei, dragging him across the cobblestones. He managed to tip him up onto the cart right as the Oakers came tromping up the opposite street.

"You! Boy! Stay right there!"

Wally hopped onto the cart. "Breeth, can you roll us out of here?"

Breeth felt too drained too move.

Wally patted the handle of the cart, which kind of felt like her ear. "I can't imagine what that was like for you," he said, trying to calm the panic in his voice, "being inside that mouse when it died. Would you tell me all about it once we're safe and sound?"

She sniffed, and the whole cart shuddered.

"We can have a funeral for the mouse too if you'd like," he said.

The idea soothed Breeth's planks a bit. "We need to bring its body, then."

Wally rubbed his lips and stared back at the mouse's body. The Oakers had almost cleared the cart. "Okay," he said.

He sprinted across the Square and had barely managed to scoop up the mouse's pieces when an Oaker called out, "You! Stay right there! We know you were the one controlling that doll! You're under arrest!"

Wally leapt back onto the cart just as the Oakers trooped into the Square. Breeth spun her wheels and hauled them down the street, easily outrunning the Oakers, who seemed very out of shape.

"I can't believe I'm saying this," Wally said, voice jostling, "but I think we have to go back to the Manor. I don't know how else to get rid of this doll and save Huamei."

Breeth could only sniff in agreement. The doll continued to pound against the compartment, like a heartbeat trying to break through her wooden rib cage.

* * *

The moment they reached Hazelrigg, Wally leapt off the cart and reached for the demon face decorating the door. His hand froze. "I don't have the knocker."

He pounded on the door. There was no response. Breeth creaked out of the cart and into the door, but all she found on the other side was a burnt-out living room.

"Hello?" Wally called. "Huamei's been hurt! And I caught the Fae-born!"

His pounding caught the attention of an old lady down the street. "Boy! What're you about? There's nothin' in that house but ghosts and ashes!"

Wally started to beat at the door with both fists now. "*Lady Weirdwood!*"

The door flew open. It was Amelia, the redheaded doctor with the eye patch.

"I caught the doll," Wally said, pointing to the pounding compartment.

Amelia saw Huamei's frozen grin and her eye went wide. Breeth creaked into the familiar floorboards of the Manor's foyer as Amelia and Wally carried Huamei inside.

Amelia flashed her one eye at the woman down the street. "You! You didn't see nothing but ghosts and ashes, yeah?"

The woman's jaw started to shake. Amelia slammed the door shut.

* * *

After swirling through some of Ludwig's carvings to soothe her aching spirit, Breeth found Wally in the War Room, dipping lemon cookies in bergamot tea. She made her way down a woolen tapestry and used a tassel to tap him on the shoulder.

He jumped, nearly spilling his tea. "Don't sneak up on me like that!"

"Sorry," she said from a woven lamb, even though ghosts couldn't really do anything but sneak.

Wally sighed and gazed at the ceiling. "I never thought I'd be happy to be back here."

"Beats being murdered by a doll, I guess," Breeth said sadly.

He reached out and gave her tassel hand a squeeze, which made her feel a bit better.

A moment later, Lady Weirdwood came swishing into the room in her wedding gown, her golden-brown snake coiled around her shoulders.

"Managed to escape my Abyssment too, eh?" she said.

Wally moved to stand.

The old woman waved him to sit down. "Finish your tea. From what I hear, you've earned it."

Wally sat, looking a little shocked. He clearly hadn't received much praise in his life. Lady Weirdwood sat beside him. The snake uncoiled from her arm and aimed its blind pink eyes at Wally, forked tongue flicking. Wally scooted away.

"So, Wilberforce," Lady Weirdwood said, "tell me how you managed to catch a Fae-born without using magic."

Between bites of cookie, Wally told her about the doll incident. Breeth was grateful that he left out details about her, claiming he'd caught the Fae-born with the first toss of his jacket.

When the story was finished, Lady Weirdwood's eyes wrinkled with concern. "A Fae-born that's immune to story weaving?"

In all her time at the Manor, Breeth had never seen the old architect so troubled.

"We'll need to find the doll's creator," the lady said. "Did it exhibit any behaviors that could provide us clues?"

"What do you mean?" Wally asked.

"That doll sprang from someone's imagination," the old woman said, tapping her temple. "There are no creatures on earth that can turn people to porcelain with a kiss. If we can find the person who dreamt it up in the first place, we can stop them from causing further destruction."

Wally had flashbacks of the events in the Square. "It . . . acted like a normal doll."

Lady Weirdwood nodded grimly. "Well," she said, slapping her knees, "considering that you *refuse* to let me keep you locked up and safe, and we don't currently have the resources to keep you under surveillance, I suppose you can return to your city. The danger should be over now. The Fae-born is caught, and Sekhmet should have the Rift sewn up shortly."

"I can leave?" Wally said, swallowing the last of his cookie. "Just like that?"

"Just like that," Lady Weirdwood said.

Wally stared at his tea and didn't budge.

"You're surprised that I'm releasing you even though you tried to steal from us?"

Wally nodded.

Lady Weirdwood breathed deep. "How is it that people

have built a system where so many children go hungry, even though there's plenty of food to go around, and yet they punish those who take desperate measures to eat? If any of Kingsport's wealthier citizens went a day without bread, they'd throw a brick through the first pastry shop they saw. And yet they're disgusted when the poor do it. It boggles the mind."

Wally studied her face. "I've never heard an adult say that before."

Lady Weirdwood smiled. "You should keep better company."

Wally looked back at his tea.

"What's on your mind?" Lady Weirdwood asked.

"Um, Sekhmet promised Arthur that we could keep any money we found in the Mirror." He cleared his throat. "We were looking to get paid, ma'am."

"Sekhmet promised that, did she?" Lady Weirdwood said, clearly disappointed in her Novitiate. "Well, your friend is in for a rude awakening. Any treasure he finds will transform and explode the moment he touches it. The only thing he'll bring back are treasures of the mind. And that's if he makes it out at all."

"Oh."

"I might be able to help you in another way," she said. "But first"—she gathered her wedding dress and stood with a grunt—"I have errands to run."

Wally tried to keep up as the old woman whisked out of the War Room and through the Manor's halls, Breeth creaking beneath their footsteps. First, the lady went to the entrance to the Abyssment and spoke to a guard with milky-white eyes.

"Is the Fae-born secure?"

"Yes, Lady," the guard said in a haunted voice.

"Good. Report back if it exhibits more strange behavior. *Other* than act like an infectious doll, that is. This one's different from the others."

Next, she visited the Manor's kitchens. "How's that antidote coming, Pyra?"

The pretty chef with the green hair poured herbs and spices into a bubbling cauldron. Her lips made explosion sounds, as if she were bombing the soup.

Lady Weirdwood nodded as if this were an actual response. "When you're finished reviving Huamei, distribute it to the rest of Kingsport's victims."

From the kitchen, Lady Weirdwood went at a quick clip to the hospital room, which was billowy white and smelled of antiseptic. Amelia was tending to porcelain Huamei.

"Once Pyra administers the antidote," Lady Weirdwood said, "tell him he's not allowed outside the Manor. His skin and scales will still be extremely fragile."

"His highness isn't going to appreciate being quarantined," Amelia said.

"Well, he won't like shattering if something hits him, either."

Amelia pulled out a scroll and unrolled it in front of Lady Weirdwood. It was a map of Kingsport with a line of *X*'s drawn along the streets. "I had Ludwig send out his birds to mark the Fae-born's attacks. It seems that doll was headed somewhere."

Lady Weirdwood traced a line through the *X*'s until she

reached a building that sat on the coast. She raised her eyebrows at Wally, as if to ask what the building was.

Wally gulped. "That's Greyridge."

Lady Weirdwood raised her eyebrows even higher.

"Oh, um," Wally said. "Kingsport's mental hospital."

Lady Weirdwood looked more troubled than ever. As they continued down the hall, her snake made a go at Wally's jacket, its tongue flicking.

The lady pointed. "What have you got there that has interested Mac so?"

Wally pulled out the pieces of the dead mouse thing. Breeth's wall stiffened. Seeing the mouse thing felt like staring at her own dead body all over again.

"I see," Lady Weirdwood said solemnly. "Was this a friend of yours?"

"Not really," Wally said. "But this mouse saved my life, ma'am. And I'd like to give it a funeral."

If Breeth could have wiped a tear from the wall, she would have.

Lady Weirdwood gave Wally a kindly smile. "I know just the place."

She led him to the north wing, through a door carved with a lantern. The hall was pitch-black—so dark it looked as if they were walking across nothing at all. Lady Weirdwood lit a candle, and Breeth seeped into it. The candle was made of fat that sputtered and crackled, making Breeth feel like her hair was on fire and her skin was growing gooey.

"I told you I might be able to help you in a way that did not involve payment," the lady said quietly. "After your demonstration today, I believe you might just be Novitiate material."

"Really?" Wally said, catching up to Breeth's orb of light. "Like Sekhmet and Huamei?"

The lady nodded. "My students undergo years of training before they can take down a Fae-born. And *none* of them catch one on their first try. You saw what happened to Huamei."

Wally glanced at Breeth's melting candle eyes. She crackled with gratitude for his not mentioning that she'd helped.

"But that isn't the only reason," Lady Weirdwood continued. "You've also got a good heart. You brought an injured Novitiate back to this Manor even after we'd held you prisoner, because you knew it was the right thing to do." The old woman studied Wally's face in Breeth's flickering light. "You could give up your life of thieving, and I could teach you magic. I wonder what your art would be . . . A painter perhaps? An architect, like me?"

Wally stared at his feet. "Thank you, ma'am. I'm honored. Really." He considered the nonexistent walls. "This place does seem better than being in the Black Feathers. Universes better." He sighed. "But I need to take care of my older brother."

Breeth's flame jittered with jealousy. Wally had never mentioned his brother. This was particularly insulting since she was dead and couldn't share his secrets.

"What's the matter with him?" Lady Weirdwood asked.

"There's nothing the matter really. He's just locked in Greyridge Mental Hospital."

"Right where that infectious doll was headed," Lady

Weirdwood said. "It sounds as if you saved your brother from a terrible fate."

Wally looked at the ground.

"That must be why you tried to rob us," Lady Weirdwood continued. "Hospital bills, hm?"

He gave a little nod.

"Changing the minds of the masses," Lady Weirdwood said. "That's what will make your brother safe. The only thing, unfortunately. But that sort of magic is difficult. Even for me. You'd have to make an entire city understand that people with mental struggles are just as human as anyone else." She gave his shoulder a squeeze. "If you ever change your mind and decide you want to try and learn that kind of magic, you let me know."

They passed a choked hallway, overgrown like a thicket, and glowing with moonlight. Just seeing the Thorny Passage leached the light from Breeth's candle. It led to the room where she was sacrificed.

"*Wally*," Breeth sputtered from her candle. "Ask her about the hall we just passed."

He gave her flame a quizzical look.

"I'm starting to trust her," she said. "If she's willing to give a funeral to a mouse, how bad can she be?"

"What happened in that tangled hall back there?" Wally asked.

The lady didn't pause in her step. "Why do you want to know about that?"

"It just gave me the creeps, is all."

She quirked an eyebrow at him. "If you become a Novitiate, you can learn all about it . . ."

Wally's jaw set, and the old woman relented.

"Ah well, if it will help convince you to join us . . . That was the Red Wing. The site of a grave tragedy."

The light of Breeth's flame flickered over the old woman's lips as Lady Weirdwood told the story. "Several years ago, one of our Wardens lost his wife in a terrible accident. She was Fae-born but preferred to live a quiet life in the Real, where she was killed by a horse carriage. In despair, the Warden climbed to the Manor's roof to say his final goodbye to her spirit in the stars. But then he spotted the door that leads to the Court of Sky, and he had an idea. He entered it, broke into the dragons' Cloud Cemetery, and stole a bone from one of their royal ancestors."

Breeth remembered that Lady Weirdwood was hoping Huamei would help mend relations between the Manor and the Court of Sky after this incident. Desecrating a dragon's grave was clearly an insult of the highest order.

"Dragons simultaneously exist in the Real and the Fae," Lady Weirdwood continued. "This grants them powers even I don't possess—powers that allow them to defy the ordinary rules of the Veil. This is why the dragon race can swap their human and scaled forms back and forth at will. And so the Fallen Warden, as we've come to call him, fashioned the stolen bone into a Quill, hoping to cheat the Veil and write his wife back into existence in the Real."

"Did it work?" Wally asked.

"It did not. When he tried to capture his wife's looks and mannerisms in ink, he could only draw from his fading memories. Instead of reviving his wife, he created a creature that merely mimicked her. Like a puppet."

Breeth's flame shuddered. She was having a hard time not feeling sympathy for this man, whom she assumed had taken her life.

"I'd rob a dragon's grave too if I thought it could bring my parents back to life," Wally said.

Lady Weirdwood gave him a sad smile. "I didn't blame him for that. I blamed him for what happened next. After his first failed attempt, the Fallen Warden grew more desperate. He knew that his wife, or the *idea* of his wife, was still alive somewhere on the other side of the Veil. He believed if he could just figure out where she went, then he could tear the Veil in that location and bring her back with little more than a daydream. A fool's errand if ever there was one. I sensed something was awry and searched his quarters. But I was too late. I found the body of an innocent girl there. It seemed he had already performed his experiment, sacrificing the poor girl so he could follow her ghost into the afterlife."

Breeth's candle wax drooped. "That was me."

She remembered the figure who had loomed over her before taking her life. The strange metal mask with the black glass visor. The ash-smeared hands. The scent of smoke and the voice as gruff as flames.

Lady Weirdwood continued. "I banished him from the Manor. I bound him from being able to speak spells or handle magical implements, and then Weston tossed him into the street. We searched the Fallen Warden's quarters ten times over, but we never did find that dragon-bone Quill."

Silence fell in the dark hallway.

"Um," Wally said, "what was the Fallen Warden's name?"

Breeth's flame wavered in anticipation.

Lady Weirdwood cleared her throat. "I think that's enough of that topic for now."

Breeth nearly extinguished with disappointment. She'd waited years to find her killer, hoping to part the floorboards beneath his feet, taking her revenge and finally ascending to see her parents. But, oh well. She'd already waited this long . . .

At the far end of the dark passage, they arrived at the most beautiful room in Weirdwood. It was vast and as dark and sultry as the night. A grass-carpet field stretched beneath a twinkling ceiling. The wallpaper was composed of thousands of swirling blue brushstrokes, occasionally interrupted by the bright burst of a star.

"The Room of Fathers," Lady Weirdwood said in reverence. "We shall hold the funeral here."

Breeth seeped into a painted cloud, its beauty nearly consuming her grief.

"We're burying the mouse *inside*?" Wally whispered.

"Normally, I wouldn't recommend it," Lady Weirdwood said, kneeling in the middle of the grassy carpet. "But while most homes are built from dead trees, my Manor is made of living ones. As the mouse reverts to its original form and decomposes, these walls will grow with its nutrients—just as a forest does."

Wally glanced toward Breeth, passing in her wallpaper cloud. She nodded, shedding rainy paint tears.

Lady Weirdwood crouched low and pulled up a loose piece of carpet. Then she took a kerchief from her wedding gown and held it out. Wally set the porcelain mouse shards inside, and the old woman held them up to the swirling ceiling. "We return this body back from where it came. May the soil delight in its nutrients just as the mouse delighted in cheese."

Breeth's cloud face contorted as she watched the mouse disappear into the floor and Lady Weirdwood fold the grassy carpet over it.

"And now," the lady said, "a moment of silence."

She and Wally bowed their heads while the night sky wall-paper swirled around them.

The door burst open. "Lady Weirdwood!"

"*Sekhmet*," the lady whispered, flashing her a severe look. "Can't you see we're in the middle of a funeral?"

Sekhmet knelt. "I'm sorry, Lady. But it's an emergency." She drew back the hood of her cloak, her long hair spilling down her back. Her face was covered in ash and there was a spot of blood on her cheek. "I couldn't locate the Rift. And that thief Arthur ran off into the Mirror sewers."

Lady Weirdwood quirked an eyebrow. "And what were you doing with Arthur?"

Sekhmet stared at the floor. "I broke the rules and had him lead me around the city."

"And promised him treasure you could not provide," Lady Weirdwood said, standing with a grunt. "Well, I can't say using a guide was a *terrible* idea. Hopefully the boy's ego will keep him alive, despite the Ogre Oakers." The lines on her face shifted like sands blown by the wind. "No Rift, you say?"

"No, ma'am."

"Stranger and stranger. How did a Fae-born get into the Real without a Rift?"

From what Breeth knew about the Veil, this was as impossible as a fish escaping its tank by wriggling through the glass.

"Tell Ludwig and Weston to hold off sending resources to the Mercury Mines," Lady Weirdwood said to Sekhmet. "They need to head into the Mirror to capture that pest Arthur before he accidentally creates any Rifts or permanently damages any of Kingsport's myths."

Sekhmet bowed. But before she could depart, the door burst open again.

"Lady Veirdvood!"

It was Ludwig, the large, baby-faced twin.

"What is it, Ludwig?" Lady Weirdwood said.

Ludwig wrung his hands. "Zere's been anozer attack on Kingsport!"

The lady couldn't hide the shock on her face. "What is it this time?"

"Corvidians. *Dozens* are svarming ze skies as ve speak. Zey seem to be attacking Kingsport's mental hospital."

Wally leapt to his feet as Lady Weirdwood swept toward the exit.

"We'll have to divide our ranks," she said. "Ludwig, tell your brother he's going to the Mirror alone to capture Arthur. Sekhmet? Gather every last staff member left in the Manor. *Now*."

Sekhmet knelt before her. "Lady Weirdwood, please send me to fight the Fae-born."

Lady Weirdwood paused and gave her a helpless look. "You're lucky we're short on Wardens after the stunt you pulled with Arthur. You are to obey Amelia's every command, do you understand?"

Sekhmet could barely contain her smile. "Yes, Lady."

With that, Lady Weirdwood, Ludwig, and Sekhmet left the room.

"Breeth!" Wally called up to her wallpaper cloud. "My brother's in that hospital!"

Breeth's paint cloud thundered. "Why didn't you tell me about him before?"

Wally looked lost a moment. "I . . . don't know. I've never told anyone about Graham. Lady Weirdwood just drew it out of me." He gave his head a quick shake. "Can you keep me safe while I rescue him?"

Breeth's cloud swirled with thought. If she had any chance of finding her killer, they would have to establish trust with Lady Weirdwood.

"Okay," she said. "But only because you buried my mouse and I like you."

13
THE GENTLEMAN THIEF

Arthur sloshed through the Mirror sewer. The stone tunnels stretched dark and endless. Every hundred yards, a slant of moonlight streamed through a drain above, lighting massive arches of ancient stonework, laced with cobwebs. The air was thick with the cold rot of death.

Yes, the sewers were as delightfully creepy as Arthur had imagined whenever he read Alfred Moore's books. But something was missing. In the stories, the gloom was banished by crackling torches, raucous laughter, and bawdy songs sung by Garnett Lacroix and his Merry Rogues. All Arthur could hear now was the gurgle of water and the shrieks of rats.

He passed a pile of bones and hesitated. If the topside of Mirror Kingsport was filled with scavengers and Ogre Oakers and living embodiments of disease, what would the sewer hold?

He had heard of people flushing their pet baby alligators down the toilet when they became a nuisance. These babies grew to monstrous sizes beneath the city. Their massive tails clogged the drainpipes, and their giant mouths hung open like caves, waiting for children to explore the city's depths. It was an urban legend, of course. But in the Mirror City, those legends came true.

Arthur hugged himself against the sewer's cold. What had he been thinking, abandoning the girl with the swords? He had to remind himself that Sekhmet had betrayed him. Conned him, in fact. Good riddance to her. Arthur could take care of himself. He'd been doing it since he was eight.

He sloshed through the ankle-high water, trying focus on more pleasant things. Instead of a titanic alligator around the next bend, maybe the Merry Rogues would be waiting with smiles and songs and a warm cup of wassail. Arthur would finally get to shake Garnett Lacroix's hand!

Tunnels branched left and right, black as pitch for their lack of drains above. He stopped and stared into the impossible darkness, his eyes wide and hungry for torchlight.

"Hello?"

Hello?   *Hello?*   *Hello?*   *Hello?*

His voice echoed down the dark tunnel. The rats fell silent.

"Garnett Lacroix?"

Silence.

That was strange. Arthur cleared his throat.

"Echo!"

Echo   *Echo*   *Echo*   *Echo*

"Lacroix?"

Silence.

Darkness seeped into his heart. The Gentleman Thief's name didn't echo in this sewer.

Every inch of Arthur wanted to run back to Sekhmet. But then he remembered a moment from *Garnett Lacroix and the Endless Forest*. The Merry Rogues had become separated in the wood and had sung "A Song for the Lost" to find one another. Arthur had memorized the lyrics and made up a melody and everything. After his mom had died, he would sing it to himself at night, hoping she would answer.

Arthur sang it again now.

> *"When your head's a haunted wood*
> *and the dark strangles the good*
> *When the world's full of falsehood*
> *Reach out for me . . ."*

Arthur stopped and listened. The song didn't echo either. It was as if neither Garnett nor his music was welcome in this sewer. Arthur gazed back toward the light of the drain he'd climbed down. He would try two more tunnels, and if he didn't find anything, he'd hightail it out of there.

He sloshed on, singing the next verse.

> *"When your heart's tangled in thorns*
> *And your will to rise is torn*
> *When all of life feels forlorn*
> *Call out for me . . ."*

Arthur stopped. The song had echoed through a tunnel to his right. He continued down it, picking up the tempo for the chorus.

> *"Oh, I'll wear my socks as earrings*
> *I'll smooch a snail or three!*
> *I'll wrestle down a mailbox*
> *And sail it down the street!*
> *I'll juggle seven toddlers*
> *And gargle cans of worms!"*

" . . . I'll do all of the silly things
to make your sadness squirm . . ."

Arthur's heart leapt. Somewhere in the darkness a voice had picked up the tune. He followed it, singing the first half of the next verse and then letting the voice finish.

> *"I'll drink a case of ginger ale . . ."*

" . . . and spray it out my nose!"

> *"I'll tame a team of grasshoppers . . ."*

" . . . and mush them through the snows!"

"I'll hop aboard a pirate ship . . ."

" . . . and clean all of their toes!"

He reached the voice just as they both finished the chorus:

"'Cause there's nothing that's too silly to save your heart from woe!"

A dusty laugh wheezed in the darkness, followed by a voice that was all charm and swagger. Or had been long ago.

"*Koff*—I haven't sung that song in—*koff*—years."

"*Garnett?*" Arthur said, eyes wide. "Garnett Lacroix?"

"The very same," the voice said.

Arthur practically ripped out his hair he was so excited. He was talking to his *hero*. His true-blue, bona fide, real-life, er, *fictional* hero.

"Oh jeez," Arthur spluttered. "I've been a fan of yours since I wet the bed! Ugh. I don't know why I told you that. Ha ha. I'm kinda nervous."

"People still . . . talk about my adventures?" the voice asked.

"Yeah!" Arthur said, trying to shake the feeling back into his hands. "I mean, *sort of*. Alfred Moore stopped writing your adventures when he disappeared. So now you're a lot less popular than you used to be." He winced. "Sorry, probably shouldn't have told you that. It's just with the Pox and star-vation and gang fighting in Kingsport, people don't feel too adventuresome these days, y'know?" He cleared his throat, trying a better tack. "But hey, I still read your adventures every day! And now you're right in front of me!" He squinted into the darkness. "But I can't see you. Do you have a torch?"

"Ah, yes," Garnett said. "Light. Light is good. There. To my right."

Arthur blindly felt his way to the wall where he found a raised stone platform and a wooden box. His fingertips recognized the objects he needed. He wrapped a bit of cloth around a piece of wood, struck the flint, and the flame came crackling to life.

When he turned around, he nearly dropped the torch. The man he'd been talking to was encased in cobwebs.

"Mr. Lacroix?" Arthur said, holding the torch closer.

The webs around the man's mouth stretched into a grin. "Yes?"

Revulsion crept up Arthur's throat. "Let's get you out of there."

He clawed at the figure, freeing him from his webbed prison. Then he stepped back, breathless. Garnett looked like a mummy, barely bones and skin. His hair, once thick and red as chestnuts, was now thin and yellow as straw. His skin, once sun-touched, was sallow and tight against his skull.

"That's, um, better," Arthur said, trying to sound positive.

Head freed, Garnett craned back his rickety neck. Torchlight twinkled in the Gentleman Thief's golden eyes, and Arthur finally recognized his hero—just as he'd always imagined him.

"What happened to you?" Arthur asked, pulling the webbing from Garnett's knees like a corn husk. "Not that you don't look *good*. Just . . ."

"*Koff koff.*" Garnett hunched over on his splintered throne. "No one has summoned me for a mission in—*koff*—I can't remember how long. The adventures dried up like an old prune, and me with them. *Koff koff.*"

Cold crept through Arthur's skin. "And the Merry Rogues?"

"In sweet slumber." Garnett pointed a mummified finger at a pile of bones. "They will wake when the next adventure calls. Isn't that right, mates?"

A femur rolled off the top of the pile.

Arthur grimaced. "I'm not so sure about that."

It was obvious why Garnett and his Rogues were in such terrible condition. Alfred Moore had ended the most recent adventure on a cliffhanger. Garnett had been encased by the Thousand Thirsty Spiders of the Thorny Throne. Hence his bloodless appearance. The three Merry Rogues, meanwhile, had been swallowed up in piranha-infested acidic quicksand. Hence the pile of bones.

Arthur remembered Gus, who was tall and skilled with knives and puns. He remembered Tuck, who was short and skilled with clubs and . . . also puns. And he remembered Mim, who was of medium height and was skilled at punching puny punks . . . but couldn't come up with a pun to save her life.

And now none of them would ever come up with a pun again.

"Thanks for visiting," Garnett said, sinking into his throne. "Come again soon."

The cobwebs started to crawl up his legs like a living blanket.

"No!" Arthur yelled, swiping the torch until the webs retreated. "You're *Garnett Lacroix!* You've been in much worse positions! Remember when you were trapped in the Haunted Hulks and didn't eat for forty days, only licking the mossy sideboards? Or how about the time you stole that jade egg, only to be pursued by a hundred and thirty-seven cougars?" He thrust the torch toward the ceiling. "The real spirit of Garnett adventure lies out *there*—on the high seas, in treasure vaults, in the eye of a storm! I refuse to accept your retirement!"

Garnett's golden eyes twinkled. "I . . . remember." He smiled at the pile of bones. "Do you remember, mates?"

This time it was a rib that rolled off the bone pile.

"Then why are you still sitting?" Arthur asked.

With some effort, Garnett hefted his skeletal head. "Is there . . . adventure?"

"An adventure unlike any you've ever seen!" Arthur leapt onto the stone platform, adventure thrumming through his veins. "There's a city of bloodthirsty beasts to escape! A friend to rescue from evil magicians! A father and a brother to break out of a mental hospital! And that's not all! An infectious doll is plaguing Kingsport's streets! The odds may seem impossible, but it's just the sort of adventure you would seize by the suspenders!"

Arthur beamed. Surely no rallying cry in history had ever been so inspired.

Garnett sighed dustily. "Just let me rest a moment," he said, and then promptly started to snore.

Arthur lowered his torch in defeat. When it came down to it, the Gentleman Thief was no more help than words on a page.

Arthur sat on the stone platform, feeling heavy. "I need to know, Mr. Lacroix."

The Gentleman Thief snorted awake.

"How did you do it?" Arthur asked. "How did you steal from the rich and give to the poor and still feed yourself? How did you stand up for the Rogues and not get caught and look so *good* while you did it? How do you be a thief . . . and a gentleman?"

"It's simple," Garnett said, blinking open his eyes. "Come closer."

Arthur put his ear to Garnett's leathery lips.

"The answer . . . lies here." The Gentleman Thief tapped the top of his head.

Arthur touched his own head. "Huh?"

Garnett gave a mummified grin and then rested his head again.

Heat rose in Arthur's veins. That was no kind of riddle! At least Graham's riddle had actual clues. What was Arthur supposed to do? Think his way out of this problem? His thinking was what had caused this problem in the first place!

Garnett gathered in his bony limbs like a dying spider. "Good night."

Arthur scowled. He wanted solid advice that he could carry back to his city—an ember that he could fan into a flame of heroism. Otherwise, he would become colder and harder over the years until he ended up like Harry.

"*ARTHUR?*" A man's voice echoed through the sewers.

Arthur plunged his torch into the water as someone came splashing down the tunnels.

"It's Weston! Weirdwood's gardener! Lady Weirdwood sent me to collect ya! Report!"

Arthur crouched in silence.

The man grumbled to himself. "Dumb kid. Crawling into the Mirror sewers. I should let him get eaten by the gray water, 's what I should do." He cleared his throat. "Arthur! You gotta come quick! Your city's under attack! Your friend's in trouble!"

Arthur knew this trick. Oakers used it all the time to try and get Black Feathers to come out of hiding. Arthur wasn't falling for it. But his only escape was blocked. And Garnett was no help. The only person who could revive the Gentleman Thief was Alfred Moore. But Arthur had no idea where the author lived.

"*Arthur!*" Weston bellowed. "Come on out now!"

A cave-sized roar answered. Arthur peeked around the tunnel's corner and found Weston scratching a building-sized alligator under the chin.

"That's a nice beasty," Weston said, tossing a beet into its giant mouth.

The alligator chomped the beet gratefully, purring as loud as a train. Arthur ducked back behind the corner just as Weston approached the tunnel where he was hiding.

"*Garnett*," Arthur whispered. "I need your help! You don't have to fight. Just . . . tell me what to do!"

Lacroix raised a skeletal finger and arched a dusty eyebrow. "Whenever I'm in a pinch, I call upon my Merry Rogues!"

Arthur frowned at the pile of bones. What was he supposed to do? Club Weirdwood's gardener over the head with a femur? But then Arthur remembered the moments Garnett had spoken to Gus, Tuck, and Mim's remains. Each time, a bone had tumbled off the top. Or had the bones *moved*?

It may have been impossible for Arthur to retrieve those Thirsty Spiders and pump the Gentleman Thief full of blood again. The Merry Rogues, on the other hand, had always followed Garnett Lacroix's commands to the letter.

In a fit of inspiration, Arthur grabbed a swath of cobwebs hanging from the corner of the Gentleman Thief's throne and wiped it off. Garnett's wide-brimmed hat had faded to the color of elephant skin. A shriveled daffodil stuck out of the brim.

He placed the hat on his head. "Listen up, Rogues!" he whispered. "I need your help, and I can't have measly acidic quicksand get in the way! I mean, if piranhas could survive in there, it couldn't have been that dangerous, right?"

The bones didn't stir.

Arthur searched his memory for smaller details of the adventure. "Besides, wasn't Gus carrying that jug full of lemon juice that he stole to make his world-class wassail? If that broke open, it would neutralize the acid, allowing you guys to swim to the top! Everyone knows quicksand is a myth anyway!"

A slight sound in the darkness. Like bones scraping.

Arthur cleared his throat, and did his best impression of the Gentleman Thief. "Gus! Tuck! Mim! I demand that you wake up posthaste! There's a scoundrel that needs fighting!"

In the darkness, the bones began rearranging themselves.

14
THE BATTLE OF THE CORVIDIANS

Wally stood outside Hazelrigg and stared up in horror.

It looked like a mistake. Like ink spilled across the sky.

But then the shape shifted, and Wally realized he was look-ing at a flock of birds . . . or *almost* birds. There were hundreds of them, each as big as he was, with a blend of bird and human features: black beaks and human eyes, wide wings and hands for feet. Their fingernails were talons of glinting steel, and when they cawed, it sounded like children crying through the throats of crows.

"Yikes," Breeth said from Hazelrigg's front door. "And I thought the goblin screamatorium was scary."

The Corvidians dove at the people of Kingsport, knife-like talons slashing at arms and faces, ripping clothes and flesh, and snagging purses and wigs, which the monster birds carried back into the sky and toward the cliffs.

"This way!" Amelia cried, and she, Ludwig, Sekhmet, and

Pyra ran toward the port where the flock cast its shadow. The birds were flying straight toward Greyridge.

Wally and Breeth followed close behind, passing people who were bleeding and sobbing, their eyes flinching toward the sky. Wally pictured his brother, helpless in his mildewed cell, and ran faster. The Corvidians would make mincemeat of Graham with those talons.

"Ludwig!" Amelia yelled, still running. "Can you blow the Corvidians away from the hospital?"

"I vill try!" Ludwig said, folding squares of paper into tiny birds with his massive hands.

"Pyra?" Amelia said. "Can you cook up something that will stun them?"

The chef giggled madly as she drew out two corked vials—one as darkly purple as a storm, another filled with electric-pink pellets. "Pluck 'em! Gut 'em! Roast 'em for dinner!"

This brought Wally some relief. With Weirdwood's staff distracting the Corvidians, he could make it to Greyridge without being sliced to shreds.

"Sekhmet," Amelia said. "You are not to draw your swords unless I say. Understood?"

"Yes, ma'am," Sekhmet said, unable to hide her disappointment.

They reached the port—a chaos of slices and screams and falling feathers. The Corvidians dove at the boats, tearing sails and swiping up oars and giant fish.

"We can't reach the flock from down here," Amelia said.

"We need to get to higher ground." She searched the port, then pointed to the fish-processing factory. "There!"

She cracked her whip and floated up to the roof as graceful as a dancer. The other staff members scaled the building's siding.

Wally left them behind, continuing up the cliffs toward Greyridge, heart pounding in his chest. "Still with me, Breeth?"

"Yep!" Breeth said, squishing through the moss that grew along the cliffside. "If those birds so much as glance your way, I'll ooze all over them!"

Wally looked straight up at the cloud of Corvidians streaming toward Greyridge. A multitude of stolen objects dangled from their claws—purses, oars, bedpans, fish, boots. The monster birds carried them up the cliffs, soared over the hospital's gate, and then dropped them onto the guards, knocking some unconscious before swooping back to the city to grab more ammo for their assault.

Why were they attacking Greyridge? Wally hoped with all his heart that it had nothing to do with Graham.

A shadow passed over Wally as a dozen Corvidians carried an entire carriage over the gate.

"Oh no," Wally said, heart sinking.

But before the birds could drop the carriage, something in the air shifted. A powerful wind blew the Corvidians and the carriage back down the cliffs. A new flock of Ludwig's paper birds had formed above the hospital's roof and were flapping up a gale, sweeping the monster birds back toward the roof of the fish factory where Amelia and the others waited, poised to knock the beasts out of the sky.

Wally sighed with relief. "Get 'em, guys."

He reached Greyridge's gate and tried to open it. It was locked.

"Let me in!" Wally shouted at the bleeding guards. "I need to check on my brother!"

The guards didn't stir. They'd been knocked unconscious.

The dead hedges lining the grounds rustled to life. Their brown limbs extended toward the gate and coiled around the bars. "I can't possess it, Wally," Breeth said from the leaves. "It's made of metal."

Wally was eyeing the spiked top of the fence, seeing if he could climb over, when a man cried out on the port.

"Oh God! Please! No!"

Wally turned around and found a man pushing a baby carriage along the docks. The baby carriage was empty.

"My son!" the man screamed, pointing at the sky. "They took my son!"

There, a hundred feet in the air, among the objects in the feathered shadow, something was *wriggling*. Wally squinted, and his stomach fell.

It was a baby, its diaper dangling from one of the Corvidian's talons. The baby squirmed and screamed, helpless as a grub. Wally looked at Ludwig's paper birds, flapping the Corvidians toward the fish factory. He looked to the factory's roof where the chef Pyra was mixing up a poison that would *pluck 'em, gut 'em, and roast 'em for dinner . . .*

"STOP COOKING!" Wally screamed toward Pyra. But his voice was lost beneath the caws and screams.

"I'll try and stop her!" Breeth said.

The moss shuddered as she zipped back toward the factory.

Wally took one last glance at Greyridge, hoping his brother was safe inside, and then sprinted back to the fish factory and the helpless baby dangling a hundred feet above it.

He reached the factory and started to climb, barely thinking about the height as he scaled the building's fire escape ladder. A stiff wind was still blowing the Corvidians overhead. The baby's screams were lost in a cloud of caws.

On the roof, Pyra giggled maniacally as she poured her ingredients and muttered violent promises of what would happen to the monster birds. Wally saw a purple cloud of poison spurt up, alive with pink lightning, and he climbed faster.

He climbed over the lip of the roof, caught his breath, and pointed. "They have a baby!"

The four staff members looked at him, startled.

Amelia squinted her one eye at the flock. "He's right. Abandon the plan! We could poison the child!"

"Good sing Pyra is such a klutz, no?" Ludwig said.

He stepped his large form aside, revealing Weirdwood's chef, who frowned at her cauldron, which had tumbled over, spilling murky purple fluid that sizzled the roof. The lightning cloud evaporated.

"I did that!" Breeth said, smiling from a cloud of chimney smoke.

In the sky, Ludwig's paper cranes had done their job of

blowing the Corvidians to the factory. The monster birds' dark eyes caught sight of the figures on the roof.

"B-but if ve cannot stun ze Corvidians," Ludwig said, "zey are going to attack us."

Amelia uncoiled her whip. "Yes, they are. And we're going to let them."

Pyra snickered eagerly.

"But—but I am not supposed to fight!" Ludwig cried. "I am ze groundskeeper!"

"How do you think I feel?" Amelia said. "I'm the bloody doctor!" She drew her whip. "But we can't let the flock fly away with the child. They could drop it. Or worse, *eat* it." She looked at the chef. "Pyra, can you cook up a new potion? Something less caustic?"

Pyra snarled in dissent.

Amelia sighed. "Ludwig. Could your birds catch the child?"

"Nein," Ludwig said. "Their paper vings vill strain under ze veight . . . Oh!" He took out his papers and started folding. "I could build a soft sort of somesing to catch him?"

Amelia nodded. "We'll keep you protected."

The Corvidians dove straight down at them, talons glinting.

"Permission to use my swords, ma'am?" Sekhmet asked.

"No," Amelia said. "You haven't completed your training. You could scald the child."

Sekhmet looked insulted, but she kept her swords sheathed.

Amelia whirled her whip, making the air resonate.

"I'm going to try and get the baby away from them. Brace yourselves."

Wally clutched his fists, taking a wide stance. With Greyridge's gates locked, the only way to protect Graham was to destroy the Corvidians.

The monster birds screeched in, consuming the Weirdwood staff in a tornado of feathers and silver talons. A cut opened across Wally's cheek. Then another over his shoulder. He swung his fists, knuckles connecting against a feathered chest and a beaked jaw. But the onslaught of talons only grew more intense and he was suddenly buried under a sea of soaring, slicing, half-human monsters.

Beneath the deafening sound of shrieks and slashes and screams, Wally heard other sounds: the baby crying itself hoarse; Amelia's vibrating whip; Ludwig's high-pitched sobbing. The attack continued to grow louder and sharper until Wally thought he might lose his mind or have every last bit of him torn away . . .

But then it was over. The Corvidians swooped back into the sky, leaving behind a mess of feathers and blood. Wally held his weeping cheek with one hand while flexing the bruised knuckles of the other.

The others hadn't fared much better. Their clothes were ripped. They bled from their faces and arms. Sekhmet tore away a part of her robe and tied it around a slash on her throat. Ludwig was missing a patch of hair, and his paper construction that was meant to break the baby's fall had been torn to shreds.

"I couldn't catch the child," Amelia said, staring up at the baby, who was screaming so loud it could barely breathe. "I was able to coax its diaper out of one of their claws only to watch it get snatched up by another."

A new scream rang out across the port. The Corvidians had taken Pyra. She kicked and punched at her captors. But the monster birds carried her higher and higher over the port . . . and then they dropped her.

Pyra's scream cut in a breathless gasp as she plummeted toward the planks.

"Ludwig!" Amelia cried.

"Yes! I see! I see!"

The giant steered his flock of paper cranes away from Greyridge and toward the falling chef. They swooped low, and with a flap of their wings, managed to create a cushion of air beneath her.

Still, Pyra hit hard. The vials in her robes shattered on impact, and a blue mushroom cloud exploded toward the sky.

"That's not good," Amelia said.

"*That's* worse," Sekhmet said, pointing.

With Ludwig's paper birds diverted, the Corvidians had managed to carry the carriage over the front gate and dropped it on Greyridge, caving in the hospital's lobby.

Caws of victory echoed across the port. Wally's heart sank. *Graham.*

"The baby!" Sekhmet said.

Before the Corvidian carrying the baby made it to the top of the cliffs, Ludwig grunted, steering his paper flock back above the hospital where they flapped another gale that sent the monster birds hurtling toward the fish factory.

"Grab hold of something!" Amelia shouted. "We can't afford to lose any more of us!"

"Wally!" A waft of coal smoke bent toward him, coiling with Breeth's shape. "I'm going to possess one of the birds. I can make its claws drop the baby safely into your arms."

"But . . . you'd have to *die* again," he whispered.

Breeth's ashen eyes searched the sky. "It's a baby, Wally. If they kill him, I'll never forgive myself."

Wally swallowed. "You're braver than I am, Breeth. Good luck."

"Get ready!" Amelia yelled.

The Corvidians swept in again, attacking even more viciously. Wally aimed his punches at their legs so they couldn't grab hold of him. But then he accidentally punched a talon, which peeled the skin off his knuckles. After that, Wally could only make a ball of himself and hold on to the railing for dear life.

The wings cleared again. A warmth trickled down Wally's neck. He reached up to find his ear bleeding. His shirt was filled with slashes, and cold slices opened across his chest. His vision blurred, woozy with pain.

He shook himself awake and studied the flock, searching for signs of Breeth. But instead he found Sekhmet and Ludwig dangling from the Corvidians' claws, clinging to chimney pots that hadn't been secured to the roof.

Ludwig, dangling in midair, dropped his pot and pulled paper out of his pocket. His trembling fingers tried folding more cranes to cushion his fall, but the Corvidians simply dropped him. The giant screamed as he fell, splatting in a crate full of fish.

"Permission to draw your swords, Sekhmet!" Amelia cried to the Novitiate.

But the moment Sekhmet grabbed her hilts, the Corvidians dropped her too. A few yards before she hit the cobbles, she slashed at the ground, creating a pocket of heat that allowed her feet to touch down gently on the docks. The Corvidians dove at her, trying to snatch away her swords, but Sekhmet deflected their talons with grace.

Wally searched the flock. *"Where are you, Breeth?"*

"I tried."

He turned and found the ghost girl's disappointed face wavering in ash smoke.

"I couldn't get inside their thoughts," she said. She hit the side of her temple with an ashen fist. "They kept squawking *Out! Out!* like they were pecking at my brain."

Wally's shoulders sank. The baby's cries were growing fainter.

The monster birds dove toward the roof again. Amelia whirled her whip while Wally raised his fists. This was it. Wally would put up a fight, but eventually the Corvidians would pluck him up and then drop him from an impossible height. Graham would spend the rest of his life in Greyridge alone, enduring an endless series of painful experiments.

The first Corvidian swept in, blood dripping from its silver claws, its hideous, half-human face shrieking. But before it could reach them, a golden object whizzed from below, pelting the Corvidian in the head, making it drop unconscious to the rooftop. Dozens more objects followed—coins, cups, and trinkets—pelting more of the Corvidians. The birds turned their attention to four figures on the docks and dove at them.

Wally peered over the roof's edge. He'd seen many strange things in the last couple of days, but none of them beat Arthur Benton wearing a wide-brimmed hat and leading a group of three skeletons, who threw fistfuls of gold from casks they'd clearly stolen from the Manor.

"Can't peck my eyeballs when I ain't got none, can ya?" the short skeleton screamed before headbutting a Corvidian. "Ya see that, Gus?"

"That ain't how you do it, Tuck!" the tall skeleton called Gus cried. "C'mere, ya glorified feather dusters!" He upper-cut two others.

"While you idiots are over there squawking," a skeleton with a woman's voice cried as she gave a Corvidian a noogie, "I've knocked out enough birds to stuff a king's mattress!"

Gus pointed a bony thumb at her. "Jeez. Who ruffled Mim's feathers?"

The skeletons had not only managed to distract the Corvidians with their makeshift golden ammunition, they also battled them with ease, their bones impervious to the bills and talons.

"Arthur!" Wally cried.

Arthur hurled a goblet and then tipped his hat upward. "Cooper!"

"You!" Amelia cried over the edge of the roof, continuing to fend off Corvidians with her whip. "Take those skeletons back to the Mirror *immediately*. We're trying to get the Fae-born *back* to their realm, not bring more over!"

Arthur pointed at her. "There's one! She's one of the bad guys that kidnapped us!"

"Got it, boss!" Tuck, the shortest skeleton, said.

He pulled off his arm and hurled it at Amelia, who ducked just in time. The arm rolled and clattered along the roof.

"Um," Tuck called up, "would you mind tossing that back?"

Amelia scowled.

"She stole Tuck's arm!" Gus cried.

"She *is* evil!" yelled Mim.

She removed her own arm and was about to hurl it when Wally held up his hands. "Amelia's not evil! She's trying to save a baby!"

He pointed at the child, high in the sky.

"Oh," Mim said, refitting her arm. "Why didn't ya say so?"

While the skeletons continued to fistfight Corvidians, Arthur tipped his hat to Amelia. "Afternoon, ma'am! My Merry Skeletons and I would be happy to help with your monster bird infestation. If you overlook this gold we nicked from your Manor, that is."

Amelia's mouth tightened. She gazed toward Pyra, Sekhmet, and Ludwig, who were still out of commission. "I don't see what other choice I've got."

"Hear that, guys?" Arthur cried. "We're hired!"

The four of them scaled the side of the building, swatting at birds as they went.

"Prepare for your swan song!" Gus cried.

"Birds of a feather get socked together!" Tuck cried.

"The early bird gets the fist!" cried Mim.

"All right, Merry Skeletons!" Arthur said, climbing onto the roof. "No more clever quips until that baby's safe, you hear me?"

"You got it, boss!"

The Corvidians swept in again. With a diminished flock and more bodies to attack, the onslaught wasn't nearly as punishing this time. But once the feathers cleared, the skeletons were left armless and legless, and one without a head.

"We've been disarmed!" cried Mim.

"And beheaded!" cried Gus.

"Aaaaaaaaauuuuuugggggggggghhhhhh!" screamed Tuck's skull in the sky.

Arthur's cheeks flooded red. "I guess you guys can't really *win* a fight without skin and muscles."

The Corvidians tried to make another sweep toward Greyridge, but the paper birds blew them back. Even though he was injured, Ludwig continued to control his creations from the fish crate. But that meant the monster birds were going to attack Wally and Amelia again. Wally didn't think they'd survive another onslaught.

He watched the Corvidians circle the roof, bones in their talons, and had an idea.

"*Breeth!*" he said, slipping behind a chimney. "Can you possess one of those skeleton arms?"

"Ooooh!" Her soot rippled with excitement. "I think so!"

He watched as her face drifted higher and higher in the smoke before dissipating into the flock. A skeleton arm came to life, thrashing and feeling around. Then another and another as Breeth worked her way toward the skeleton arm closest to the baby.

"What's happening?" Amelia asked, staring at the flock. She turned to the Merry Skeletons. "Are you doing that?"

Mim shrugged her armless shoulders. "I don't know what my arms get up to when they're not on me."

In the sky, one of the arms felt around until its bony fingers managed to seize hold of the baby's diaper. With a swift tug, it wrenched the baby loose from the claws.

"I'm gonna drop him now, Wally!" Breeth screamed.

"Get ready to catch!" Wally yelled, holding out his arms.

Arthur held out his arms too. The flock passed over the roof, the skeleton hand released the diaper, and the baby fell screaming from the sky. Amelia cracked her whip, which gently coiled around the child, twirling him right into her arms.

"There, there," she cooed, patting the baby's back.

Just then, two hands slapped the edge of the roof. Pyra climbed up, huffing, her hands, face, and robes dyed a bright blue.

"Pyra!" Amelia said. "Do you still have the poison ingredients?"

Pyra peeked inside her cloak and grunted assent.

"Start cooking. You won't have the luxury of Ludwig's wind control, I'm afraid."

Pyra snagged her cauldron and poured in the ingredients, eyes shining wickedly. Soon, a purple cloud spurted up from the rooftop, squirming with pink lightning. It enveloped the Corvidians, and Arthur and Wally covered their heads as birds and skeleton limbs rained onto the roof and the streets below.

"I have to admit, thief," Amelia said, "you and your skeletons did good."

Arthur doffed his ridiculous hat. "Glad to be of service, ma'am."

Gus scoffed. "I didn't see *you* lose any limbs in that tussle."

Breeth's face rematerialized in the ash cloud. "The ghost girl never gets credit," she said. But she was smiling.

The air had barely cleared of purple smoke when Amelia started shouting commands. "Pyra! Head to the docks and make sure Ludwig and Sekhmet are okay. You two"—she pointed to Arthur and Wally—"put those skeletons back together and get them to the Manor!"

The skeletons leapt from the roof to collect their missing limbs and head while Arthur tossed stray bones down to them.

"That's *my* femur!" Gus cried. "Give it back!"

"Is this a funny bone?" said Tuck.

"If it is, it ain't yours!" Mim said.

Wally stepped to the roof's edge and eyed the damage to Greyridge. His heart settled in his chest when he saw that the hospital was still standing. Graham was safe. From the Corvidians, at least.

Amelia stepped to the roof's edge with the baby. "After I return this child, I'll bring these Corvidians back to the Mirror and find out where these Fae-born are coming fr—"

She was interrupted when the sea began to rumble.

They all peered over the roof's edge as the planks of the port strained and splintered. The water shot up in great sprays as an enormous hole opened up in the swell like a whirlpool, swallowing two large ships. The dock exploded as dozens of tentacles burst through. The tentacles were huge, the size of ship's masts, and as black as nightfall. They flopped their way across the port, coiling around whatever they found and dragging it into the ocean. This included the skeletons and treasure chests.

"Wait!" Gus said, dragging his bony fingers. "I haven't put my foot on yet!"

"Ain't you gonna buy me dinner first?"

"*Gaaarneeeeeeeeett!*"

Arthur removed his hat in reverence for his skeleton friends. And probably his gold.

The tentacles blindly felt their way up the cliffs toward Greyridge. They coiled around the outer wrought iron fence and tugged, making the metal strain and squeak.

Wally watched, helpless. He'd thought it was over. That Graham was safe . . .

Amelia stared at the giant tentacles and shook her head. "The moment one Fae-born is snuffed out, another rises. What's happening?" She drew her whip. "I'll have to return to the Manor for backup and get Lady Weirdwood's input. There's no use defeating this monster if another is going to take its place."

"Wait!" Wally said. "What about my—"

But Amelia had already leapt off the roof, whip singing.

Wally stiffened with fear. How was he supposed to rescue Graham without Weirdwood's staff and their magic?

15
ALFRED MOORE

reeth billowed in a million bits of swirling ash, rising over Kingsport. A fog rolled in from the sea, flooding the streets. Through the mist, she could see massive glistening knots of tentacles—like dozens of giant squids had crawled onto the port and then exploded.

It was a spooky sight. Even for a ghost.

Breeth turned her ashen eyes to the rooftop. Arthur sat on the edge, staring at his garish hat. Funny, Breeth could have sworn the daffodil in the brim had been shriveled when he'd arrived. Now it was in full bloom.

"I was *this* close," Arthur said, making an inch with his finger and thumb. "I could see the title in my head: *The Adventures of Arthur Benton and His Merry Skeletons*."

"I'm sure it would've been a bestseller," Wally said, clearly annoyed.

"More than a bestseller!" Arthur said, leaping to his feet. "A best *life*! Garnett Lacroix is *real*, Cooper! A little cobwebbed maybe, but he and I had a conversation and *everything*!"

Wally did not look impressed. He pointed a thumb over his shoulder. "If you want to go back to the Manor for protection, you should follow Amelia."

"Where are you gonna go?" Arthur asked.

"Nowhere."

"To Greyridge to save your brother?"

Wally's jaw set. "How do you know about my brother?"

"I, um, met him when I visited Harry. Well, I met his *hand* anyway." Arthur mimicked a puppet. "I might have laughed if I hadn't been so nervous."

Wally's expression softened. "You just described my entire childhood." He gazed toward Greyridge. "Harry's really in there too?"

Arthur nodded. "The Rook's holding him ransom until I pay off his debt."

Wally headed to the fire escape ladder. "Let's go get them."

"*Now?*" Arthur said, staring at the tentacle-infested port. "How will we get through?"

Wally quirked an eyebrow at Breeth. "We'll figure something out." He stepped down a rung. "Aren't you the one who throws himself into adventure, no matter how dangerous?"

Arthur looked lost, like he was trying to remember how to be brave. And then he slapped his forehead. "Cooper! So much has happened, I almost forgot! Your brother isn't in Greyridge!"

Wally froze, hands on the top rung. "What?"

"He's in Mirror Kingsport! I saw him there when I was with Sekhmet. He was putting on a puppet show in the Slopping District. His story needed a little work, but it wasn't shabby."

Wally shook his head. "There's no way Graham could have

escaped his cell, made it all the way across the city, through the Manor, and into the *Mirror*."

"I'm as confused as you are," Arthur said. "But he's there."

Wally narrowed his eyes. "I'm not falling for this."

"What do you mean?"

"This is what you *do*, Arthur. You use stories to manipulate people's emotions and then you take advantage of them."

"Why would I lie about this?" Arthur asked.

"*Hmm*," Wally said sarcastically. "Maybe so you can get me to go back to the Manor and help you replace all the gold you just lost?"

Arthur looked hurt. Breeth could sense both boys' heartbeats pounding in the ash swirling around them.

"I'm not lying this time, Wally," Arthur said. He pointed at the tentacles that had stolen his gold. "I was going to share half of that take with you. I owed you after what happened on our last heist."

Breeth's ash rippled with sympathy. This was the first time she'd heard Arthur use Wally's first name. Maybe she hadn't given this Arthur a fair shake.

Wally searched Arthur's face and then sighed. "I have to go see for myself."

"Then I'm coming with you," Arthur said, refitting his garish hat. "I have to make sure the old man's still alive anyway." He stepped to the roof's edge and stared at the sea of tentacles. "But how do we get through?"

Breeth took that as her cue to creak down the side of the fish factory and into the destroyed port. Flexing as hard as she could, she curled the broken boards around the few tentacles closest to them, clawing them aside. The tentacles struggled against her, thrashing and flexing, but Breeth curled more boards, managing to pin the tentacles to the beach. Maybe she was good at arm wrestling after all.

Arthur's mouth dropped open. "No fair!" he said to Wally. "Did that Huamei guy teach you magic? Sekhmet wouldn't even let me hold one of her swords!"

Wally only shrugged. "The tentacles must be afraid of us since we defeated the Corvidians."

The boys climbed down from the roof, and Breeth continued to clear a path for them up the cliffs, using whatever organic material she could to sweep the tentacles aside. Back in port, Pyra laughed maniacally as she sprayed a potion that made the tentacles retreat like slugs touched with salt.

"This is so weird," Arthur said, kicking a restrained tentacle. "The doll, the ravens, and now this giant tentacle monster."

"I'll say," Wally said.

"I mean it's weird other than the obvious reasons. These monsters are all straight out of Garnett Lacroix adventures. *The Case of the Doll with the Sapphire Eyes. The Night of the Ravens.* And now *The Thing from the Belly of the Sea.*"

"Okay," Wally admitted. "That *is* weird. What do you think it means?"

"Only one way to find out," Arthur said in an embarrassingly heroic voice.

They reached the top of the cliffs, and Greyridge's outer fence came into sight. They strained under the tentacles' pull.

"Harry's safe, right?" Arthur asked. "Those gates are impenetrable . . . right?"

More tentacles slithered out of the ocean and coiled around the fence. They jerked once, then twice, then a third time until the fence buckled with a shriek. The tentacles slithered in, wrenched open the portcullis, and then squeezed through the entrance with a great squelching sound.

Arthur winced. "Maybe not."

Wally's panicked eyes sought Breeth's face in the moss. She could tell he was asking her to zip ahead and check on her brother. But before she could ooze so much as an inch, something strange happened. The tentacles slurped out of the hospital and fell limp.

"Huh," Breeth said, using Greyridge's hedges to sweep the tentacles aside as easy as cooked noodles. "They aren't fighting against me anymore."

The boys climbed over Greyridge's collapsed fence and made their way past the broken portcullis. The foyer was in darkness, its electrics fizzling. Paperwork and glass littered the floor, and the walls glistened with slime. The broken carriage lay in the corner, and a man lay beside it, blood trickling from a gash on the side of his head.

"That's Graham's doctor," Wally said, his voice shaking.

Arthur looked like he might be sick.

"They just slithered in," a voice said. "They slithered in and—" The nurse at the front desk stared blankly, a wisp of hair standing up directly from the top of her head.

Wally ran to her desk. "Is my brother okay?"

She gave him a dazed look. "Brother?"

"*Graham Cooper!*" Wally said.

Breeth winced in the broken portcullis.

The nurse mindlessly rustled her paperwork. "I don't think we have a . . . Gran Copper."

Breeth grew impatient. She seeped into the floor's moss and oozed to the door leading to the cells. Feeling inside her wooden self, she found the lock and twisted it.

"I unlocked it, Wally!" she said, creaking open.

Wally sprinted down the hallway. Arthur followed slowly, eyes still fixed on the wounded doctor. Breeth was about to follow them, but then she heard a voice.

"*Oh. Oh my.*"

But this wasn't just any voice. It had a certain resonance to it, felt through the hospital's wood and moss. It clearly belonged to a woman. And yet instead of echoing down the hallways, it carried through the *materials* of the hospital.

The voice was like Breeth's.

Breeth followed the resonance, seeping down a tunnel clogged with a lifeless tentacle, and arrived at a cell that had been wrenched open. Inside was a ghost. The woman was blue as a candle flame. She floated in the middle of the air and stared at something on the floor.

Breeth seeped up the mossy wall to get a better look.

Oh, she thought, piecing together the gruesome scene.

The ghost lady was staring at her own dead body.

The ghost and her body were slim, with silvery hair and liver spots on their hands. The only difference between them was that the ghost was still in one piece, while the body . . . Well, it didn't take much detective work to realize that the tentacles had slithered into the hospital, broken into this cell, and then pulled this woman apart.

Breeth gulped, and the ghost woman's pearly eyes shot up in fear.

"Are you the angel of death?" the woman whispered.

"Um, no?" Breeth said. She doubted her moss looked very deathly. Or angelic.

The woman sighed, relaxing a bit. Her pearly eyes studied her own dead body. Then she scoffed. "I've heard of artists sacrificing their lives for their work, but this is ridiculous."

"You're an artist?"

The ghost woman nodded. "An author. Or I *was*, at least." She shook her head and laughed without humor. "Killed by my own pen name."

Breeth's mossy nose wrinkled in confusion. She knew pen names were something authors made up when they didn't want to use their real ones. But how could someone be killed by a made-up name?

The ghost lady's pearly eyes flashed to the hallway. "I warned them he was coming for me. The nurse tried to assure me that I was safe in this cell. But I knew better. He would bend heaven and earth to finish the job."

"Who's *he*?" Breeth asked.

"Alfred Moore," the woman said.

Breeth's moss bristled in recognition. That was the author Arthur was obsessed with.

"The guy who writes those adventure books?" Breeth asked.

"*I* wrote those books," the ghost lady said, annoyed. "I never was able to sell my work under my real name. My publishers claimed the public wouldn't be interested in stories by a *female* writer." She cleared her throat and did an impression of a male voice. "*We simply can't sell adventure tales bearing a woman's name. But with a pen name . . .*" She sighed. "What choice did I have? If I wanted The Adventures of Garnett Lacroix to be read by the masses, then I would have to adopt a male nom de plume." She stared at her body. "Little did I realize the monster I created the day I came up with *Alfred Moore*."

Breeth's thoughts were all in a tangle. A pen name was nothing more than a name, right? As harmless as ink on paper.

"Wait, how did a guy you came up with *kill* you?" she asked.

The ghost lady opened her hand and stared through her ghostly fingers. "I was sick of writing those silly adventures. And I was sick of writing as a man, not receiving the credit I was due for my work. So I shut my quill away in a drawer, swearing never to write as Alfred Moore again." She closed her ghostly fingers into a fist. "But Alfred didn't want the stories to end."

Breeth felt a tingle of understanding. Of course. Whenever someone imagined something in the Real, it appeared in the Fae: a unicorn. A goblin screamatorium. Even a male pen name . . .

"I never met my pen name," the ghost lady continued. "Not in person. But after I retired Alfred, stories started to appear on my desk. Stories I had not written. It seemed Alfred had learned of my existence—the woman who created him—and was convinced that the only way to take control of his destiny was to kill me." Her form flickered with fear. "Someone had given him a Quill. To use his somewhat flowery description, 'a magical Quill of black bone, veined red, and as gnarled as an old knuckle.' Alfred started to write monstrous stories with this Quill, and those stories appeared on *my* pages." The ghost lady sought Breeth's eyes. "But words cannot harm us, right?"

Breeth nodded her moss uncertainly.

The ghost lady's voice grew haunted. "That's what I'd hoped. But then Alfred's stories started to come true. His words described objects coming to life in my apartment. And that's just what happened. My bedsheets tried to strangle me. My letter opener tried to stab me. One night, I found the arsenic pouring itself into my soup."

Breeth's mossy eyes widened. That was almost as scary as her own death.

The ghost continued. "I narrowly managed to survive Alfred's attacks. I carried his stories with me, reading wherever I went. Whenever they described something ghastly, I was ready. I dodged the letter opener that flew at my heart. I took the bedsheets to the cleaner's and never picked them up again. I never sipped the soup."

Breeth looked at the body on the ground. "How did you end up in Greyridge?"

The woman sighed. "I made the mistake of telling my cousin that I suspected my pen name was trying to murder me." Her pearly gaze drifted around the cell. "Naturally, he had me committed."

Where she could no longer avoid danger, Breeth realized.

The ghost lady continued. "Alfred managed to reach me in this hospital by pulling monsters from my own Garnett Lacroix adventures. I heard whispers of the doll after its porcelain victims were committed here. Next came the ravens.

And finally the tentacles." She frowned at her own dead body. "Third time's a charm, I suppose."

"I'm sorry you were killed," Breeth said. "It's not fun."

"No," the woman said, her pearly eyes shining on Breeth's. "It isn't, is it?"

Breeth was about to ask more questions—about the author and the monsters and whether the ghost lady wanted to be friends—but then a crack formed in the cell's ceiling, as luminous as an exploding star. Breeth recognized the light, soft and cool on her moss. She'd seen it the moment after she was killed, right before she was absorbed into the knife hilt.

The ceiling continued to peel open like burning paper, catching the ghost lady's attention.

"I guess this is it," she said. She hugged herself and looked at Breeth. "Please, do me a favor? Check on my cat? I had to leave her when I was committed."

An invisible force drew the ghost lady upward, like a tissue lifted by the wind.

"Wait!" Breeth said. "I want to come with you! My parents are up there!"

She tried to leap from the moss into the open air, so she too could be drawn upward . . . but the light didn't seem to want her.

"My name is Valerie Lucas!" the ghost lady called. "I live on the corner of River Road and Will—"

And then she was gone—absorbed into the light. The bright tear in the ceiling closed like a zipper, and the cell fell dark and empty, save the dead body all in pieces.

Breeth oozed miserably between the stones, feeling as helpless as the moss she inhabited.

* * *

After taking a few moments to herself, Breeth seeped into the hallway, listening for familiar voices.

"Stop arguing and grab the bloody guard's keys!" a man snarled.

Breeth followed the voice and found Arthur standing outside of a cell, staring at a man through the barred window. The flower on Arthur's hat was wilted again.

"Last time, you told me to leave you in here," Arthur said.

"That was before the guards was attacked by ravens and giant squids! You can't *buy* luck like that!"

"If a tentacle doesn't grab you on your way through port, the Rook's men will kill you the moment you set foot in the city!"

The man scoffed. "I never thought I'd see the day when my son wanted to be more Black Feathers and less Garnett Lacrotch."

This was Arthur's *dad*? Breeth thought. They sure didn't act like father and son.

"You're safer in here!" Arthur shouted. "All right? I've never felt so relaxed knowing you were behind bars!"

This was too complicated for Breeth. She saw another figure at the end of the hallway and seeped up to Wally.

"Holy cow," she said. "Do I have something to tell you."

"Not now," Wally said.

"Uh," Breeth said, "you're *really* gonna want to hear this."

Wally stared through the bars. "He was right."

"Who was right?"

"Arthur. My brother's not here."

Breeth seeped through the moss and under the door. Moonlight streamed cold and pale through the cell's window onto an empty bed and a strange drawing on the wall.

"Every time I've walked down this hall," Wally said through the bars, "Graham has stuck his hand out to greet me with a smile and a riddle. This is the first time that hasn't happened."

Breeth searched for clues. How could a person just disappear from a locked cell? She examined the drawing. Parts looked quite realistic, as if she could float right through it into the Mirror. But the middle had been smeared with an *X*.

Out of curiosity, Breeth seeped into the cobwebs of the drawing . . . and every bit of her ignited with dark flame. An explosion of power and magma coursed through her, howling with the darkness between the stars, twisting and contorting her spirit like she was caught in a black hole—

Breeth wrenched herself free, fleeing back to the moss. If she'd had breath she would have panted. "So, um," she said, "I think he went through that weird drawing."

Wally stared at it. "*Practicing his portals,*" he whispered. His eyes leapt to Breeth. "Can you help me get to the Mirror?"

Breeth was all too familiar with the look on his face. It was the ache of a missing family. But she'd already helped Wally so much. She'd died as a mouse thing and been pecked in the brain by a flock of bird monsters and fought off a slippery swath of tentacles. What if it took weeks or even months for her to help Wally chase after his brother? How long would it be before they could find her killer?

"Wally," she said. "I think I may have sensed my parents a few minutes ago. A patient died in another cell, and I watched her ascend into this light. I felt them in there. I need to find a way back to them."

Wally stared into her knotted eyes. "You've been so helpful, Breeth. I don't know how I'll ever thank you." He looked at the painting on the wall. "But my brother might be in trouble. Once he's safe and sound, I promise I'll help you find your killer."

"Got it," Breeth said, trying to smile through her sadness. "First save the living guy, then help the dead girl."

* * *

By the time they returned to Arthur, he'd found the keys and was releasing his dad.

"Attaboy!" the man said, ruffling his son's hat, whose daffodil was in full bloom again. "Glad to see the Rook's claws ain't sunk too deep."

"Go hide somewhere in the city," Arthur said. "And *don't drink*. I'll find you once I have enough money to pay off your debt."

The man raised his right hand. "Black Feathers' honor."

Breeth doubted a gang of thieves possessed much honor.

Arthur's dad trucked down the hallway and vanished.

"You weren't lying," Wally said to Arthur. "About Graham."

"I never lie!" Arthur said.

Wally looked like he wanted to argue but thought better of it. "I need to get back to Mirror Kingsport and find him."

"How?" Arthur said. "Those weird people took their door knocker back. Hazelrigg will be nothing but a burnt-out shell."

"I got in once by yelling Lady Weirdwood's name," Wally said. "Maybe it'll work a second time."

They exited the hospital into the evening. The port was eerily quiet. The tentacles writhed like beached fish. It was dinnertime, when people would usually be flooding the docks, but now the only sounds were ocean waves. Even the seagulls had been frightened away by the Corvidians.

A robed figure waited for them on the cliffs. Arthur and Wally froze, ready to fight or run. But then the figure drew back its hood.

"You saved my life, thief."

Huamei was still looking a little stiff around the shoulders, but his porcelain skin had softened for the most part.

"Oh," Wally said. "That. It . . . just seemed like the right thing to do."

Huamei bowed. "I owe you a boon."

He didn't seem too pleased about it, Breeth noticed.

"Is this some kind of honor-bound dragon thing?" Arthur said.

Huamei flashed his ocean-deep eyes at Arthur.

Arthur gulped. "I'll take that as a yes."

"Can you take us to Mirror Kingsport?" Wally said.

Huamei considered this a moment, clearly weighing the risks. "You have proven you can keep yourself safe, thief." He looked at Arthur. "You, on the other hand . . ."

A sound from the docks caught their attention. Sekhmet and Pyra were making splints for Ludwig so they could get him back to the Manor.

"This way," Huamei said. "If Sekhmet sees you, she'll detain you."

He led them along the collapsed fence and they ducked behind the hedges.

Huamei studied Greyridge and wondered aloud to himself. "Why would the Fae-born break into a hospital?"

"Oh! Oh!" Breeth said, stretching one of her hedge branches. "I know! Wally, raise your hand for me!"

"Um," Wally said, raising his hand.

Breeth described everything she'd seen and heard: the ghost lady, her body pulled apart by tentacles, the fact that she was the real author behind Garnett Lacroix and that Alfred Moore was just her pen name, and finally, that he had received a magical Quill that helped him kill her with a story. Wally repeated it all.

Arthur removed his ridiculous hat. "Alfred Moore is . . . dead?"

"He never existed," Wally said. "But yeah, it sounds like the woman who used that name to write Garnett Lacroix was killed. Sorry, Arthur."

Arthur's head hung heavy. "So Moore was never a recluse. He was just invented by a woman . . ." He sniffed, tearing up a little. "No wonder those books handled emotions so well."

"Describe that Quill again," Huamei said, eyes narrowing.

Breeth quivered her branches, and Wally relayed the information. "Black as night. Red veined. Gnarled like an old knuckle."

Huamei stroked his braid in thought. "I believe, thief, you may have just solved the mystery of how the Fae-born made it into the Real without a Rift."

"Actually, *I* solved it!" Breeth said.

"What do you mean?" Wally asked Huamei.

"By inventing a pen name and placing it on the cover of a book, a book that was embraced in the imaginations of people all across Kingsport, Valerie Lucas breathed life into an author located in the Mirror."

"Alfred Moore," Arthur whispered.

"Correct." Huamei sat on a lifeless tentacle, thinking. "That Quill had to have been fashioned from one of my ancestor's bones. Dragon-bone quills don't abide by the rules of the Balance. Fae-born usually require Rifts to find their way into the Real. Dragon-bone quills, on the other hand, allow *anyone* to bring creatures to life, in the Real or the Fae, by simply writing words on a page. Those with strong imaginations can use the Quill to powerful effect."

"Especially if they have a *bone* to pick," Breeth said. "Eh, Wally?"

He ignored her, and her branches drooped. She always felt better after making someone laugh, and she still hadn't shaken the chill of seeing the ghost lady's dead body.

Huamei studied Greyridge, considering. "It sounds as if Valerie Lucas's Mirror pen name got his hands on this Quill and has been writing monsters into Kingsport."

"Why didn't Moore just write, *Valerie Lucas drops dead* and be done with it?" Wally asked.

"Dragon bones have their limitations," Huamei said. "They cannot be used to directly take life or revive the dead in the Real. The wielder must come up with more *creative*, indirect ways to kill. For example, sending a tentacle monster to do his bidding."

"Or do his *squidding*," Breeth said.

Wally didn't so much as crack a smile.

"Wait, wait, wait." Arthur held his head as if it was about to explode. "Let me get this straight. My favorite author *doesn't* exist because he was actually a pen name for a writer named Valerie Lucas. Except he kind of *does* exist, but he lives in the Mirror City. And now he's used a dragon-bone Quill to write monsters into the streets of Kingsport in order to kill the woman who created him?"

Huamei nodded. "He has become a sort of backward author. A work of fiction that can create things in the Real."

"This sure is a *novel* situation," Breeth said. "Get it, Wally? Say that joke for me. You can have it. It's yours."

Wally pursed his lips.

She rustled her branches. "Well, you're no fun."

Arthur shook his head in disbelief. "This is *way* more complicated than Moore's books. Sorry—*Lucas's*. No wonder I didn't solve it."

"This explains why I couldn't send the doll back to the

Mirror by adding to its story," Huamei said. "By using the dragon-bone Quill, Moore disturbed the Veil, making it weak in your city." He was lost in thought a moment. "The only place he could've gotten that Quill is from the Fallen Warden."

Breeth's branches tensed at the name.

"Who?" Arthur asked.

"The Wardens don't speak his name," Huamei said. "But he's one of Lady Weirdwood's ex-employees. He stole that bone from my people's Cloud Cemetery in order to bring the Veil crashing down and locate his wife's spirit in the hopes of bringing her back to life. Lady Weirdwood was too foolish to stop him before he desecrated my ancestor's grave."

Wally cleared his throat. "Didn't she banish and bind him so he could no longer perform magic or handle magical implements?"

"It's possible that he has an accomplice," Huamei said. "But she should have had better control over him in the first place. My kingdom has been at odds with Weirdwood ever since. One dragon bone is priceless—worth more magic than exists in that entire Manor."

"Wait," Arthur asked Huamei. "If you're royalty, why aren't you living it up in a dragon castle right now?"

Huamei's cheeks flushed and he looked at the ground. "I am a descendant of the Tian Empire. My fa—*step*father is a duke in the Court of Sky. I was meant to inherit his position when I came of age. But last week, Mother had a moment of weakness and was overcome by guilt. She told the duke, the man I believed was my father, the truth about my origins. It seems she met my real father in a traveling market and was wooed by him. That's how I came to be. My *step*father wasted no time in banishing me from the Court of Sky and enrolling me as a Warden Novitiate to avoid political embarrassment."

"So you're a bastard?" Arthur asked.

"What I *am*," Huamei said with sudden heat, "is the first dragon to serve the Wardens in over a century. It's a humiliation. Of course, Lady Weirdwood had no choice but to accept me. She owed my kingdom a debt ever since the Fallen Warden desecrated my ancestor's grave." He stood and stared at the hospital. "If I find that Quill and the Fallen Warden, I could restore honor to my family and return to the Cloud Kingdom."

Breeth's leaves fluttered with hope. "I could take revenge on my killer and get back to my parents."

Wally finally looked at her and smiled.

"Um, Wally?" Arthur said. "Could I, uh, speak to you privately for a moment?"

Before Wally could protest, Arthur dragged him into the hedges. Breeth flickered through the leaves behind them, ready to poke Arthur in the forehead if he started being obnoxious.

"I think Graham is involved in this," Arthur said.

Wally remained expressionless, listening intently.

"When I met him," Arthur said, "he told me this riddle. I couldn't solve it at the time because I didn't know how all of this worked. I thought the solution was a theater curtain. But I just realized he was talking about the fall of the *Veil*."

Wally's head grew heavy. "Yeah. That sounds like Graham."

Arthur swallowed. "He also gave me that Golden Scarab that disappeared in the Manor . . . I didn't want to tell Huamei about any of this because I don't want the Wardens going after your brother."

Wally was quiet a moment. "Thank you, Arthur."

Arthur put his hand on Wally's shoulder. "I want to help you find Graham. I know you have every reason not to trust me, but I want to change that. Life's hard enough without being able to rely on your friends."

As Arthur spoke, Breeth watched the daffodil on his hat bloom. Again, he didn't notice.

"I think you should trust him, Wally," Breeth said.

Wally took a deep breath. Then he extended a hand. Arthur shook it.

"Aw," Breeth said, embracing them with her branches. "Reunion!"

Arthur quirked an eyebrow toward the sky. "And so it was that Arthur Benton started on his track to becoming a *real* Gentleman Thief."

Wally rolled his eyes and exited the hedge.

"I was kidding!" Arthur said, following after.

"What was that about?" Huamei asked.

Arthur stood tall. "Cooper and I have decided to help you track down that Quill and restore your dukedom. And we won't even charge you! You might be wondering what kind of selfless thieves would make such an offer. But we're doing it for the sake of Kingsport!"

Huamei was unmoved by this speech. "There are still many things we don't know. Like where the Fallen Warden and Alfred Moore are hiding. We'll need to track down Valerie

Lucas's house to search for that story that wrote itself on her desk. It may contain clues."

Arthur shook his head. "That's gonna be tricky. I've spent *years* trying to figure out where Moore—er, *Lucas*—lives."

"Wait!" Breeth said. "The ghost lady asked if I would check on her cat! She told me she lives at the corner of River and Will-something. She didn't say what her cat likes to eat though."

"River and Willow," Wally said. "I robbed a house there once."

"How do you *know* all this stuff?" Arthur said.

He hadn't heard Breeth. He'd only heard Wally spit out an address he'd been trying to find for years.

Wally avoided his eyes. "A true thief never reveals his secrets."

Arthur sighed and then smiled. "River and Willow it is!"

They set off down the cliffs, and Arthur breathed deep. "This feels like something straight out of Garnett Lacroix!"

"I can't believe I'm saying this," Wally said. "But this is *literally* something out of Garnett Lacroix."

16
THE MURDEROUS TALE

This is it," Wally said, gazing up at the brownstone house, which glistened in a light drizzle.

The house had clearly been abandoned. Trash and leaves piled around the steps. The windows that weren't shattered were speckled with dust. The front door had been kicked open by looters.

Arthur swept off his garish hat. "I can't believe I'm actually here."

"Didn't you meet the *real* Garnett Lacroix?" Wally said.

"Yeah, but he was kind of disappointing." Arthur's eyes shined on the house. "Miss Lucas's stories made me who I am."

He reverently scaled the steps and disappeared through the front door. Wally and Huamei followed. All was quiet inside. The house had gone untended for weeks. Everything was covered in dust. Most of the valuables had been stolen, and rats and spiders had taken over the kitchen.

Wally and Huamei walked down a side hallway, while Breeth creaked through the floorboards. *"Here, kitty kitty kitty!"*

They searched the bedroom, washroom, and kitchen. In every room, something was out of place. Sheets were missing. Candlesticks contorted in unsettling ways. Poisons spilled out from under the sink. Wally shuddered when he remembered that Valerie Lucas's own household items had tried to kill her.

Breeth screamed as a calico cat chased her across the floorboards.

"I forgot I was a mouse for a while!" Breeth cried. "I hate cats now!"

Huamei watched the cat chase nothing, likely thinking this was normal feline behavior. "How did you really come to know all this information about Valerie Lucas?" he asked Wally. "I would hate to have to tell Lady Weirdwood that you're a spy for the Order of Eldar."

"Oh, um," Wally said, feeling suddenly vulnerable. "I found her file when I was looking for my brother and just . . . put it together."

Huamei gave him a skeptical look but didn't press the issue.

Down the hall, Breeth scared the cat away by tipping over a stack of pots and then creaked back. "Miss Lucas's cat is a jerk and a demon and an all-around terrible person, and his breath smells like death."

They scaled the staircase to the second floor and entered Valerie Lucas's office. The walls were stacked to the ceiling with books and papers, all scrawled and disorganized. The desk was spattered with ink and held quills in different states of distress. Arthur sat in the middle of the floor, holding a single page.

"*Chapter one,*" he read. "*The night was as purple as ink, and the owls were hooting their enchantments, waking the bats and wolves, and giving them a taste for blood.*" He traced the handwritten letters. "This is the first page of the first Garnett Lacroix story. This book was my safe haven after Mom died. Whenever the world felt cold and unfamiliar, I could always escape into this world." His eyes shined with tears. "Now that Valerie Lucas is dead, those adventures are finished forever."

Huamei stepped past him. "We need to start searching."

Arthur carefully folded the page and stuck it in his vest pocket. Then he, Huamei, and Wally flipped through the stacks of paper in silence, searching for the story that had tried to murder Valerie Lucas. Wally noticed a flutter in one of the stacks, riffling from the bottom upward, like an invisible finger running along their edges.

Breeth squealed. "Wally! If I possess a page, I can read the letters on me! I never realized I could do this!" She ruffled more. "It isn't exactly *easy*, though. The letters feel upside down or backward, like trying to figure out what the freckles on your back say."

Wally snorted.

"What's funny?" Arthur asked.

"Nothing," Wally said, wiping his nose. "Just the dust."

Something wet slapped against the window, making them all jump. A giant tentacle plunged and slurped against the pane. Huamei looked from the window to a piece of paper on the desk, which was quickly filling with cursive text, as if written by an invisible pen.

"Moore knows we're here," Huamei said.

"I got this!" Arthur said, grabbing the page and tearing it into small pieces.

But the writing simply leapt to another blank page. Then another. And another.

Wally gulped as the window strained against the tentacle's efforts.

"You two find the manuscript," Huamei said, drawing out his paintbrush. "I'll handle the tentacles." He started to paint a symbol in the air. "It's a good thing the humans are hiding in their homes, otherwise I wouldn't be able to do this."

With each brushstroke, Huamei's skin grew blue and scaly, his eyes large and cold as ice. Fangs extended from his lips as his shadow grew long across the wall. Wally looked away, heart pounding. Lady Weirdwood had said that Huamei's skin would be fragile as he recovered from the porcelain. But Wally wasn't about to argue with a dragon.

Huamei snarled, and Wally felt a spray on the back of his neck, as chilling as ocean waves. He slipped through the door and slithered down the stairs. Something large shrieked outside, and the giant tentacle was ripped from the window with a great squelch.

"Gah!" Arthur slapped his forehead. "I'm missing out on all the action!" He grabbed a letter opener off the desk and brandished it like a sword. "You keep searching, Cooper. I'll guard the front door!"

Before Wally could argue, Arthur thundered downstairs.

"Breeth?" Wally said to the empty room.

"I got this stack!" she said, ruffling pages.

Wally examined papers at random. "This stack seems to be all about Garnett Lacroix."

"This one looks like journal entries," Breeth said.

"These are fan letters addressed to Alfred Moore."

Something heavy thudded against the roof and Wally ducked. The walls trembled. Towers of paper spilled across the floor. Downstairs, Arthur screamed, "Bring it on, you oversized toilet plunger!" His voice cut short as the floor canted to the side, the entire house tilting on its foundation. Wally widened his stance to keep balance.

Breeth giggled. "*Eww!* This stack is in Miss Lucas's handwriting, but it says it's written by someone named *Montana Marshes.* Listen to this. *He steamily hefted her into his arms and hungrily sniffed along the glistening nape of her—*"

The front of the house buckled and splintered as the tentacles squeezed.

"Breeth!" Wally cried. "In case you hadn't noticed, *giant tentacles* are trying to break in and kill us!"

"Right! Sorry. You kind of forget about danger when you're dead."

Wally braced himself against a shelf and took stock of the room. It would take them hours to scan every page. He wouldn't be surprised if the tentacles crushed the house like a matchbox in the next five minutes.

"Maybe Miss Lucas hid the story before she was committed," he said.

"Ooh!" Breeth said. "Smart!"

He watched her ruffle out of the pages, creak through

the floorboards, and then thump into the writing desk. "Found it!"

"Really?" Wally said, running over. He tried the desk's drawer. It was locked.

"Yep!" Breeth said. "This handwriting is different from the other pages. The first line says: *I met the Jangling Man among the lilies, and he offered me an object that would alter my life forever.*"

The house bucked again, sending Wally sprawling. "Can you open the drawer?"

The drawer jiggled. "Sorry," Breeth said. "Lock's made of metal."

Wally tried to force it open. It refused to budge.

"I'll keep reading!" Breeth cleared her throat, swirling dust from the keyhole, and put on her best male voice. "'*My boss wants to save your life,' the man said, drawing a strange Quill from his pocket, 'by giving you something that can destroy your creator.' I stared at my hands, grown spotted with age. Over the past few months, I had felt myself aging at an accelerated rate, my hair and fingernails shedding like autumn leaves.*"

The house made a terrible crunching sound. The room buckled and splintered, compacting to an uncomfortably cramped size.

"This is taking too long!" Wally said, ducking. "Can you skim for clues?"

"Sure!" Breeth said.

Another inhuman screech came from outside as more tentacles slapped against the pane, blocking out the light. The roof groaned, ready to collapse. Downstairs, the front door splintered open. "En garde, slithering infidels!" Arthur shouted. "*Wait.* Ow! Ow! Stop!"

Wally slammed the office door. They had to get out of there.

"Here's something maybe," Breeth said from the drawer. "*I returned to my office in the ferns, wielding the strange instrument, which seemed to grow warm in my ha—*"

The window exploded. A tentacle whipped into the office, catching Wally by the ankle and dragging him toward the window.

"Breeth!" he screamed.

Wally felt the cool air of the outdoors on his ankle before a piece of the broken ceiling came piercing down like a guillotine, impaling the tentacle. Wally scrambled away.

"*Pleh!*" Breeth said, her splinters dripping tentacle slime. "That was *disgusting*!"

The feeling crept back into Wally's face as he realized she had left the desk to save him.

"Now will you *annoying* tentacles stop interrupting my reading?" she said, and thumped back into the desk.

Seven more tentacles wriggled through the broken frame and into the room. Wally backed up until he hit the desk.

"*Breeth*," Wally whispered. "There are more. A *lot* more."

"I can't read and fight tentacles at the same time!" she said. "If they get this manuscript, we won't find any clues about my killer!"

"Okay," he whispered. "Keep reading."

"Ew!" Breeth said. "Moore was so focused on writing monsters, he ran out of ink and started using his own *blood*!"

"That information is *not* helpful right now," Wally whispered, eyes on the tentacles.

"Sorry," Breeth whispered back. "It doesn't say anything about where he's hiding in the Mirror. But he did mention lilies and ferns, so he's clearly *outside*, but . . ."

The tentacles blindly felt their way across the floorboards. Wally held his breath. He stepped up onto the desk before a tentacle reached his foot. And he stepped off just as quickly as it slithered up and around the desk, coiling it in its grip.

"Um," Breeth said as the tentacle pulled the desk from the wall. "Am I moving?"

Wally was too horrified to answer. A giant mouth had

appeared in the window. It was slimy and circular, with hundreds of rows of bristling teeth.

"*B–B–Breeth!*" Wally finally managed to whisper. "Get out of there!"

"No! We have to solve this!"

Wally grabbed hold of the desk and tried pulling in the opposite direction. But it was no use. The tentacle was a thirty-foot muscle.

"*Pull*, Wally!" Breeth shouted. "We don't have enough information!"

Wally strained. "Huamei! Arthur!" he cried. "I need your help!"

No response.

"I'm flipping to the end of the story!" Breeth said.

The office door burst open and a tentacle from the hallway slithered in. It wrapped around Wally's waist and pulled. More tentacles swarmed through the window and grabbed the desk, wrenching it from Wally's grip.

"Breeth!" he screamed. "Quick! Possess something else!"

As the desk slid toward the hole in the wall, Breeth read as fast as she could. "*My doll and my ravens defeated, I summoned the one thing I knew would defeat her. The world ender. The krak—*"

Her voice broke off when the desk reached the tentacle monster's mouth. Its teeth made short work of the wood—like a rotating saw, flinging sawdust and bits of paper—and the desk vanished into the abyss of its throat.

The manuscript consumed, the tentacle monster slithered off the brownstone.

"Breeth!" Wally called after it.

There was no answer. He checked the rooftops for signs of the ghost girl. In the sky, dragon Huamei spewed seawater, washing the tentacles back into the sewers. But the tentacles retreated willingly, taking Alfred Moore's manuscript and Breeth with them.

"*Cooper!*" Arthur limped through the splintered door and clapped Wally on the shoulder, laughing with relief. "It was close, but I managed to scare the foul beast away. Did you find the story?"

Wally was doing his best not to cry.

Breeth hadn't so much as screamed.

17
THE FOOL DREAMER

nd then the tentacle was like, *Oh no!* And *I* was like, *Oh yes!* and I jabbed at it like this! *Ya!* And then all of the tentacles retreated in fear, slurping right back into the sewer!" Arthur lifted his golden blade over his head in triumph. "That monster will rue the day it ever messed with Arthur Benton and his trusty letter opener!"

Wally's eye twitched. He seemed drained. Like the tentacles had dragged a piece of his soul into the sewer with them.

"C'mon, Cooper!" Arthur said, jostling his shoulder. "We just survived not one but *two* real-life monster attacks! I mean, sure, those ravens and tentacles will haunt our dreams for years to come, but we *defeated* them!"

Wally stared at his hands. "I lost Moore's story."

"Curse it!" Arthur said, not feeling particularly cursed at all. "I suppose this means that the adventure continues! Did you manage to read any of it?"

Wally relayed what little information he had gleaned in the chaos: the Jangling Man who had given Moore the Quill, the lilies and the office in the ferns, even that Moore had started writing with his own blood.

"A Jangling Man?" Arthur said. "Who *jangles*? A key maker? A man who swallows treasure? And I'd always imagined Moore would be in the city. Not *outside*."

Wally didn't respond, still deflated.

Arthur started to feel concerned. "Come on. Let's get to the Mirror and search for your brother."

They exited Valerie Lucas's destroyed house. Dragon Huamei was perched on a mailbox, head bowed. His scales shed like leaves into the gutter. A boy's silhouette took shape in his belly.

"I wonder if that hurts," Arthur said.

"Well, this is fortunate," a voice said behind them.

They turned to find Sekhmet, swords drawn.

Arthur's heart skipped a beat, but he managed to smile. "I know, I know. You're impressed to see me. You didn't think I'd be able to survive the Mirror all by myself."

Sekhmet's swords glowed white-hot. "The others may be too busy to arrest you for bringing Fae-born skeletons into the Real, but I'm not."

Arthur stepped behind Wally. "Magic her, Cooper! Like you did with the tentacles! Smack her over the head with that beam! Tie her up with that rope!"

"I . . . can't," Wally said, only growing more deflated.

Sekhmet raised her glowing swords. She was about to slash downward when a gruff voice stopped her. "*Not Wally.*" Huamei limped toward them, spine hunched, long fingernails tapping against the stones. "*I owe him a boon.*"

"*You*," Sekhmet said, pointing a sword at him, "aren't supposed to be out here. Amelia told me to bring you back to the Healing Room *immediately*. She said you're still fragile after—"

"Amelia is not my authority," Huamei interrupted. He cleared the salt water from his throat, then cracked his neck back into place and stood upright. "And Weirdwood Manor has always underestimated how difficult it is to kill a dragon."

"It's true!" Arthur said. "You should've seen him battle that tentacle monster!" He flipped the letter opener in his hand. "Should have seen me too, for that matter."

Sekhmet rolled her eyes at Huamei. "It's your funeral." Then she went after Arthur.

"Wait!" he said. "You need me! I know things!"

She froze and gave Huamei a questioning look.

"He's right," Huamei said. He told her all of the information that had led them to realize that Kingsport was being destroyed by someone's pen name.

Arthur pointed a thumb at his chest. "And I know more about Alfred Moore than anyone, so I'm the only one who knows where he's hiding." He hoped she didn't realize this last part was a lie.

Sekhmet gave him a look. "The answer's obvious, isn't it?"

Arthur gulped. "Is it?"

She pointed to the street signs. "If the author who created the pen name lives at Willow and River, then all we have to do is find their Mirror counterparts. Wallow and Reaper or something."

"You're wrong," Arthur said. "Valerie Lucas dreamt up a far more romantic and appropriate location for Alfred Moore."

Sekhmet crossed her arms. "Where is he, then?"

Arthur felt his cheeks flush. "I can't just tell you that information! You'd leave me in the dust!" He gestured down the street. "If you want to waste time at the bookstore, reading all of Garnett Lacroix's adventures to figure it out, be my guest."

Sekhmet suddenly looked less confident. "We can't access the Mirror anyway."

"What do you mean?" Huamei asked.

"I wasn't going to mention this in front of the thieves, but the Manor has been compromised. The doors to the Fae have been sealed. Lady Weirdwood is in a coma."

"What happened to her?" Wally asked, coming out of his funk a bit.

Sekhmet shook her head. "Amelia couldn't figure it out at first. But then Weston returned from the Mirror, bruised and beaten from those skeletons Arthur sicced on him. He ventured into the Abyssment and found the carcass of a Golden Scarab."

Arthur's eyes widened, but he tried to play it off as surprise, like he'd never heard of such a thing.

"The Scarab stung the Manor's roots, injecting them with poison," Sekhmet continued. "Because Lady Weirdwood is linked to the Manor, she collapsed. Amelia believes the Order of Eldar sent the Scarab. But until we figure out where it came from, Pyra can't cook an antidote."

Arthur stared at the ground, thinking. If he told Sekhmet that he brought that Scarab into the Manor, she would slap another pair of those magma manacles on him. Besides, he had promised Wally he'd keep Graham's secret safe.

Arthur kept his mouth shut.

Huamei took out his calligraphy brush. "I don't need the Manor to get us to the Mirror."

"Put that thing away," Sekhmet said. "I want to go and bring down Moore as much as you do. But we should wait until the Wardens return from the Mercury Mines and let them go instead."

Huamei shook his head. "If I return to the Manor, Amelia will lock me in the Healing Room. I won't let that happen. I have reason to believe that the Quill Alfred Moore has in his possession is one of my ancestor's bones. I'm going to track it down, retrieve it, and restore honor to my family and return to the Cloud Kingdom." He stared at her with the ocean depths of his eyes. "If we solve this ourselves, it may be enough to earn your precious Wardenship."

Sekhmet sighed. She stared in the direction of Hazelrigg, considering. "The Wardens *are* in over their heads in the Mercury Mines. And the staff *is* still recovering from the Corvidians and tentacles . . ." She breathed deep. "Fine."

The entire time Huamei and Sekhmet had been talking, Arthur had been trying to puzzle out a solution to Moore's whereabouts. He knew that Valerie Lucas loved anagrams, frequently scrambling the letters of important clues in her adventures. In *The Mystery of the Gilded Thread*, the Merry Rogues had learned about the Gentleman Thief's past by unscrambling the letters in his name. *Garnett Lacroix* was actually an *Ex-tailor* named *Grant C.* That's why Garnett's outfits were so impeccable.

If the name *Alfred Moore* was made up, it just might be an

anagram. But by unscrambling the letters, all Arthur had come up with was *Fool Dreamer*. That was certainly true of Moore . . . but it didn't give Arthur any clues.

Sekhmet stared at him. "You're trying to solve it right now, aren't you?"

"*No!*" Arthur said, stalling for time. "I'm just trying to decide whether or not I trust you to take me with you if I give you the answer."

Sekhmet lifted her hand and made a symbol. "I swear on the grave of my mentor Rose that I will let you come with us if you know where that author is hiding."

Arthur swallowed. "Okay," he said. "I'll tell you the answer. Right . . . *now* . . ."

Sekhmet, Huamei, and Wally stared at him. Arthur had always been good under pressure. All of those eyes staring at him had always unlocked a fear in him, making his thoughts spark like fireworks . . .

And then it clicked. It was the emerald of Sekhmet's staring eyes that did it. Arthur did a little letter juggling and then cried out, "Lucas, you subtle *genius*! I know where he is!"

Sekhmet crossed her arms. "So you *were* figuring it out."

"I was just building suspense!" He beamed. "By unscrambling the letters in *Alfred Moore*, you get *Emerald Roof*!" He clapped Wally on the shoulder. "All that talk of lilies and ferns threw me off at first, but now it makes perfect sense. Moore isn't writing outside! He's hiding in the city's greenhouse!" He removed his hat and showed them all the daffodil. "Right where Valerie Lucas came up with the inspiration for Garnett Lacroix's signature symbol!"

Sekhmet did not look impressed. She merely glanced at his hat. "Your flower's wilted."

* * *

Arthur led Wally, Huamei, and Sekhmet through Huamei's paint portal and down the oddly slanted streets of the Mirror City, hoods drawn over their faces. Wally's cloak was still drying after Huamei had painted it on him.

They ventured down Gloom Avenue, through Stench Park, and past the unsettling marble statues of the Bleary Estate, keeping to the shadows and alleys.

"We have to prepare for battle," Sekhmet said. "Moore could summon an army of porcelain dolls or a flock of Corvidians so thick it chokes the sky."

Arthur slowed his pace a little. This was starting to feel less like an adventure and more like a suicide mission.

"Huamei," Sekhmet said, "is there any way you can neutralize the author so he doesn't have a chance to use that Quill?"

"I can flood the greenhouse with seawater and wash him out."

"Better yet," Sekhmet said, "fill it up and seal the exits."

Arthur's heart clenched at the thought of watching his beloved author drown before his very eyes. "Jeez. Why don't you just blow up the greenhouse while you're at it?"

"Magicians don't use gunpowder," Sekhmet answered simply.

"I was being sarcastic!" Arthur said.

He refused to believe that Alfred Moore was completely evil. After all, Moore had created Garnett Lacroix. Kind of.

"Don't you think a flood is a little extreme?" Arthur asked.

"Not as extreme as unleashing monsters on a city in order to murder an innocent author," Sekhmet said.

Arthur blushed. "You have a point there."

A few blocks later, they arrived at the greenhouse, its emerald roof gleaming in the strange starlight. Arthur squinted through the fogged glass walls. There was a silhouette, flickering and distorting with candlelight. The man was hunched, scribbling furiously.

"Ready?" Sekhmet whispered, drawing her swords.

"Psh," Arthur said. "Ready is our middle name. Right, Cooper?"

He turned back, hoping to see his friend at least smirk through his painted hood.

Wally was nowhere to be seen.

18
GRAHAM

Wally crept through the Mirror streets, slipping into an alley when a herd of Ogre Oakers trundled his way. His senses were alert, but his pulse wasn't pounding like it had the first time he'd come to this place. Everything in his life was so mixed-up and turned around, it was hard to feel as afraid in this place as he once had.

Wally felt guilty for abandoning Arthur, Huamei, and Sekhmet. But he needed to be alone when he saw Graham. He'd never done it any other way. Besides, Wally felt useless to the Novitiates now. He wanted to help save Kingsport, but without Breeth to guide and protect him, he didn't have anything to offer. He was just a sneak thief without his lock picks.

The sun rose like a silver coin over the inky sea, giving the Mirror City a touch of normalcy. But the light seemed to disturb the Mirror citizens, who closed their shutters and slammed their doors. Black snow dusted the streets. Somewhere, children sang a dark hymn.

Wally arrived at the Slopping District where beastly sellers packed up their strange wares for the day. The cobbles glowed in the silver sunlight. He found the puppet theater—right where Arthur said it would be. But its shutter was closed, the puppets tucked away in their drawers.

"Graham?" he said softly.

The street was silent. Then . . .

"Brother?"

Wally turned around and found a hand sticking out of a second-floor window.

"Graham!" His eyes filled with tears of relief. "What are you doing here?"

Graham's hand craned down as if looking right at him. "Punch and Judy."

"Huh?"

"Punch and Judy. Have you seen them?"

Wally huffed. Of course he'd seen them. They were the loud, obnoxious puppets that performed on the docks for thrown copper pieces.

"Graham, we're in a dangerous place. This is no time to talk about *puppets*."

Graham's hand smiled. "Perhaps, dear brother, now is the perfect time to talk about puppets."

The doctor at Greyridge had told Wally never to humor his brother's delusions—that it would only make them worse. But Wally found that conversations with his brother went more smoothly when he just let Graham be Graham.

"Fine," he said. "What about Punch and Judy?"

"Do they realize they're on a stage?"

"Of course not," Wally said. "They're made of fabric and wood."

The hand shook its head sadly. "And here I had hoped my brother had learned something since his adventures began."

"What are you talking about?"

"The world is as real to humans as the stage is to Punch and Judy. People and puppets alike go about their day, unaware of the wonders that lie just beyond the walls of their reality—be it a cardboard stage or the sky above them. If they could just *step* outside themselves, they would experience the more interesting parts of the universe." Graham's hand sniffed, breathing in the Mirror City's silvery air. "If all the world's a stage, little brother, then you and I are currently *backstage*."

"Fine," Wally said. "I get it. You've left the stage. Can we go home now?"

"This *is* my home," Graham said.

"No," Wally said. "Kingsport is your home."

Graham clucked his tongue. "Kingsport is as dull to me as a miniature set glued with cotton ball clouds." He gazed around the Slopping District. "Until recently, I knew you weren't ready to know of this place's existence. Too many curtains in your brain, blocking the view. But now that you've been through the Manor . . . you're finally ready to understand."

Wally hugged himself against the Mirror's cold. "This city is evil, Graham. The creatures here have escaped into Kingsport and hurt people."

Graham's hand nodded sadly. "Every city has its dark side. You know better than most that the people of Real Kingsport don't need imaginary creatures to find ways to hurt one another. They have their own methods: stealing, starvation, gangs that take advantage of kids." The hand gazed up at the golden clouds, the green, morning lightning. "The Mirror isn't all Ogre Oakers and murderous authors, you know. Why, just this morning I watched a giant and his pale blue ox chop down a forest of hissing trees."

Wally marched to the door below Graham's window. His brother may have been older, but he ate very little and didn't get much exercise. Wally would carry Graham back to Kingsport if he had to. The door was locked, of course.

Graham's hand grinned above. "Now that you can visit me whenever you please, there's no reason for me to return to that foul city." His fingers tilted lovingly toward the crooked horizon. "I've wanted to live in this place since I was very young. And now I'm finally here."

Wally stared at the cobbles, following clues back through their childhood like bread crumbs. "Wait. You just *happened* to draw pictures of other worlds before a Manor that borders the worlds just *happened* to show up?"

The hand shook its head. "Don't be silly. That would be too great a coincidence. Too many coincidences spoil the story. No, I first dreamt of the coming of the Manor when I was six years old. And I saw the specific location in Kingsport where the Veil would grow thinnest, allowing me to enter the Mirror City with my portals." Graham's hand smiled toward the cliffs. "Of course it would happen at the mental hospital. The patients there are more willing to bend their views of so-called reality in ways the city dwellers are not."

"You saw all of this coming?" Wally said. "You couldn't have *warned* me?"

"Oh, but I did. How many times did I tie you up when you were younger? Did you think I was being cruel? I was preparing you to escape that Manor's tower when the time was right."

Wally felt manipulated. Like his brother had been pulling his puppet strings since the beginning. "If you could see the future, then why didn't you warn Mom and Dad about the Pox? You could've saved them! We could still be a family!"

Graham's fingers curved in an impression of a sad smile.

Wally's heart took a tumble. "You did try and tell them . . . But they didn't believe you because—because who'd believe a kid who says a third of the city's going to die?"

The hand sighed. Then it vanished in the window.

"Graham?" Wally called up. He tried forcing the handle. He pounded the door, bruising his fists. "*Graham!*"

The door opened. Graham stepped out. He wore a cloak, his hands tucked in his pockets, no longer mimicking puppets. "Now you know why I don't tell people about the future. Instead, I just try and prepare them for it."

Wally hadn't felt prepared for anything that had happened over the last few days. But he wondered what would have happened if his brother had never tied him up when he was younger. Would he have even survived the Manor?

Graham touched Wally's arm. "I'm sorry, little brother. I've been used to the idea of the Mirror since I was very young. It must be overwhelming for you."

"Yeah," Wally said. "It is." He set his jaw and took Graham

by the wrist. "Come on. We need to get you back to Greyridge. Maybe they've cleaned it up by now."

He turned to leave.

"*Wally*," Graham said softly.

Wally stopped and studied his brother's face. Graham was finally free from the hospital. The bill no longer had to be paid. Wally's greatest dream had come true . . . So why did it feel like a nightmare?

"What about me?" Wally asked. "What am I supposed to do?"

"You, little brother, have to go back."

Wally suddenly felt lost. Like a balloon with a cut string. He no longer had to pay off the hospital bills, but he was still at the mercy of the Rook. Wally would return to Kingsport and try to find a way to pay off his tribute to the Rook, then eke out a life for himself with the Black Feathers. That somehow scared him more than being stuck in the Mirror. With no family to look after, what would he fight for?

"What are you going to do?" Wally asked his brother.

"Oh, you know," Graham said, rocking toe to heel, "watch the sky flora. Relish the inverted doughnuts." He stared at the sky. "I also hope to teach the people of the Real how to leave their puppet stage and enter the Mirror. If they refuse—and they probably will, humans are nervous creatures—then I will break their stage so everyone can see the wonders that await them on the other side."

A horror crept through Wally. "What are you saying?"

"I'm talking about the fall of the *Veil*, brother!" Graham

said with feverish excitement. "The merging of the *Fae* and *Kingsport*. Just think of it! Your wildest fantasies filling the city. A cake the size of a skyscraper! A drake cub curled in your lap. Children chasing their escaped eyeballs down the street. And that's just on the *Real* side. The sugar in Kingsport alone could feed the starving elf children in the Fae for decades!"

Wally took a step away. "But . . . that's what that evil Order is trying to do."

Graham nodded. "The Order of Eldar."

"They want to overthrow Lady Weirdwood and the Wardens so they can control the border," Wally continued. "If they tear enough Rifts, the Veil will fall, destroying Kingsport and the rest of the world. It would be an *apocalypse*."

Graham chuckled. "*Apocatastasis*."

"Whatastasis?"

"A return to how the world was before humans mucked it up and drove all of the myths and dreams away. The rise of the Great Slumbyr."

Wally's head felt heavy. These things didn't sound as scary when his brother described them . . . But Wally was so new to all of this. He didn't know what to believe.

"The Order of Eldar is greedy," Graham continued. "On that much Lady Weirdwood and I agree. But if the Veil falls, then *no one* can control it. Both the Order and the Wardens will be powerless. When the Order succeeds in overthrowing the Manor, they will help me realize the potential of both realms." He placed a hand on Wally's shoulder. "As will you."

"Overthrow the Manor?" Wally said, feeling sick.

He remembered the Golden Scarab Graham had given to

Arthur. The mechanical insect had *poisoned* Lady Weirdwood, leaving her in a coma. Graham's eccentricities had always felt harmless, but now . . .

Graham squeezed Wally's shoulder. "It's the only way."

Graham suddenly looked like a stranger. Wally could barely recognize him.

"But if more creatures pour into Kingsport," Wally said, "then more people are going to die."

Graham nodded sadly. "As in any revolution."

Wally pulled his shoulder away. "I refuse to be a part of this. I'm not going to help bring down the Veil or whatever it is you want me to do."

"Haven't you been listening, brother? You don't have a *choice*. I've already seen it happen. Call it genes. Call it fate. Call it the great puppet strings that make the world spin round. You'll make the Veil fall simply by being *you*."

Wally felt frozen. He didn't dare move a muscle.

"Your intentions are good, Wally," Graham said. "That's what matters. You're going to try and help people. And that will make all the difference in the end."

Fear pumped cold through Wally's veins. "How will I bring down the Veil?"

Graham got a glazed look in his eyes.

"*Huh?*" Wally said. "Answer me!"

Graham stared over the rooftops. His face fell slack. "Oh."

"What?" Wally said. "What is it?"

"The dragon is about to die."

Ice touched Wally's heart. "Huamei?"

"Yes."

"*What?* Why didn't you warn me?"

"Because you might have saved him," Graham said. "The Veil cannot fall without Huamei's death. It's tragic. But that's how this story goes."

"I have to save him!" Wally said, backing away.

"You can leave whenever you want," Graham said. "It won't help."

Wally was torn between dragging his brother back to Greyridge and rescuing Huamei.

"Don't worry, little brother," Graham said with a smile. "I'll be here. I'll always be here."

Wally ran back toward the greenhouse.

"Farewell, Wally!" his brother called. "I wish you the best of luck and all of the strangeness I can muster. And remember! What goes best with Graham?"

Wally kept running. He didn't have time for riddles.

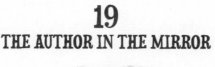

19
THE AUTHOR IN THE MIRROR

I'm going after him," Sekhmet said the moment they realized Wally was gone.

"I'm coming with you," Arthur said. "I don't want a warthog or something turning my friend into a pet."

The moment he was done speaking, he smelled a pleasant scent, as if his words were as fragrant as flower petals.

Sekhmet pointed her sword at the silhouette in the fogged greenhouse wall. "You and Huamei need to stay here and keep an eye on Moore. If he could track our actions in the Real, he may know we're here and try to escape." She looked at Huamei. "You keep an eye on Arthur."

Huamei sneered. "I wasn't aware babysitting was part of my Novitiate duties."

"Just do it," Sekhmet said, holstering her sword. "I'll be back."

She ran down the street, and Arthur studied Moore's silhouette behind the fogged glass. The Mirror writer was still writing. Arthur knew that Valerie Lucas was the actual creator of Garnett Lacroix, but he couldn't help but have an attachment to Moore. When Sekhmet returned, she was going to lead a full-on attack against his favorite author. Arthur couldn't watch that happen.

He stared at the scribbling silhouette. "He doesn't *look* harmful."

"Few things in the Mirror do at first glance," Huamei said. "Think of the porcelain doll."

Sure, Arthur thought. But that doll didn't write the greatest adventure stories ever told.

Garnett Lacroix would never just up and murder one of his enemies, no matter how evil they were. He would use charm and cunning to disarm them. And if that didn't work, only then would he defeat them with a battle of wits over a poisoned cookie or something.

"I think we can handle this ourselves," Arthur said. "Without a flood."

Huamei narrowed his eyes. "Are you trying to save the life of someone you've never met? Let alone never existed?"

"I've never met Little Red Riding Hood either, but I don't want the wolf to eat her."

Huamei's lips coiled, like he was trying not to laugh. He considered the silhouette. "Dragon bones aren't to be trifled with. A mere scribble of that Quill could summon creatures that—"

"Yeah, yeah," Arthur said. "I know."

He needed to find the thing that would get Huamei on his side. Arthur studied the dragon boy's face—his flared nostrils, his raised chin. *Pride*. That was the key.

He nodded toward Sekhmet, now a small figure in the distance. "Do you usually take orders from her?"

"I do not," Huamei said, clearly annoyed.

"Then why start now?" Arthur said. He nodded toward the greenhouse. "I could go in there and try to reason with Moore. If he summons a wave of chain saw crabs or something, then you can turn into a dragon, swoop in, and rescue me. We can secure the Quill and get you back to the Cloud Kingdom. And you won't have to take orders from a mere human. Whaddaya say?"

Strangely, the pleasant flower scent faded.

Huamei narrowed his eyes at Arthur. Then he took out his calligraphy brush. "I'll be on the roof. It's foggy enough, and my scales will camouflage with the sky. If you're in trouble, send a signal, and I'll break through."

"Perfect," Arthur said.

With great swooping arcs, Huamei began painting a coiling blue body in the air. Arthur stared at the greenhouse and tried to formulate a plan. He remembered an unsettling detail from the story that had tried to murder Valerie Lucas and knew just what he needed.

"*Wait*," Arthur said to Huamei, who was partway through his transformation. "Can I borrow your ink?"

Dragon Huamei wrinkled his scaled forehead.

"Trust me," Arthur said.

Huamei reached a clawed hand into his robes, which were slowly transforming into his mane, and drew out an ink bottle. Arthur pocketed it.

Soon, Huamei was no more—vanished within his own

dragon painting. Using his coral-sharp claws, he scaled the greenhouse.

"Okay," Arthur whispered to himself as he entered the glass door and pressed through the coils of purple and green vines. "Here I go. Into adventure. All by myself. This is great. This is what heroes do."

It was warm and dark in the greenery. The air felt sweaty. The plant life stretched so wide and deep, Arthur felt as if he were lost in a jungle. Anything could part the leaves and attack him at any moment.

Arthur took a breath and relaxed his shoulders. It was important, he knew, to maintain a confident air when the world was crumbling around you. When your city was attacked by monsters. When your childhood hero was little more than bones and cobwebs. When the author who created him was an imaginary pen name who killed innocents. When you didn't have a single coin to pay off the gang leader who wanted your father dead.

That last thought made Arthur hold his stomach.

He was wheezing by the time he reached the back of the greenhouse. Not out of exhaustion but out of fear. He tried to remind his quaking heart that he was an expert on everything Moore and not just a twelve-year-old kid in a strange land that he barely knew anything about.

Candlelight flickered behind the leaves. The dragon-bone Quill scratched. Arthur took a deep breath. "Hello?"

The Quill stopped scratching. "Who is it?" The voice was quiet. Haunted.

Arthur cleared his throat, hoping to banish the butterflies

in his stomach. Then he opened his lips and let the words flow. "Door-to-door sales, sir!"

Another silence. "In a greenhouse?"

"We're specialized, sir! Only selling to the most imaginative artists deserving of our wares." Arthur took out the bottle of ink. "You wouldn't happen to be a writer, would you?"

Silence.

Arthur gave the bottle a shake. "I have in my hand the finest ink you've ever dipped quill in," he continued, summoning the voices of the Market Square sellers. "Ten out of ten writers call it a *necessity* to finish that pesky manuscript. Whether writing your hero out of a death-defying predicament or penning a gruesomely believable monster, this ink will serve you."

More silence. Arthur waited, heart pounding in his head.

"*Well* now," the man finally said. "That *is* intriguing."

Arthur parted the leaves. Wind whistled through the plates of glass, ruffling the pages on a small desk. The desk was nearly empty. No leftover plates of food. No tea. Nothing but pen and paper and the flickering candle.

And there was the man. Alfred Moore. The author's face looked ravaged by sleepless nights. His eyes were puffy, and his nose was filled with broken blood vessels. Gray streaked his thinning hair. His fingernails had not been trimmed in ages, and his fingers were stained with blood. This was not how Arthur had imagined his favorite author.

Moore studied Arthur and grew more relaxed. "Why, you're only a boy! And you sound as if you've read more than a few adventure stories, hm?"

Arthur smiled. "Devoured every one in sight."

In Moore's hand was the Quill. As Wally had said, it was gnarled and black as night, with red veins as bright as starlight. Arthur eyed it warily, imagining all of the terrible things it could do to him.

"How much is this ink of yours, then?" Moore said.

"F-for a dedicated writer such as yourself?" Arthur said, trying not to stumble as he held up Huamei's paint bottle. "We're, um, running a deal." He said the first number that came to mind.

He expected Moore to use the Quill to write gold into the room. But instead the author patted his pockets and searched his desk drawer for coins. It was as if the Mirror author didn't know the power the Quill held . . .

Moore looked disappointed. "I've nothing to pay."

"That's all right," Arthur said, taking a step forward. "I'll give you this free sample. That way when your books start flying off the shelves, you'll be a return customer."

Moore unscrewed the bottle's cap and dipped his Quill. He wrote a sentence, dark blue beside the bloodred letters. Arthur tried not to wince. Every word Moore wrote was another potential death in Kingsport.

Arthur leaned in, trying to steal a peek at the page. He noticed a piece of paper on the corner of the table that read *the tentacles slurped back into the sewer, dragging the precious manuscript and the whereabouts of the author's hiding place with them.*

Moore thought his enemies had been diverted.

Arthur turned his attention to Moore's current work. "What are you writing? If I may ask?"

Moore smiled. "Recently, I've been dreaming up something quite fiendish! Imagine if the brains of the dead grew ivy like pumpkins, dragging the bodies out of the Kingsport Graveyard and into the city!" He started to scribble again. "That's sure to put me back on the bestseller list!"

Arthur paled. His mom was in that graveyard. He couldn't let Moore write one more word. He tried to think of how Garnett would handle this situation, but all he could think of was the Gentleman Thief tapping the top of his own head, which was no help at all. For all of Arthur's talk about protecting the poor and being a hero, he was never able to pull it off. He'd spent the last few years trying to score enough money so he could start acting like Garnett. But his methods had been anything but gentlemanly.

Arthur removed his hat. "Sir, I came here under false pretenses."

Moore stopped writing, the Quill hovering over an unfinished sentence.

Arthur swallowed. "I've been a

fan of yours since I was eight years old. Your Garnett Lacroix stories inspired me to become the person I am today. To stand up for the poor. To respect the human spirit more than money. To be a hero in the face of adversity."

Moore chuckled and pointed. "You've even re-created the Gentleman Thief's hat!"

Arthur looked at the hat and noticed the daffodil was in full bloom. He didn't know what to make of it.

Moore sighed a lonely sigh. "I don't get out much, and so never meet my adoring fans. You're actually the first."

Arthur glanced around the plants. He had always imagined Moore locked away, scribbling away the hours. The author had probably never stepped outside this greenhouse. He didn't even know that his own Gentleman Thief was wasting away in the sewers below this building.

Arthur studied the man's upside-down handwriting. "Why did you stop writing adventure stories? Why turn to horror?"

A shadow passed behind Moore's eyes. "I hadn't been feeling like myself. I was exhausted. I lost my hair and appetite. I felt as if I was disintegrating—like an old scarecrow left to rot in the rain." He held up the Quill and brightened. "But then a stranger showed up and gave me this fine instrument."

The Jangling Man, Arthur thought.

Huamei suspected this was the Fallen Warden—the man trying to bring down the Veil.

Moore continued. "He told me that a witch named Valerie Lucas had put a curse on me—a curse that would slowly but surely make me disappear. If I wanted to reverse it, all I had to do was use this Quill to cast a spell—to write her out of the equation."

By pulling Miss Lucas apart with tentacles, Arthur thought, trying not to let the disgust show on his face.

Moore took a deep breath, brightening. "Now that the witch is dead and buried, I've started to feel more myself." He tapped the page with his Quill. "So I've continued down this wonderfully haunted path. If I'd known how enthralling horror stories were, I'd have started a long time ago. Gives one a *chill* in the bone marrow."

Arthur realized that the real reason Moore couldn't write Garnett Lacroix was because Valerie Lucas had retired, drying up the Mirror author's imagination. Now that Lucas was dead, Moore would never write another word about the Gentleman Thief. He could only repeat gruesome versions of the old adventures. His mind was as twisted as Parasite Lane was to Paradise Lane.

Arthur hesitated, wondering how to proceed. "Readers also need comfort and heroes to look up to. Things have grown bad in Kingsport, what with the gangs and the starvation. The Pox left a scar that won't heal any time soon."

Something shrieked above, like a claw scraping glass, and Moore's gaze leapt to the greenhouse's ceiling where the shadow of Huamei's whisker just managed to whip out of sight.

Moore flinched, then frowned at Arthur. "Are you hiding something, son?"

"Not at all, sir," Arthur said, forcing his quivering lips into a smile. "Unless you're talking about my hope to get an autograph."

Moore turned his scowl back to the glass ceiling.

Arthur tapped the bottle of paint, trying to draw the

author's attention away from the window. "When was the last time you wrote about something nice?"

Moore gave the page a blank stare, as if he wouldn't know where to start.

"May I?" Arthur asked, reaching for the Quill.

Moore pulled away. "I'd rather hold on to this."

Arthur smiled. "I'll dictate, then."

Moore dipped the Quill in the paint and gave Arthur an expectant look.

"What Kingsport could use," Arthur said, "is a vacation. I'm thinking of a field, speckled with dandelions. A softly gleaming sun. A brook trickling somewhere nearby."

Moore wrote the words . . . and his expression started to change. He breathed as if smelling a soft rain. Candlelight sparkled in his eyes like morning dew. The author even wiggled his feet, like his toes were tickled by grasses.

Moore smiled. "This ink of yours is quite smooth."

"I'd never hock a bad product," Arthur said. "What nice things can you come up with?"

Moore tapped the paper with the Quill, thinking. But when it came to pleasant things, the Mirror author was at a loss.

"How about . . ." Arthur said. "A new suit on Lacey Lane?"

Moore raised his eyebrows. "People do like new suits."

He dipped the Quill into the paint and began to write. Arthur breathed a quiet sigh of relief. He wished Sekhmet was there to see what he'd accomplished. All it took was a little explaining. No floods or explosions or violence required.

Moore continued to write. "It'd be charcoal gray with

purple piping . . ." He dipped the Quill and got a wicked expression. "And when men try it on, the collar will *strangle* them."

"No!" Arthur said.

Moore stopped, confused. He slashed a line through the sentence. Somewhere on Lacey Lane, Arthur imagined, a man clutched at his throat, breathing with relief.

"We're trying to lead *away* from horror," Arthur said.

Moore frowned. "And vanish again? No. The Jangling Man told me I had to keep writing successful stories, otherwise I'd fade like that witch intended. The things you're describing are pleasant but *boring*. They'll never sell."

Arthur bit his lip. He would have to take a new track. A more honest track.

"The Jangling Man deceived you," Arthur said. "That Quill you're holding can do more than reverse a witch's curse. It's way more dangerous and powerful than he led you to believe."

Moore listened. Arthur smelled flowers once again. Almost like his words had activated the scent.

"In fact," he continued, "the monsters you've been dreaming up have come to life in my city, turning people into porcelain and dropping them from great heights and pulling them apart. Not just characters. *People*. With families."

Arthur picked up a blood-inked page from the desk and showed it to Moore.

"That witch you were talking about was a normal woman named Valerie Lucas," Arthur said. "She was an author. She created you. And yes, when she stopped writing about you,

you became a shell of your former self. But she didn't deserve to die for that."

A shadow crept across Moore's brow. "What evidence do you have for this?"

Arthur pulled out the page he'd taken from Lucas's house and handed it to Moore.

Moore read it in silence, brow furrowed. "How do I know you didn't just copy this from my first book?"

"My handwriting's not that nice," Arthur said.

He did his best to explain everything. The Fae. The Real. The Veil that separates them. The Quill made of dragon bone. He told Moore that he was a backward author. Just as Valerie Lucas wrote words that created him in the Fae, Moore was writing words that created monsters in the Real.

Moore looked suddenly lost, and Arthur knew he had to tread lightly.

"I know what it's like to be mistreated by your creator," Arthur said. "My dad uses me to make money, just like Valerie Lucas accidentally did with you . . . That doesn't mean we have to follow in their footsteps."

Moore stared at his work. "Are you telling me I don't exist?"

Arthur swayed on his feet. "I, um, guess so . . . yeah."

Moore looked at the Quill. "But this instrument creates whatever I want it to?"

"Yes. But that's why you should really only be writing about things like meadows. And suits. Only ones that don't strangle. We want to *help* the people of Kingsport. Not hurt them."

But Moore was no longer listening. His eyes were fixed

over Arthur's shoulder, growing wide with horror. Arthur followed his gaze. A giant sea foam eye filled the glass wall.

"Get back!" Arthur yelled at the dragon. "I didn't give the signal!"

"The man who gave me this Quill warned me about you," Moore whispered. "You're from that Manor, aren't you? You've come to kill me."

Arthur turned. "That dragon isn't with me. I mean, he's nice. He's—" The scent of flowers snuffed out.

Before Arthur could explain, Moore began to write, mumbling to himself. "If what you say is true—that Valerie Lucas stopped writing and I started dying—then I regret nothing. I choose life over death. At any cost."

Arthur's heart pounded. "*Wait!* We can find another way!"

But Moore only wrote with more ferocity. "I need somewhere safe. Somewhere my work won't be interrupted."

Huamei's beak smashed through the glass wall. He tried to squeeze his massive head through the frame, but it wouldn't fit. His beak thrashed and snipped a foot away from Moore's arm, but it couldn't reach.

This was up to Arthur.

He lunged to snatch away the Quill, but Moore drove it clean through his hand before pulling it back out. Arthur screamed and stumbled backward, pressing into the bleeding wound.

The author continued to write, and a monstrous roar reverberated from the port. Something enormous tromped down the streets.

"Please," Arthur said, bleeding on the floor. "We're here to help."

Alfred Moore looked at him with madness in his eyes. "You can help me by dying." He stabbed the Quill down, placing a period at the end of a sentence.

A shadow darkened the greenhouse's glass ceiling. It wrapped a wrought iron claw around Huamei, tearing him from the building. The Fae beast was made of stone and had a rattling portcullis for a mouth. It seized the entire greenhouse with its claws. The glass cracked, the frame buckled, and the floor heaved upward. Arthur tumbled at breakneck speed through the plants. He saw one last look of victory on Moore's face before the author vanished in the leaves.

Arthur struck the front entrance so hard it burst open, spilling him onto the street. He leapt to his feet as the greenhouse was ripped from its foundation, leaves and glass shards raining into the street. It was being devoured by another building, wrought iron claws feeding the glass into its portcullis mouth.

Alfred Moore had used the Quill to transform Mirror Greyridge into a monster.

Arthur watched as the author leapt from the greenhouse into the hospital. The building shrieked with the screams of its patients as giant bat wings unfurled from its sides. With three great swoops, Monster Greyridge took flight over the roofs of the Mirror City.

Huamei flew after it, coiling and thrashing, his seashell fangs helpless against the stone.

Arthur removed his hat and watched the battle in the sky.

What had he done? He'd tried to solve the problem with peace, but instead he'd brought disaster. By telling Moore about the power of the Quill, Arthur had given the author control over his own destiny.

Alfred Moore was writing his own story now.

Huamei turned his fangs to the monster hospital's giant wing. The hospital didn't like this at all, so it swung itself like a stone club, cracking the dragon in the head with the weight of a thousand stones. Huamei's body went limp, and the dragon fell, unspooling through the air before crunching through a nearby roof.

Arthur expected the bat-winged Greyridge to fly away now that its enemy was unconscious. But instead it crashed down like a giant hammer, landing right on top of the dragon's unconscious body.

"Huamei!" Arthur sprinted toward him, mumbling to himself. "Please be okay. Please be okay. Please be okay."

Dragons were powerful, Arthur assured himself. Huamei had said so himself. He'd be fine. Just fine.

With a great swoop of its wings the monster hospital flapped away. Arthur crawled into the wreckage and found the dragon. He stared at the wounds in the scales. Like cracks through porcelain.

Huamei was dead.

20

THE DRAGON'S WAKE

Wally ran into Sekhmet on his way back.

"Huamei's in trouble!" he yelled before she could draw her swords.

He ran past her, and she followed. By the time they got back to the greenhouse, it was too late. The dragon's eyes were open. Blood pooled from his beak.

On the ground beside the body, a goblin mouth doorway led into the warm glow of the Manor's War Room. With his last breath it seemed Huamei had used his claw to scratch a portal back to Weirdwood.

Sekhmet's eyes burned bright with tears. Then she drew her swords, and with a great gust of air, lifted the dragon's body. Wally bent and picked up Arthur's garish hat. The daffodil in the brim had wilted completely.

* * *

Wally found Arthur in the Healing Room, which was white and billowy and quiet. Ludwig and Pyra lay in two of the beds, healing from the battle with the Corvidians. Little paper animals stitched up Ludwig's leg wound, while Pyra had a slab of beef resting on her face, her skin still blue from the explosion. Neither looked up when Wally passed. They were grieving.

Arthur lay in a corner bed, as still as the blankets that covered him. His face was turned toward the wall, his right hand wrapped with bloody bandages.

"Hey, Arthur," Wally said, hanging the hat on the bed's poster. "How you holding up?"

Arthur didn't budge. "It was my fault."

"No," Wally said, remembering Graham's words, "it wasn't."

Arthur covered his face with his good hand. "You weren't there."

Wally sighed. What was he supposed to say? *Actually, my brother told me he can see into the future, and it seems everything that happens is more out of our control than we'd like to believe. We're all just puppets.*

Wally sat on the foot of the bed and looked around the hospital room. "This place reminds me of the day we met."

Arthur only sniffed.

It had been after the great Battle of the Barrows between Kingsport's rival gangs. The fight that would ultimately make the Rook the underground leader of the city. The gangs had fought with brickbats, steel bars, and broken bottles, so the hospitals were packed with people, bloodied and broken.

Wally and Arthur were the only kids in their ward who received no visitors. Wally's parents and Arthur's mom were buried in the graveyard from the Pox, while Harry had been noticeably absent.

While Wally healed, Arthur made up a story about an afterlife called the Great Elsewhere where they would be able to walk in, rescue their parents, and bring them back to the land of the living. It had brought Wally a little comfort, and he had thought this was the beginning of a long friendship. But then he had gotten to know Arthur and his ego. And he'd decided it was wise to keep the kid at a distance. Now, after everything they'd been through, Wally wasn't sure how he felt about Arthur Benton.

Arthur's head lay heavy on the pillow. "Every time I've tried to do something heroic, I've only ended up hurting people. I should just go join stupid Garnett and rot with him in his stupid sewer."

Before Wally could respond, the door to the Healing Room opened. Wally stood as Arthur sat up. Sekhmet entered and walked straight toward them.

"Go ahead," Arthur said. "Do what you need to. Beat me up. Lock me in the Abyssment. I deserve it."

But when Sekhmet reached the bed, she threw her arms around him, pulling him into a tight hug. Arthur looked shocked a moment, then he hugged her back.

Wally went to the other side of the room to give them some privacy.

* * *

Once their tears were spent, Sekhmet pulled away and wiped her eyes. For the first time since they'd met, Arthur waited for her to speak first.

"It was my first mission as a Warden," she said. "We were in the Neon Pastures, fighting demon-possessed lambs. I was told to guard my mentor Rose's back." She sniffed. "I was new and hungry for the fight. I saw a lamb hissing on the other end of the pasture, and I knew I could take it. My swords were thirsty. So I went after the lamb. I exorcised it. And when I came back, Rose was—"

Sekhmet's voice broke. Arthur waited for her to continue.

"Rose, my mentor, whom I swore to protect . . . was dead. She didn't realize her back was undefended . . . and she died. Because of me." Sekhmet stared at the ceiling, trying to keep more tears from spilling. "Rose had a son who died when he was very young. At least now they're reunited . . . somewhere."

Arthur touched his chest. The warmth of Sekhmet's hug was still there. So much about her made sense now. Her brooding. Her cutting way of speaking. Her insistence on following the rules—locking him up and being as brutal as possible with her enemies.

Sekhmet sniffed. "When we returned to the Manor, I hid in the darkest corner I could find. But Lady Weirdwood found me, of course. You can't keep secrets from her in this place. I thought she was going to banish me from the Manor. But she only hugged me. She said I may have been promoted from Novitiate a little too soon, and she told me to return to my duties."

Arthur placed his uninjured hand on Sekhmet's and squeezed. They were so much more similar than he'd realized—both trying to rise in the ranks of a punishing system, constantly tumbling back down because of their imperfections.

"After that," Sekhmet said, staring at Arthur's hand over hers. "I started following every rule of the Manor. But I wanted nothing more than to be a Warden and fight again. I got greedy and let the rules slip. And now, because of my actions, Huamei is dead."

It took Arthur a moment to realize what she was saying. "Wait," he said. "It's *my* fault Huamei died. I'm the one who insisted on talking to Moore and then made him realize what that Quill could do!"

"No." Sekhmet pulled her hand out from under his. "I abandoned the mission. A mission I shouldn't have been on in the first place. I left two people who are new to this stuff alone in the Mirror. If I'd brought you with me to find Wally, none of this would have happened. With my swords, Huamei's magic, and your Wordcraft, we might have restrained Moore together."

Arthur grew a different kind of teary. It sounded as if she actually valued his presence.

Sekhmet sniffed. "I have to remind myself of what Lady Weirdwood told me in that dark corner of the Manor. She told me I didn't kill Rose. The demon sheep did." She stared at Arthur. "We didn't kill Huamei, Arthur. Alfred Moore did."

"But—" Arthur began.

"We did not kill Huamei, Arthur," Sekhmet said again slowly. "It was Alfred Moore."

Arthur closed his mouth and looked away. She didn't understand.

"If Moore had killed you instead," Sekhmet said, "would you want me and Huamei blaming ourselves?"

It finally sank in then. Arthur shook his head.

"Besides," Sekhmet said, wiping her cheek, "Huamei knew he was still fragile from turning into porcelain. But he chose to go into battle anyway. He was stubborn. But he was honorable." Sekhmet stood from the bed with purpose. "We'll grieve for our fallen comrade. And when the Wardens return from the Mercury Mines, we will bring Alfred Moore down."

Arthur suddenly felt overwhelmed. "But how? Moore has the dragon-bone Quill. And I taught him how to use it. He's invincible, and we're just a bunch of—"

Sekhmet grabbed him by the chin, angling his eyes toward hers. "We need solutions. Not self-pity." She whisked toward the exit. "Let me know if you come up with anything."

And with that, she was gone.

Something white caught the corner of Arthur's eye. He looked at Garnett's hat, hanging on the bed's poster. The daffodil was in full bloom. Arthur connected all of the moments the flower had wilted or bloomed, and he finally understood what the Gentleman Thief had been trying to tell him in his sewer hideout.

When Arthur asked Garnett how he managed to be a gentleman *and* a thief, Garnett had tapped his head, too drained to realize he wasn't wearing his hat. The daffodil in his brim was a living moral compass. When it bloomed, it meant Arthur was on the path of becoming a Gentleman Thief. When it wilted, it meant his lies had led him astray.

He just wished he'd realized this before trying to take on Alfred Moore.

After Sekhmet left, Wally wandered back to Arthur's bed. "Did you hear that? Sekhmet wants our help."

Before Arthur could respond, the door opened again, and Amelia entered.

"I've contacted Huamei's family," she said quietly. "His mother will arrive shortly to collect his body. Normally, we would bury one of our own in the Manor, but dragon bones are sacred, powerful things, and they must return to the Cloud Kingdom."

Arthur gave a miserable sigh, drawing Amelia's eye to him.

"I think it would be best if you boys don't mention how Huamei died," she said. "I'm worried the duchess of the Tian Empire will hold the Manor responsible for her son's death. Lady Weirdwood is our diplomat, but she's still comatose from the Golden Scarab's venom. If she doesn't wake soon, I'm afraid Huamei's death will trigger a war with the dragons."

Wally sat in shock. A dragon war? As if things weren't bad enough.

"I have something to confess," Arthur said. "That Scarab came from the Temple of Kosh." He twirled the bloomed daffodil between his fingers. "And it wasn't from the Order."

Amelia gave him a severe look. "How do you know that?"

Arthur avoided looking at Wally. "I . . . can't tell you."

Wally softened. Arthur really did want to keep Graham safe. Even if it got him in trouble.

"I'll have Pyra mix up an antidote," Amelia said. "If it works, then you'll have some explaining to do." She grabbed the door handle. "If you want to say goodbye, Huamei's body is in the Room of Fathers on the second floor. The wallpaper weather is quite pleasant today." With that, she closed the door.

Wally felt a tingle of recognition. The Room of Fathers was where Lady Weirdwood had buried the mouse thing. His heart squeezed when he thought of Breeth's smiling wooden face. Two of the three people he'd connected with since he came to this Manor were gone now. The last was in a coma. And that was his own brother's fault.

Arthur's eyes twitched toward the ceiling. "Just knowing that Huamei's mom is about to see her son's dead body . . ." His face broke and he turned away.

Wally wanted to yell at him. To ask why he didn't wait for Sekhmet. Why he always had to dive in and be the hero. But it seemed their fates were set in stone. And there was nothing Wally could say that would make Arthur feel any worse than he already did.

Wally patted Arthur's leg. "You were trying to do the right thing."

"Do you really think that?" Arthur asked.

"Yeah," Wally said. "Yeah I do."

* * *

After heading to the Room of Fathers and saying goodbye to Huamei, whose body was being closely guarded by Weston and his doorknobs, Wally and Arthur returned to the Healing Room, where Arthur collapsed from exhaustion.

But sleep eluded Wally. He tried closing his eyes, but his

thoughts writhed with tentacles and puppet strings and cracks through scaled skin. So he watched shadows dance on the ceiling instead.

How were they going to bring down a mad author who could create anything with a scribble of his Quill? He and Arthur could return to Kingsport, leaving Weirdwood's staff to solve this problem themselves. But if the staff failed, Moore would continue writing his horrors, and there might not be a city left to live in. If that happened, maybe Wally would take Lady Weirdwood up on becoming a Novitiate. Maybe she'd let Arthur join too. No more days as lowly pickpockets.

A tiny squeak made Wally sit upright.

Lady Weirdwood's caramel-colored snake slithered into the Healing Room, making S's across the checkerboard floor. Its head swayed back and forth, tongue flicking toward the beds to its left, then to its right. Wally pulled his knees in tight. Lady Weirdwood wasn't awake to feed the snake, and now it seemed to be hunting.

As the snake wound its way toward the far corner of the Healing Room, its movements grew slow. Its tongue flicked. It had spotted something. Wally squinted at the dark space between two beds. There, at the base of the wall, was a drawing of a mouse. It resembled an ancient hieroglyph that you'd find inside a pyramid . . . only it had purple stripes—just like the mouse thing Breeth had possessed.

The snake coiled its body, poising to strike. Then it lunged at the hieroglyphic mouse. To Wally's surprise, the picture of the mouse bounded to safety at the last moment. It scampered along the baseboard, leaving the snake to shake off the pain of biting into solid wall. Having failed in its hunt, the snake slithered out of the room.

Wally blinked. He remembered what Lady Weirdwood had told him during the mouse's funeral—how the Manor was a living thing that would absorb the bodies buried in it. He never thought it would manifest as a picture in the *wallpaper*.

Wally leapt out of bed and chased after the mouse. It hopped down a series of dark passageways, leading him to a room as bright and sultry as a desert. The walls were slanted sandstone, converging in a sharp point. Fires crackled in wide bowls, making more hieroglyphics waver. The walls were covered with images of people with the heads of birds and jackals, holding pots and spears and pieces of fruit.

A coiled image at the top of the pyramid caught his eye. He looked up . . . up . . . up . . .

"Oh," he said. "Hi, Huamei."

21
FIGHTING A FICTION

Wally sprinted back to the Healing Room, nearly slipping on the tile.

"Arthur! Wake up!"

Arthur sat bolt upright. "What? What is it? Is Huamei's mom here to eat me?"

"No! I know how to stop Moore!"

"What?" Arthur rubbed the sleep out of his eyes. "How?"

Wally held up the thing he was holding.

Arthur's face went pale. "What is that?"

"It's . . . Huamei's claw."

"*What?*" Arthur grabbed the claw, stuffed it under the pillow, and hissed, "You heard what Amelia said! Huamei's mom will pick her teeth with our bones!"

"Calm down, okay?" Wally said. "Huamei gave it to me."

Arthur gave him a dumbfounded look. "He . . ."

Wally nodded. "I talked to him. In this weird pyramid room. He's in the walls of the Manor. Or, he was."

"Can I see him?" Arthur said. "I need to apologize. I need to tell him that—" His voice faltered.

"I think I'm the only one who can see him," Wally said. He remembered Graham telling him about all of the things people couldn't see just because they didn't have words for them. "My brother—I think he cast a spell on me. Not the sort of spell you read about in books with a wand and weird chanting. A real spell. With regular words. A spell that opened my eyes to ghosts."

Arthur swallowed. "Did Huamei mention me?"

Wally gave Arthur a sympathetic look. "I think because he died as a dragon, he's stuck that way and can't speak human languages. But I'll bet if he could've said something, he—"

Arthur held up a hand. "Don't try to make me feel better."

Wally reached under the pillow and pulled out the claw. "Huamei's ghost looked more like a painting than anything. Like something he would make with his brush. I told him that his mom was so upset about losing him that she's threatening a war with the Wardens. He cried when I told him that. His tears leaked down the walls like paint. I think he died believing she didn't care about him."

Arthur's eyes filled with tears. "That's really sad."

"Yeah." Wally sighed. "He led me down a secret passage to the Room of Fathers. That gardener Weston was standing guard over Huamei's body with an army of doorknobs. Huamei pointed his ghostly whiskers toward his body's claw. Then he rattled the doors, distracting Weston and his doorknob army, while I snuck in and took the claw. It came off easily because it's still kind of made of porcelain."

Arthur took the claw and rubbed his thumbs across it. "We can turn this into a quill and write anything we want into the Mirror."

"We'll be evenly matched with Alfred Moore. We can save Kingsport."

"All because of Huamei's sacrifice."

The two fell silent.

"What will we write?" Wally asked.

Arthur breathed deep and thought a moment. "We could write an army of steel soldiers. Or an army of armored lizards."

Wally snorted. "An army of steel soldiers *riding* armored lizards! Moore won't know what hit him."

The boys smiled, but then concern crossed Arthur's eyebrows. "Moore's been writing adventure stories for years. He'll come up with better ideas than we will. He could write a volcano that melted our steel soldiers. It'll be like sword fighting a fencing master."

The boys were considering this problem when the door opened, making both of them jump. Wally quickly hid the dragon claw under the covers as Sekhmet entered the room.

"You guys look suspicious," she said.

Wally and Arthur looked at each other. Arthur nodded.

"Can you keep a secret?" Wally asked Sekhmet.

"That depends," she said.

Wally showed her the dragon claw. Her mouth fell open.

"Before you say anything," Wally said, "I talked to Huamei."

He told her the story. When he was finished, Sekhmet took the claw, holding it gently. A confusion of emotions played across her face. She and Huamei had always seemed at odds, but they were still partners.

"If Huamei's mom knew we had this . . . ," she said.

The three imagined the awful fate that could befall them.

What good was having a magical quill if the odds were still hopeless and merely having the thing could get you eaten alive?

"Should we show this to Amelia?" Wally asked.

Sekhmet sighed. "No. She would confiscate it and turn it over to the dragons. If you think *I'm* a stickler for rules . . ."

There was a commotion outside the Healing Room. Wally, Arthur, and Sekhmet snuck to the door. Wally had the terrible feeling that Alfred Moore had discovered their plans and was already storming the Manor with a nightmarish assault.

As they exited the room, they almost bumped into Ludwig, who limped down the hall in his leg cast.

"Sekhmet!" he said. "Ze tentacle monster is here! At ze entrance!"

Wally covered his mouth. The monster was going to squeeze Hazelrigg like it had Valerie Lucas's house, making it and the Manor inside splinter to pieces.

Ludwig rubbed his head. "Amelia left me in charge vhile she and Veston try to smooze sings over vis ze dragons."

"Is the monster trying to break in?" Sekhmet said.

He gazed toward the entrance. "*Nein.* It just . . . *gurgled* at me vis zat awful mous and zen it *tickled* me under ze chin." Ludwig's cheeks shook with fear. "It vas *horrible!*"

Wally's eyebrows leapt. He sprinted to the entrance, and the others followed. The tentacle monster's toothy mouth filled the doorframe. Sekhmet went to draw her swords, but Wally stopped her. "*Wait!*"

The monster's mouth started to shudder and choke, spitting gouts of green saliva onto the carpet. And then it coughed up a pulp of digested paper.

Sekhmet approached the beast with caution, swords raised. She knelt and slowly picked up a slimy page of Alfred Moore's manuscript. The ink was illegible, running with saliva. "So much for getting more clues on how to beat Moore."

Wally barely heard her. He was too busy hugging one of the monster's tentacles.

"Guys?" he said. "I want you to meet Breeth."

* * *

Once Breeth had squeezed her tentacles through the entrance, like an octopus fitting itself through a space no bigger than its beak, they brought her to a cave-like room where they piled wet towels on her slimy body so she wouldn't dry out. The tentacle monster's toothy mouth gurgled with contentment.

"This is your . . . *friend*?" Arthur asked.

"Uh-huh," Wally said.

"But it's also the tentacle monster we fought?"

"Kind of. It's hard to explain."

"And it's going to help us fight Alfred Moore?"

"*She*. And only if she wants to."

"Who is *she* again?"

"A ghost I met in the forest wing."

Arthur threw up his hands. "Well, that answers all of *my* questions."

Breeth lifted two tentacles and tapped them against another tentacle over and over again.

"Two?" Wally said. "You need two of something?"

She shook her mouth back and forth, continuing to tap her two tentacles.

"Charades!" Arthur said. "It's trying to play charades!"

"*She*," Wally said.

"Right," Arthur said. "*She's* playing charades."

Breeth's fanged mouth dipped up and down. Wally guessed that meant *yes*.

Arthur rubbed his hands together and studied what Breeth was doing. "Okay, two syllables."

Breeth nodded. Then she held up one tentacle.

"First syllable."

Breeth rolled onto her side, flopping her tentacles to the floor.

"Dead," Arthur said. "You're dead. Yeah, we knew that already. You're a ghost."

Breeth shook her head. Remaining on her side, her toothy mouth made a vibrating sound.

"Snoring!" Arthur said. "Sleep!"

One of the tentacles wiggled back and forth as if to say "sort of." Then she pointed toward the ceiling.

"Oh, um—" Arthur said. "Ceiling? No, *sky*. Sleepy sky!"

Breeth continued snoring, and Wally snapped his fingers. "Oh! *Night!*"

Breeth nodded enthusiastically as she rolled upright. She held up two tentacles.

"Second syllable," Arthur said.

Breeth froze a moment like she was thinking. Then she bundled four tentacles together and walked them around the floor.

"Uh . . ." Arthur said.

"Slime?" Ludwig guessed. "No, no, *suction cups!*"

"Ludwig," Sekhmet said, "you're terrible at this. Stop being so literal."

Ludwig blushed, and Sekhmet took out Huamei's claw. "How about instead of distracting us, you do us a favor?"

Ludwig's pink cheeks paled. "Is zat . . . ?"

"Yes," Sekhmet said. "I need you to fashion it into a quill. And keep it hidden. If anyone finds out we have this, the dragons will attack Weirdwood."

Ludwig swallowed, took the claw, and excused himself.

Wally watched Breeth's four tentacles walk back and forth. "Is it an animal?"

Breeth nodded enthusiastically.

"Cow!" Arthur said. "Sheep! Pig! Dog! Goat! Llama!"

The tentacles flopped to the ground, exasperated.

Wally gave Arthur a look. "Do you really think she's trying to say *Night Llama*?"

"I don't hear *you* guessing," Arthur said.

"Horse?" Sekhmet guessed.

Breeth nodded fervently and pinched two tentacles together as if to say "*You're* this *close.*" While continuing to walk her imaginary tentacle animal around the floor, she pointed two tentacles at Arthur and Wally and shook her head. Then she pointed to herself and nodded.

"Girl!" Sekhmet said. "Girl horse! *Mare!*"

"*Nightmare!*" Wally and Arthur cried out at the same time.

Breeth threw all of her tentacles into the air as if they had just scored a goal.

"*Oh,*" Wally said, smile fading. "It's a nightmare being in there?"

Breeth shook her head, then pointed a tentacle into her mouth.

"You . . ." Wally tried, "are a nightmare?"

She nodded fervently.

"Aw, you don't look that bad," Arthur said. "Right, Cooper?"

"I don't think that's what she's trying to say," Wally said. He thought a moment. "Oh! You're *Moore's* nightmare."

Breeth made a gurgling shriek of success as every one of her tentacles wrapped around him in a big, slimy hug.

"Of course!" Arthur said. "This monster came straight from Alfred Moore's nightmares! She's a twisted version of Garnett's adventures!"

"We can attack him with the very thing he's been hurting other people with," Sekhmet said. "Give him a taste of his own medicine. Scare him into submission."

Wally rested his hand on Breeth's side. "Are you sure? You might die again."

Her tentacles went limp, but she nodded.

Wally understood why she would make this sacrifice: Moore could tell them the identity of her killer. Besides, it was probably no fun living life as a tentacle monster.

"I hate to be the bearer of bad news," Sekhmet said. "Moore will try to kill anything that enters that monster hospital. She wouldn't make it through the portcullis."

Everyone paused. The only sound was Breeth's dripping teeth.

"What if we save his life instead?" Wally asked.

"I hate to break this to you, Cooper," Arthur said,

"but we're trying to *defeat* the evil Mirror author, not rescue him."

"I mean *pretend* to save his life," Wally said. "He doesn't trust us right now. But what if we were to make him believe he was in mortal danger from the tentacle monster and then swoop in and rescue him at the last moment?"

"He might kill us anyway," Sekhmet said. "If his greatest fear shows up, he'll throw everything he can at it."

A grin crept across Wally's face. "Puppets."

Arthur's forehead wrinkled. "I'm not following you."

About time, Wally thought.

Usually he was the one left in the dark while Arthur rattled off some nonsense that didn't have any bearing on reality. Of course, it had been Graham who'd slyly given Wally the solution in the Mirror City. Wally was starting to embrace his brother's way of looking at the world.

"We can't set foot in Moore's hospital without getting destroyed by some horrible creation," Wally said. "So what if we send in someone he won't destroy?"

"Who?" Arthur said.

"Garnett Lacroix."

Arthur's eyes went wide.

Wally continued. "We can use Huamei's claw to revive Garnett Lacroix by adding to his story like Huamei tried to do with the porcelain doll. Breeth can get him past Monster Greyridge's defenses and then attack Moore. The Gentleman Thief will save his creator from the tentacle monster and then convince Moore to hand over the Quill."

"Cooper," Arthur said, "you're a *genius*."

Wally blushed. "We'll need a writer who knows those stories inside and out."

Arthur searched Wally's eyes. "Valerie Lucas? But she's dead."

"I'm talking about *you*!"

"*Me?*"

"Of course! You've quoted nearly every single line of those books to me! All you have to do is ask yourself '*What would Garnett do?*' and then write it down like Alfred Moore—er, Valerie Lucas would."

"But . . . what would he do in *this* situation?"

Wally tapped his lips. "Could you give Garnett sword hands and impenetrable skin or something?"

Arthur scoffed, insulted. "I wouldn't believe it if I wrote it." He held his head. "I don't even know how to bring Garnett back from the dead! All of his blood is gone!"

Wally smirked. This was the first time he'd ever heard Arthur admit all the things he *couldn't* do. He patted his friend's shoulder. "I'm sure you'll come up with something."

Sekhmet cleared her throat. "Did either of you want to ask the expert on magic whether this plan will actually work?"

Wally and Arthur stared at her.

"If you write with a dragon claw," Sekhmet told Arthur, "then your soul will be drawn into the body of Garnett Lacroix."

"Oh," Arthur said, swallowing.

"Wait," Wally said. "That didn't happen to Moore when he wrote his monsters."

"Moore doesn't have a soul," Sekhmet said. "He's a

figment." She placed a hand on Arthur's shoulder. "If Garnett dies, then your spirit will become lost forever."

"Better and better," Arthur said, rubbing his face.

"Still," Sekhmet said, "I haven't heard a better solution. The Manor is spread so thin between the dragons, the Faeborn, and the fight with the Order that Amelia is considering sealing off Mirror Kingsport, trapping the imagination of its citizens, and letting Kingsport fall into Daymare."

"Daymare?" Wally said, heart sinking.

"Melding with the Mirror City," Sekhmet said. "All of Kingsport's worst fears will come true. Like a living nightmare no one can wake up from."

Wally and Arthur went quiet.

"Then we do it," Arthur said. "For Kingsport."

"There's more," Sekhmet said. "You can't stay here. Amelia knows this Manor almost as well as Lady Weirdwood, and she's way less forgiving. If she finds you with a dragon claw, she'll lock you up. She might even turn you over to Huamei's mom. And it would be foolish to send you back to the Mirror. Too many risks. In order to write without interruption, you're going to have to return to Real Kingsport."

"Where more of Moore's monsters are going to attack me," Arthur said.

"I'll come with and defend you," Sekhmet said, flipping a sword over her hand. "Wally, you and Ludwig can head into the Mirror to help once Garnett is revived."

"How are we going to get Garnett and Breeth up to Greyridge?" Wally said. "She's huge, and the building's flying in circles hundreds of feet up in the air."

"I sink I can help vith zat."

Ludwig stood in the doorway. He held the newly fashioned Claw Quill in one hand, and in the other, his squares of paper.

"Your birds can get an entire tentacle monster to fly?" Sekhmet asked skeptically.

"She vill require a *boost*," Ludwig said, examining Breeth. "But once she is up in ze air, I can get ze vind under her. Like, vhat you say . . . a *kite*."

Sekhmet frowned at the paper cuts on her fingers. "Guess I'm folding more cranes."

"How will we boost Breeth?" Wally asked.

Arthur snapped his fingers. "Underwear."

Wally rolled his eyes. "Tell me this doesn't involve removing pants."

"Nope! We can build a sling out of stretchy underwear bands. There's got to be underwear on Licey Lane, right? They might be a little itchy, but still."

"How much time do you spend thinking about underwear?" Sekhmet asked.

Arthur's ears turned red. "You have to get creative when you're an author." He thought a moment. "It will take time to build the sling. If only we had more help . . ."

At that, Breeth started to gurgle and choke. Her tentacles heaved and then her toothy mouth hocked up three skeletons.

22
ARTHUR THE AUTHOR

Kingsport was in darkness, the lamplighters too afraid
to light the lamps. Windows were shattered. Roofs
were caved in. Rubble littered the sidewalks.

Arthur watched the skies and sewers for signs of an
impending monster attack. But all was quiet. Alfred Moore
must have been too busy fortifying the bat-winged Mirror
mental hospital that Arthur would have to break into as
Garnett Lacroix. The thought was less than comforting.

"What's the plan?" Sekhmet whispered.

"Right," Arthur said. "The plan."

Now that he'd finally earned Sekhmet's respect, his tongue
felt tied in knots. It wasn't easy coming up with a way to revive
your childhood hero and send him on an adventure when an
unspeakable monster could be waiting around the next corner.

But there was one place in the city where Arthur always felt
safe—where the adventure always flowed through him.

"Okay," he said, "we're going to head to the rooftop where
I've read Moore's stories for the past several years. I'll nestle
myself between my trusty chimney pots and—"

Arthur heard the sound of drawn steel, a sizzle, a clink, and then a thunk. He turned around to find Charlie, the Rook's bodyguard, dumping Sekhmet's unconscious body in an alley, having just clubbed her over the head. His shirt smoldered where Sekhmet had tried to cut him, but his chain mail gleamed unbroken underneath.

Charlie brushed off his hands. "Boss wants to see ya."

Arthur tried to dash away, but Charlie seized his arm and dragged him toward Paradise Lane.

"Charlie!" Arthur said, forcing a smile. "I got that treasure the Rook wanted. Stashed it in Cobbler's Alley." It was the only place Arthur could think of that was so crowded with packing crates he might have a chance at escape. "If we could just head that way, I'm sure the Rook will remember this when he chooses his successor for the Black Feathers."

Charlie plodded silently ahead, hand clamped tight as a manacle around Arthur's arm.

"But if you *don't* take me to the treasure," Arthur said, "the Rook will probably demote you to the Stormcrow's dishwasher."

Charlie only snorted.

Arthur started to panic. Again, his heroic plans had been foiled in the span of a breath. Why didn't things ever work like they did in adventure stories?

Charlie shoved Arthur through the Stormcrow's entrance and then patted down his pockets while Arthur frantically searched for an escape. The pub looked small and quaint compared to the maniac pub of the Mirror. There were no snarling scavengers. No smoky steins. The lamps flickered yellow. Usually, the Stormcrow would be bustling, but it seemed a tentacle had smashed through the side wall, forcing the pub to close for repairs.

In the corner, Liza swept shattered glass. Arthur caught her eye, flashing her a desperate look, but she quickly glanced away. When it came down to it, Liza must've been as afraid of her father as everyone else.

"What's this?" Charlie asked, pulling the claw Quill out of Arthur's pocket.

"*That*," Arthur said, thinking fast, "is petrified mammoth's dung. If you look really closely, you can see bits of undigested corn."

Charlie gave the claw Quill a disgusted look but held on to it. He forced Arthur through the back door, painted with the screeching rook. The office's cherry wood walls were high and wide. A desk sat in the middle, stacked with gold and accounts.

The Rook sat on his feathered throne. "Hello, Arthur."

A few days ago, Arthur would have been elated to be invited into the Rook's office. But that was before he knew about the opportunities that awaited him in Weirdwood Manor—opportunities that would give him a life far more adventurous and noble than the one he would lead as a Black Feather.

Charlie held up the claw Quill. "He had this in his pocket."

"What do we have here?" the Rook said.

He smiled, revealing his tattooed tongue. His yellow eyes shone as he studied the Quill's blue veins, but he did not take it.

Arthur stiffened when he realized he'd brought the one thing that could defeat Moore straight to the most dangerous man in Kingsport. If the Rook found out how it worked, he could level the city. Arthur had to get it back. He searched for excuses: *That Quill is made of mammoth's dung. It was dipped in blood. It's infected with the Pox . . .*

But before he could come up with a reasonable excuse, the Rook stood from his desk and went to a sheet-covered figure in the corner. He pulled off the sheet, revealing a woman. Arthur couldn't tell if she was alive or dead. Her cheeks were pinched pink, but her eyes were glassy and unblinking. She stood all by herself, but she didn't seem to be breathing. Her expression was as dull as wax.

The Rook ran his fingers down the woman's pale throat. "Soon, my love," he whispered.

My love? Arthur thought.

He looked at the Rook and his black-swirled tongue. He saw his tattooed hands, which hadn't reached out for the claw Quill. Huamei had said that Lady Weirdwood once bound someone from speaking spells or handling magical implements . . .

Arthur could have kicked himself, it was so obvious. If he had read it in a book, he would have rolled his eyes.

The Rook was the Fallen Warden.

"Lock our errant thief in the cellar," the Rook said, brushing the air with the back of his hand.

Before Arthur could protest, Charlie grabbed him by the back of the neck and dragged him behind the Rook's desk, kicking a rug aside and hauling open a barred trapdoor, leading to the cellar.

"The Rook is my king!" Arthur cried. "His feathers my nest! I am encompassed in the black of his eye and protected in the claws of his talons! I will serve him as the earth serves the sun, as the worm serves the rook!"

Charlie hesitated. The Rook raised his eyebrows. He was listening.

Arthur's mind worked quickly, weaving together the separate threads of the Rook and the Fallen Warden. If Lady Weirdwood was able to bind the Rook, then that meant she was more powerful than he was . . .

"The Wardens are onto you," Arthur lied. "They caught Alfred Moore and locked him up in the Abyssment. They're headed here right now."

The Rook's eyes narrowed.

"Lady Weirdwood told me to come ahead and betray you," Arthur continued. "To lead you into a trap. I pretended to follow her orders, but I have remained loyal to the Black Feathers." He nodded to the claw Quill in Charlie's hand. "That's why I stole that thing from her. To give to you. Sekhmet, that girl with the swords that Charlie knocked out, didn't know I had it."

The Rook sneered. "Taught you some Wordcraft in that creaky old Manor, did they?"

"They tried, but I resisted," Arthur said. He held up his right hand where Moore had stabbed him and tried to think of the most violent person in Weirdwood. "I got this from Pyra when I disobeyed."

The Rook sneered at the claw Quill in Charlie's hand. "Where did that come from then? Dragon bones are rarer than diamonds."

"That?" Arthur said, thinking fast. "That's Moore's Quill.

You don't recognize it because he used its magic to fashion it into something more comfortable to hold."

Arthur had no idea if dragon bones could change themselves, but he stood tall and unblinking as the Rook stepped close, his nose inches from Arthur's.

"How do I know you aren't lying, boy?" the Rook asked.

Arthur hesitated. He had to find the Rook's weak spot. He glanced at the dull woman in the corner. This must have been his failed attempt at bringing his wife back to life.

"Because I know you haven't done anything wrong," Arthur lied. "You aren't a bad person. You just miss Liza's mom. I miss mine too."

The Rook's expression softened slightly, giving Arthur another moment to think.

The gang leader had needed someone else to handle the dragon-bone Quill. Someone creative enough to tear big holes in the Veil so that he could be reunited with his wife's spirit. He'd found Alfred Moore in the Mirror, giving the pen name author the one thing that would kill his creator and set him free, while also getting him to unleash monsters on Kingsport.

But Moore had written that he'd received the Quill from a *Jangling Man* . . . Of course. That had to have been Charlie, whose chain mail was always clinking. As with the Black Feathers, the Rook kept his dirty business several people removed from himself so the Wardens wouldn't be able to track him.

More importantly, with his magically bound tongue and hands, the Rook was unable to use the Quill. It seemed he couldn't even touch it with his tattooed hands.

"The Wardens will be here any moment," Arthur said. "We need to come up with defenses. *Now*."

The Rook considered him a moment, then frowned at Charlie.

No, Arthur thought. *Don't let him use it.*

"And here I am with a bodyguard who never learned how to bloody write," the Rook said.

Charlie blushed and shifted.

The Rook's eyes glanced to his office door, clearly considering his daughter.

"You don't want Liza to get involved in this," Arthur said. "The Quill's too dangerous." He held out his hand to Charlie. "Let me do it."

The Rook's mouth grew tight. "If it turns out you have deceived me, I will feed you and your sorry excuse for a father to one of Moore's rabid nightmares."

Arthur gulped as Charlie slapped the Quill in his palm. Arthur considered bolting out of the pub, but he wouldn't make it two steps before Charlie snapped his neck.

Arthur sat on the feathered throne while the Rook laid a clean piece of paper in front of him. The Rook glared over Arthur's shoulder, watching his every move.

"Write *precisely* what I say," the Rook said.

Arthur nodded and dipped the Claw Quill, using his left, uninjured hand.

The Rook said, "The Mirror Rook glided in from the silver city and alighted on the Real Stormcrow Pub in order to defend it."

Arthur fought down a shiver. He remembered the

deafening BOOM behind the back door of the Mirror pub. If he summoned that creature to the Real, the Rook would become unstoppable. Sekhmet wouldn't be able to come and rescue him. But if Arthur wrote anything other than exactly what the Rook asked him to, Charlie would break him within seconds.

Arthur began to write.

The Mirror Rook glided in from the silver city and . . .

"Um, how do you spell *alighted*?" he asked, trying to buy more time.

The Rook told him, irritation in his voice. Arthur wrote the letters slowly, thinking. When Wally had told him to write a portal to escape the Manor, Arthur had foolishly written *magical* Kingsport. All it had taken was a single word to change everything.

. . . alighted on the Real Stormcrow Pub . . .

Arthur wrote the Rook's words even more slowly, as if afraid to misspell something.

He had time enough to change one word. One very important word.

. . . in order to . . .

It wasn't until the very end that the answer came to him. A tiny change. Just a few letters. He smiled to himself. And then Arthur finished the sentence, writing as quickly as he could. The Mirror Rook would not be swooping in to *defend* the Stormcrow Pub but to . . .

. . . destroy it.

"No!" the Rook screamed.

He seized the Quill, but his tattooed hand started to sizzle, and he cried out and let go. With his other hand, the Rook shoved Arthur out of the feathered throne and then stomped painfully on his arm, making Arthur's grip release and the Quill clatter under the desk.

Charlie picked up Arthur by the shirt and hurled him through the trapdoor. Arthur hit the cellar floor hard. The trapdoor fell shut, and Charlie locked it with a *click*. Arthur could still see the men through the trapdoor's bars.

"Cross it out!" the Rook screamed at Charlie. "*Now*, you fool!"

Charlie crouched, frantically searching under the desk for the Quill, but it was too late. The pub's walls began to tremble. Outside came a sweep of wings as big as ship's sails and a grawk as loud as thunder.

"Dad?" Liza's voice echoed, scared and hollow from the pub.

A deafening shriek pierced the night as a talon the size of a scythe sliced through the ceiling. Liza screamed, but it was lost in the collapse of the pub's walls. The office filled with talons and shrieks and splintered wood. A giant feather fell over the bars of the trapdoor, so Arthur could only see bits and flashes of the attack. He heard a wet sound, and Charlie grunted. Blood dripped down the steps. The ceiling continued to wrench apart as a beak, as black as tar and as long as a ship's prow, clacked through.

"I am your master!" the Rook screamed at it. "I created you in all of your glory through my power and for—"

The beak snapped, and his voice cut short. Arthur watched as the massive head of the Mirror Rook retreated through the

hole in the roof, the Rook's feet kicking like a helpless insect in its beak. As the Mirror Rook took flight from the roof, the feet fell still and did not move again.

* * *

When the sound of flapping faded in the distance, Arthur collapsed to the floor, dust settling with his pounding heart. He had summoned the Rook's Mirror counterpart, and it had devoured the Rook. Arthur felt neither guilty nor victorious. Only fear.

Arthur blinked at his surroundings, blood pounding in his eyes. The cellar was not filled with fingers or skeletons, but that didn't make it any more pleasant. The air felt like the cold, damp armpit of a corpse—thick with the stench of festering cheeses. He hugged himself. This is where Black Feathers came to die. And there was no one left upstairs to let him out.

Arthur could have sat there all night, staring. But then he remembered. Sekhmet was unconscious in an alley. Wally was waiting for him in the Mirror City.

"Come on, Arthur," he said, forcing himself to his feet. "You can figure this out."

He climbed the ladder and reached through the bars of the trapdoor, brushing aside the giant feather. Through the debris, he spotted the claw Quill, blue veins glowing. He grabbed a splintered piece of wood and used it to pull the Quill toward him. Huamei's claw was still warm, thrumming with the power of having summoned the Mirror Rook.

Arthur had been hesitant about writing before, but now his fear had grown into mind-numbing dread. If he wrote one wrong word, it could destroy him. He searched the cellar and realized, with no small amount of relief, that he couldn't write if he wanted to. He didn't have paper or ink.

The relief quickly turned into guilt. Were Wally and the others cursing Arthur's name? Was Wally telling them that this was typical Arthur Benton—running away from danger to serve himself?

Rats scrabbled and squeaked in the cellar's dark corners. But beneath them was another sound. Snores. *Familiar* snores.

"Harry?" Arthur said, blindly feeling his way through the darkness. His hands found a large belly, and Arthur patted his way to his father's cheeks, which he lightly slapped. "Harry, wake up! We gotta break out of here!"

Harry didn't stir. He had all the telltale signs: pungent breath, bottomless snores, drool dripping down his cheek. It seemed that the moment Arthur had released his dad from Greyridge, Harry had gotten drunk. He was so far gone, he'd even slept through the Mirror Rook's destruction of the Stormcrow.

Arthur went to the corner, cupped some water from a hissing pipe, and dribbled it over Harry's lips. Harry snorted awake, sitting up with a start and then rubbing his head. "Where are we?"

"Stormcrow's cellar," Arthur said. "Not that having you awake does any good."

"What do you mean?" Harry said, squinting.

"Do you realize how much more difficult you make everything?" Arthur yelled. "Like life isn't hard enough! You drink all my earnings away so we can barely feed ourselves, let alone starving orphans! No wonder I've never felt like a Gentleman Thief! I've taken after you, and I hate it! Leaving Wally behind! Stealing treasure from good people just to save you from being *killed*!" Arthur sat on the ground in defeat. "I hate it."

Harry was silent a moment. "Son, I ain't touched a drop since you released me." He nodded to the trapdoor. "Charlie up there conked me over the head."

"But . . ." Arthur said, "your breath. The drool."

"I was eating cheese and onions when he got me!" Harry wiped the slobber from his chin. "And I'd like to see *you* not drool after getting knocked unconscious!"

Arthur's surge of anger dissipated when he saw the bump shining on Harry's forehead.

"Oh," Arthur said. "Sorry, Dad."

Harry climbed the ladder and tried to force open the trap-door. It barely budged.

"This is a pickle, eh?" he said.

Arthur squeezed the Quill. "If only we had some paper and ink . . ."

Harry gave him a confused look. Then he reached in his back pocket and pulled out several eviction notices. They must have been nailed to their apartment door—one for each day Harry failed to pay rent.

Arthur snatched the pages. "Dad, you're a lifesaver!"

He made a small desk beneath the light of the trapdoor by setting a cask lid between two barrels. Now he just needed ink. He found a barrel of oil and dragged it sloshing over to his makeshift desk. The liquid inside was sludgy black. Using his left, uninjured hand, Arthur dipped the Quill and wrote *Garnett Lacroix*. It was messy, but it would do.

Arthur's hand trembled. His heart pounded. He needed to come up with a way to revive Garnett Lacroix. Something that he as a reader would believe. But nothing came to him.

He squeezed his eyes shut and tried to imagine a perfect start to the story. Maybe he'd describe the stars of the Mirror City. They were like . . . *ninja stars made of light*. Wait, no. They were like *sea anemones of fire* . . .

Bluch. This was harder than he thought. He didn't sound *anything* like Valerie Lucas. Arthur tried not to think about the fact that Kingsport's fate was at stake and that his spirit could be lost forever.

"What're you doing, scribbling at a time like this?" Harry asked.

"I need to write a story about Garnett Lacroix," Arthur said. "I can't explain why right now. Just . . . let me focus."

"Ah. Right," Harry said, leaning against the ladder. "*Lacrotch*."

"*Lacroix*," Arthur corrected.

"*Lacwaw*," his dad said. "That's the one. You used to sit in my lap while I read you those stories. You'd giggle and gasp and smile up at me like I was your hero. You remember that?"

"Of course I remember. Mom gave me those stories."

"*Pbbbb*." Harry fluttered his lips. "Nah. She was sick at the hospital. She told me to pick out somethin' special for Christmas, and that's what I picked."

Arthur stared at his father. "*You* bought me Garnett Lacroix?"

Harry grinned. "Sure did."

"Those books changed my life," Arthur said, seeing his dad in a whole new light.

"'Course they did!" Harry said. "I'm not as big a fool as you like to think."

Arthur remembered something important then. Every hero had to have a dark night of the soul before things grew bright again. And things didn't get much darker than the Stormcrow's basement . . . or lighter than the memories of a beloved childhood story.

Maybe life was more like adventure stories than Arthur gave it credit.

He stared at the blank page. "Dad, do you remember any of the stories?"

Harry rubbed the bump on his head. "I think I might. You always did like that one about saving the orphans."

"Would you tell me that one?" Arthur asked. "Like you used to?"

Harry cleared his throat. "Once upon a time there was this thief who dressed better than just about anybody, if I remember correctly."

Arthur listened until he felt inspired. Then he told his father to hush and placed Quill to paper.

Garnett Lacroix woke with a start. He clawed the cobwebs from his eyes and gazed around the sewers.

"What the devil?" he said, his voice echoing down the dark tunnel.

Arthur found he was no longer self-conscious about what to write. He simply let the adventure flow through him. Just like when he was little.

Garnett opened his vest and peeked inside at the many empty bags of blood that lined his shirt. "Good thing I was carrying those blood transfusions for that orphanage!" the Gentleman Thief said. "The spiders drank those instead of me!" He tore out the empty bags and discarded them. "I'll have to track down more blood for the orphans after this adventure is through!"

Arthur wasn't sure that was how Valerie Lucas would've resurrected her hero, but he hoped she'd be proud of him.

Garnett touched his cheek, which was quickly transforming—papery as mummy skin to soft and prickly. Blood coursed through his fingertips.

"Where are my Merry Rogues? Gus? Tuck? Mim?"

There was no response. ~~The sewers rang hollow with the desperation of a man who~~

Arthur crossed out the line. "Get to the action, Benton."

Garnett picked himself up and brushed the last of the cobwebs from his pants. "Wherever they are, they probably need my help!"

Arthur wrote the Gentleman Thief out of the sewer and

into the tangled Mirror streets. Arthur briefly worried that he was only *imagining* his hero walking up Parasite Lane. What if in the Mirror, nothing was happening? What if Garnett was still covered in cobwebs?

But it felt so natural to write that Arthur continued.

Garnett Lacroix blinked up at the strangely glistening sky. The stars looked like bright sparkling fangs that dripped glittery horror onto the rooftops.

"Beautiful!" he cried. "But now is no time for sightseeing!"

He walked until he heard a familiar sound. The joyful voices of his Merry Rogues! Garnett followed the music and came to the Ghastly Courtyard. But instead of his Rogues, he found a group of skeletons standing on the gallows, snipping away underwear bands and sewing those bands together.

"Gus? Tuck? Mim?" Garnett said. "What happened to you?"

"Just a little bone tired is all!" Tuck said.

"Too many skeletons in our closet!" said Mim.

"We haven't got the guts to tell you!" said Gus.

Garnett wiggled a finger in his ear. "Please, leave the puns to me." He clapped them on their shoulders, rattling their bones. "It's good to see you."

The skeletons went back to work, sewing the stretchy bands of underwear together.

"Arthur!"

A boy ran up to Garnett and handed him his wide-brimmed hat with the daffodil tucked in the brim. The boy was clever-looking. A little on the short side, maybe, but could probably pick a lock better than most.

"Who is this Arthur of which you speak?" Garnett said, putting on his hat and feeling whole again.

"Sorry, Mr. Lacroix," the boy said and shook Garnett's hand. "I'm Wally. We weren't sure you were going to show."

Back in the Stormcrow cellar, Arthur grinned. He hadn't

written those last words. They had appeared on the page all by themselves.

"*Of course I showed!*" Arthur wrote. "*Wherever there's a bat-winged hospital on the loose, expect the Gentleman Thief!*"

"*That's oddly specific,*" Wally said, then smiled. "*I'm glad you're here.*"

As Wally's words scratched themselves on the page, the cellar started to melt away.

"Arthur?" Harry said, panicked. "Son, what's happening? Your eyes are going white . . ."

Arthur blinked and found that he was staring through the eyes of Garnett Lacroix.

23
MONSTER GREYRIDGE

We sure this is gonna work?" Wally asked as he tied one end of the underwear sling so it dangled between two gallows.

"Of course it'll work!" Tuck said.

"We're dead shots!" said Mim.

"Besides, what's the worst that could happen?" said Gus.

Wally secured the knot and dropped to the planks. "Um, we could all die?"

Mim threw a bony arm around his shoulder. "Ah, lovey. Being dead's not so bad."

Wally shrugged her away and went to talk to Arthur/ Garnett, who stood on the edge of the Ghastly Courtyard, hands planted on his hips, gazing into the sky. Wally had to admit that the Gentleman Thief did look heroic. Strong chin. Powerful frame. Gold-laced jacket and bright blue pants. Wally finally understood what Arthur imagined he looked like whenever he struck a pose in his tattered rags.

"Ready?" Wally said.

Garnett breathed deeply. "As ready as a crocodile in a petting zoo."

Wally smiled and shook his head. Arthur really needed to work on his lines.

"Just be careful up there," Wally said.

"Fear not, young thief," Garnett said. "Alfred Moore has brought me back to life dozens of times—from being shot in the heart to falling off a waterfall to that time my head was shipped to the Far East."

"Well, now he's trying to do the opposite," Wally said.

Garnett only winked at him.

Wally watched Monster Greyridge flap its way across the horizon. It flew the same circle above the city, over and over again, taking about an hour to make a complete rotation. They would have to time their launch perfectly to make sure Garnett broke through the hospital's portcullis. The skeletons had aimed the elastic sling at the moon. The hospital was nearly on target.

"Four minutes, everyone!" Ludwig shouted, madly folding paper cranes.

Wally's stomach lurched. He approached Breeth, whose tentacles were nestled in the saddle at the base of the underwear sling.

"Ready, Breeth?"

When she didn't respond, he climbed her tentacles like slimy tree roots and sat next to her toothy mouth.

"I said, are you ready?"

The mouth shook back and forth.

Wally patted her mucus-covered cheek. "I don't blame you."

If the tentacle monster died, Breeth's spirit could possess some nearby organic matter. But she would still feel every second of its death.

Breeth's tentacles gave a sudden jerk, and Wally grabbed hold to steady himself. The Merry Skeletons were hauling back the sling, stretching the underwear bands tight to wrap around a stake in the ground.

Wally's heart started to pound. "Do you remember what you need to do up there?" he asked Breeth. "Grab on to the hospital, squeeze through the portcullis, and then *pretend* to attack Moore. Garnett will come in and defeat you in battle. Gently, of course."

The mouth nodded.

"After you get back," Wally continued, "we'll have Pyra mix up some food that will make the tentacle monster go to sleep and never wake up again. It'll be peaceful. Then we'll demand that Moore tell us who gave him that Quill and we can find your killer. Okay?"

A curt nod.

"Vun minute!" Ludwig called.

Bat-winged Greyridge had nearly reached the center of the moon's light. The skeletons strained, pulling the sling as taut as possible.

Garnett stepped to the base of Breeth's tentacles, then turned to salute the Merry Skeletons. "Wish me luck, my boneheaded companions!"

"Good luck!"

"Glued duck!"

"Lewd guck!"

The sling stretched as far as it would go, Tuck began securing it to the stake.

Wally gave Breeth's side one last pat. "You've got this. I believe in you."

Breeth gurgled miserably.

"That's not how you tie a knot!" Gus said, trying to wrench the sling from Tuck's bony fingers.

"It's not *not* how you tie a knot!" Tuck said, pulling it back.

Gus huffed. "That is *not* the knot that will not fail us. Now stop being naughty and give it here!"

The skeletons played tug-of-war with the rope, yanking it back and forth until . . . it slipped out of their bony fingers.

A scream tore out of Wally's lungs as he and Breeth were launched into the atmosphere.

"Sorry about that!" Tuck cried.

"Hold on, Cooper!" Garnett screamed.

Wally clung tight to Breeth's tentacles, trying desperately not to fall as they soared into the sky. The wind flattened his ears and sent his tears streaming. Two panicked breaths later, Wally and Breeth reached the height of their ascent. Then they started to fall back toward the ground, hundreds of feet below. Wally tried to scream again, but his breath was stolen by the fall. He closed his eyes, his stomach lifting and pressing into his throat.

But then a new gust of wind relieved the falling sensation.

Ludwig's paper cranes flapped below, carrying him and Breeth in dips and rises toward the flapping hospital.

"Get ready to grab on!" Wally called to Breeth.

Her tentacles hit the stones with a slimy *SMACK!* and Wally fell hurtling toward the ground. But then he jerked to a stop, his hat sailing off his head. Breeth lifted him by his ankle and set him in a nook between two of her tentacles.

Wally hugged the hospital's side, trying to catch his breath. "We're alive. I can't believe it. We're alive."

It was only then that Wally felt the weight of the situation. He was supposed to stay on the *ground* while Garnett, the *hero* was launched into the sky. But the Gentleman Thief was a thousand feet below while Wally and Breeth were all alone atop the monster Greyridge.

They needed to get indoors before they were blown right off the hospital. He studied Greyridge's outer wall, trying to avoid looking at the ground, a thousand feet below.

"There's the entrance!" he called over the screaming wind and the giant, flapping wings. "Breeth, can you get me over there?"

Breeth clung to the building like an octopus to the side of a boat. One of her tentacles hesitantly inched like a caterpillar across the wall. Wally sidestepped across it, cheek pressed tight to the stone.

The portcullis was locked. And he still didn't have his lock-pick set.

Flustered, he searched his surroundings. The dizzying height made his vision blur. Where could he find a lock pick this high up in the sky? And then he saw it, flapping and glistening in the moonlight.

"Breeth," he said. "Can you snap off one of those thinner bat claws for me?"

Breeth slowly peeled one of her tentacles off the tower. The moment the wing flapped downward, she lashed out and caught hold of its claw. But the claw didn't come loose. The wing struggled to flap upward, and the building careened to the side, bringing them parallel with the ground. Wally squeezed tight to Breeth's tentacle, feet dangling, eyes shut, trying not to lose his stomach.

As the hospital started to fall, Breeth's tentacle gave a twist and a jerk, and the tip of the claw snapped off. Monster Greyridge shrieked in pain, but then its wing unfurled, flapping again, and the building righted itself.

Wally opened his eyes, took the claw, and picked the lock. Breeth hauled open the portcullis, and they both slipped inside. The Mirror hospital was cold and howling. Black flames flickered in the marble hallways, which echoed with giggles and murmurs from the cells.

Someone clapped in the darkness. "I see you've managed to make it all the way up here." Alfred Moore stepped into the light, grinning. "But let's see how long you survive." The color drained from his face when he saw Breeth and her tentacles. He started to back away. "You stay away from me! Stay away!"

Trembling, he scribbled something on his notepad with the Quill, and the rug beneath Wally's feet started to bend and contort, like a giant tongue. The portcullis began chomping up and down like rusted teeth as the tongue rug tilted Wally toward it.

"Whoa, whoa!" Wally said, trying to keep his balance.

The second before the portcullis teeth chewed him to bits, Breeth lashed out and pulled him to safety. Wally stared, wide-eyed, at the entrance. Monster Greyridge had tried to chew him up and spit him out.

"Very well," Moore mumbled. He sounded calm, but he kept darting fearful glances at Breeth. "I have more tricks up my sleeve. This hospital is *filled* with terrible things that have ignited my imagination!"

He ran down the hallway, writing as he went. The corridors lengthened and twisted like bamboo shoots, turning into a tangled mass of catacombs.

Wally hesitated. He considered waiting in the lobby for an hour until the skeletons could launch Garnett up there. But with the hospital twisting itself into mazes, they might lose the Mirror author forever. Kingsport would fall into Daymare and Breeth would never find her killer.

Wally cracked his knuckles. "Let's go get him."

Breeth picked Wally up and chased after the author, using her many tentacles to suction the wide walls and propel them forward at great speed. The deeper they ventured, the more impossible the mental hospital became. Staircases flipped. Passageways steepened. Halls split in half, then fourths, then eighths, then sixteenths.

But they managed to catch up with Moore, who was winded. Breeth set Wally down.

"We just need that Quill," he told the author. "And for

you to tell me who gave it to you. Then I'll call off the tentacle monster."

Moore's face twisted into a scowl. "I refuse to be beaten by my own creation."

He scribbled something new, and one of the cells filled with a sound like fluttering moths.

"What is that?" Wally whispered, not really wanting to know.

The cell burst open, and a flock of straitjackets flooded the hallway. Wally was able to dodge the first few, but then one of the jackets wrapped around his chest, binding his arms and squeezing so tight he couldn't breathe. The rest of the jackets wrapped around several of Breeth's tentacles.

Fortunately, the moment Wally's jacket had squeezed, he had instinctively flexed his muscles—just as he had with Graham's binds. Wally loosened his muscles now, making the jacket momentarily fall slack, and Breeth used her free tentacles to tear it off him. Wally regained his breath and then checked on Breeth. The straitjackets were designed for human arms and so looked like mere boxing tape on the ends of her tentacles.

"They're not squeezing too hard, are they?" he asked her.

Breeth shook her mouth no.

"That's goo—"

He was interrupted by the scratch of Moore's Quill. The sound quickly faded under what sounded like electric wasps. Another cell burst open, and a swarm of drills flew out toward Wally and Breeth, threatening to fill them with holes.

"Breeth!" Wally shouted. "Use the jackets!"

Breeth's jacket-wrapped tentacles seized the drills by their business ends. The drills smoked and jittered, until they shorted out, falling in dead thunks to the floor.

Wally rested his forehead against Breeth's side. "Boy, it feels good to have a tentacle monster on your team."

"Yes, I imagine it does," Moore said, backing down the hallway. He glanced left and right at the cells, thinking. Then he saw something and wickedness crept back across his face. "Ah well. Nothing good lasts."

He wrote again, and the hallway filled with a blinding, frantic light.

Wally knew what this new terror was before it formed. Moore was bringing to life the experimental treatments the doctor had threatened against Graham: the straitjackets, the

drills. There was only one experimental treatment left . . .
shock treatment.

The crackling thing formed in the center of the hallway. It
was a goblin. Made of electricity.

Moore cackled. "Good luck stopping this one!" He disappeared down the hallway.

The moment the electric goblin spotted them with its wild,
bending eyes, it struck like lightning. Breeth shrieked in pain.
Her tentacles jerked and flopped as she started to sizzle. The
hallway filled with the stench of cooked fish.

Wally watched, helpless. If he touched her, he'd be electrocuted too.

"Breeth! I don't know what to do!"

Just when he thought the tentacle monster was done for,
an explosive splintering sound echoed from somewhere far
down the corridor.

"Ha *ha*!" a heroic voice cried.

"Garnett?" Wally screamed, his voice echoing.

"Cooper?" the Gentleman Thief's voice echoed back.

"Garnett, *help*!"

How would Arthur find them? The halls had divided more
times than Wally could count.

But somehow, moments later . . .

"Oho!" Garnett cried. "Hello there, massive tentacle butt!
How do I get around you?"

"Don't touch her!" Wally cried. "She's being electrocuted!"

"Got it!" Garnett said.

Through the jittering tentacles, Wally watched as Garnett

used a board from a busted cell door to pry Breeth off the floor. Wally found another board and did the same on his side, lifting tentacles. The moment Breeth was off the ground, the flow of electricity ceased, and the electric goblin snuffed out.

Breeth stopped sizzling, and Wally threw his arms around her. Garnett squeezed himself between the tentacles and the wall.

"Arthur!" Wally said. "I mean, *Garnett*! How did you know to do that?"

"From one of Garnett's—I mean *my* past adventures!" the Gentleman Thief said. "The Merry Rogues saved my life from the Lightning Queen by making sure the electricity couldn't be grounded!"

Wally smiled, then gave the tangled hallway a quizzical look. "How did you get here so fast? And how did you find us? We must've made a hundred turns down these halls!"

"Gus, Tuck, and Mim reversed the sling!" Garnett said. "The moment the hospital circled to the opposite side of the horizon, they shot me up here! As for how I traversed this impossible hospital"—he patted Breeth's side—"this beautiful creature left a perfectly legible slime trail!"

Wally was so relieved he almost forgave Gus and Tuck for launching him preemptively. Breeth stroked Garnett's shoulder, thanking him for saving her.

Garnett smiled at the dead drills and straitjackets. "It seems you've managed to defeat the hospital's monsters! Without weapons nonetheless!" He bowed, and then drew his sword. "Onward!"

They traveled deeper into the hospital and arrived at a marble staircase.

"The doctor's office is up there," Wally said. "That must be where Moore is hiding."

They started to climb. And climb. And climb. The staircase wouldn't end. A draft turned Wally around. Behind them, the stairs were unmaking themselves, stone by stone, floating around the outside of the hospital and building more stairs ahead. If they went back, they would fall a thousand feet. If they kept climbing, they would continue into the sky forever.

"How are we supposed to defeat Moore if we can't even reach him?" Wally asked.

Before Garnett could respond, something came wheezing and rattling down the stairs.

"Pardon me a moment," Garnett said, lifting his sword.

Graham's zombie doctor came loping toward them, holding bottles of smoking pills. Garnett stifled a yawn and then slew the doctor with a single stroke.

"Back to the problem at hand," he said, holstering his sword. "Breeth? Can you prevent these stones from flying to the top?"

She tried, but the stones nearly dragged her out into the sky with them.

"Curse it!" Garnett said. "I was certain that would work!"

Wally squeezed his temples. They couldn't think the way they did back in Kingsport. The buildings here had rules all their own. A giant wing whooshed past a barred window, and Wally had an idea.

"What if we were to tickle the building?"

"You're *mad!*" Garnett said.

"I'm *not,*" Wally said. "You—er, *Arthur* personifies buildings all the time back home. He says Manors think and dresses weep with jealousy." He pointed out the window. "If this hospital has wings, then it has to have, y'know *armpits* or something. My idea isn't any weirder than—"

"You misunderstand," Garnett said, laying a hand on Wally's shoulder. "*Mad* was meant to be a compliment."

"Oh," Wally said, blushing.

"Madam?" Garnett said to Breeth, gesturing out the window. "Could you lend us one of your long appendages and tickle this flapping monstrosity?"

Breeth slipped one of her tentacles through the bars and wiggled it under the bat wing. The entire hospital began to jitter with uncontrollable shrieking giggles.

"Its defenses are down!" Garnett said.

They sprinted the rest of the way up the staircase, finally arriving at the doctor's office. They paused and stared at the door. The floor swayed with the beat of bat wings.

For once, Garnett seemed at a loss for words.

"What happened to your humorous quips?" Wally asked Garnett.

"I'm scared, Wally," Garnett said, instinctively flexing the hand that had been stabbed on Arthur.

Wally nodded. "Glad I'm not the only one."

Garnett drew his sword. "You should stay here."

"No," Wally said. "I don't want you to have to go alone.

Besides," he said, patting Breeth, "we've got a tentacle monster on our side."

Garnett smiled. "And each other." He grabbed the door handle and looked back at Breeth. "Ready, tentacled madam?"

Breeth nodded.

Garnett threw open the door.

* * *

Breeth squeezed through the doorway with a great squelch, flinging out her tentacles to seize the author. Moore didn't so much as flinch. He scribbled a giant shaker of cayenne pepper into the air. It sprinkled over Breeth, and she shrieked in pain, retreating into the corner.

Moore chuckled from behind the doctor's desk. "I was briefly put out by seeing my own nightmare. But then I realized . . . I know its every weakness!"

In the hallway, Arthur looked at Wally through the Gentleman Thief's eyes. "It's true. Cayenne is how Garnett—er, *I* defeated the tentacle monster in my adventure."

If Moore could defeat Breeth that easily, then their plan to rescue him wouldn't work. Arthur peeked through the doorway as the Mirror author continued to scribble. Terrors shimmered to life in the doctor's office. Snails made of sewage. Hulking were-gators. Floating eyes with tears of flame. Impossible monsters Garnett had faced in his adventures . . . only much more horrifying.

"You fend off the monsters with your sword," Wally

whispered to Garnett. "While he's distracted, I'm going to grab the Quill."

"Wally, *no*, you'll die."

"It's better than losing Kingsport," Wally said. "Besides, Graham is the one who compromised the Manor. I'm responsible for his actions." He gazed deep into Garnett's eyes, as if seeing Arthur beneath the surface. "And I don't have a family to return to."

Arthur stared back. "What's it like? Always taking the fall for everyone else's mistakes?"

Before Wally could answer, Arthur drew Garnett's dagger and brought it plunging down, pinning Wally's pant cuff to the floor.

"Arthur, no!" Wally said, trying to pull the dagger free. "What are you doing?"

"The right thing for once," Arthur said.

Before Wally could argue, Arthur stepped with Garnett's feet into the doctor's office. Moore looked up from his writing.

"Do you know me, sir?" Garnett asked.

Moore squinted. Then he shook his head.

"*The Great Bicycle Heist*?" Garnett said, stepping into the candlelight. "*The Night of the Swamp Singers*? *The Man-Eating Daisies of Doom*?"

The madness in the author's face melted, giving way to shock. He drew a line through his writing and the forming monsters snuffed out like extinguished flames.

Moore stared at the Gentleman Thief, jaw trembling.

"G-Garnett? I thought you were gone. I—I couldn't think of any more stories. That witch *stole* them from me."

"On the contrary, sir," Garnett said, doffing his hat. "Here I am. In the flesh."

Moore remained skittish, Quill hovering over the page.

Arthur racked his brain of everything he knew about the author. His lonely lifestyle. His adventures. His desire for fame and fortune.

"You were once an adventure writer," Arthur said with Garnett's lips, "leading a swashbuckling life—albeit from the comfort of your writing desk. But then you were forgotten. And now you have an emptiness in you. A need to be loved and celebrated. Believe me when I say that I know this feeling all too well."

As Garnett spoke, the daffodil on his hat bloomed. And Arthur knew he wasn't talking about the Gentleman Thief, but about himself.

Moore squeezed the Quill so tight his knuckles turned white. "You know what it's like for your creator to discard you? To cut off the ink that is your lifeline?"

The Gentleman Thief laid a hand over his heart. "Look who you're talking to. I've been lying bloodless in a sewer for years."

A sadness fell on the author. "You were *my* invention. But now you're here to skritch me out like nothing more than a clumsy sentence."

"Quite the opposite," Garnett said. "I'm here to write the grand ending to your story."

Moore's hand started to shake. He pressed the tip of the Quill to the page, ready to summon more monsters.

Garnett laid his hat on the ground. Then he laid his sword and dagger beside it. "If you intend to replace heroism with nightmares in Kingsport"—he opened his palms toward the author—"then I'm afraid you're going to have to kill me, Mr. Moore."

"Arthur, *no*," Wally whispered from the doorway. "Your soul will be lost!"

Garnett gave him a sad smile, eyes sparkling as bright as the sun. "Who is this Arthur you speak of?"

Wally bit his lip.

Garnett turned back to Moore. "With the world what it is today, people are forgetting our adventures. Perhaps it's time you and I made one last grand gesture, saving Kingsport from the monsters and unrealistic expectations we've created. Perhaps, Alfred, it's time you and I retire."

Moore's expression softened. "Is it as simple as that?"

"It's as simple as that." Garnett took another step forward. "You're afraid to discover what happens when a character retires? So am I. What if we were to find out together?" He held out his hand. "You need only give me that Quill. And I can write a fitting conclusion for the both of us."

Moore's face began to tremble. Arthur continued to smile with Garnett's lips, even though he could feel his own lips shaking with fear back in the Stormcrow's basement.

The moment seemed to stretch into eternity. But then Moore lifted the Quill from the page, leaving nothing but a harmless dot. Arthur used the Gentleman Thief's fingers to reach out and take the Quill. A cold wind made him blink . . . and Arthur found himself enveloped in the stale air of the Stormcrow cellar, staring at words on an eviction notice.

"Arthur!" Harry said, hugging him. "What happened? You went into some sorta trance like—"

"*Shh!*" Arthur hissed at his dad.

He stared at the page, which continued to fill with words.

Garnett rested his hand on the author's shoulder and began to write. "Having performed their great work in the city of Kingsport, inspiring one young thief at least to become a better person, Mr. Alfred Moore and his marvelous creation, Garnett Lacroix, the one and only Gentleman Thief, walked arm and arm into the sunset."

Arthur blinked tears. The moment Garnett Lacroix touched Moore's Quill, he had taken over his own destiny.

The air around the author and his creation began to glow. The light grew so bright, Wally closed his eyes. Even Breeth's tentacles shrank away. The light grew and grew like an exploding star, enveloping Garnett Lacroix and Alfred Moore . . .

And when it faded, the author and his creation were gone.

Arthur set down Huamei's Claw Quill. And he collapsed into his father's arms.

* * *

Back in Mirror Greyridge, Wally blinked at the space where Garnett and Moore had just been—now mere sunspots in his vision. A splattering made him peer around the corner just in time to see the tentacle monster melt into a wave of ink. Breeth's shocked face appeared in the doctor's desk.

"I'm sorry, Breeth," Wally said. "I couldn't get him to tell me who gave him the Quill."

Breeth giggled. "*That's* what you're thinking about right now? We just won a sky battle against a freaking monster hospital!"

Outside, the whoosh of bat wings fell quiet. The objects in the room—the chair, the paper, and Breeth's desk—started to lift, weightless. Wally lifted with them. Now that Moore was gone, so were his imaginings. The hospital was just a hospital floating in the sky.

And now it was falling.

Wally's pant cuff tore from the dagger as he flew upward, slamming into the ceiling. He covered his face as the objects in the room rushed up and struck the boards around him. Everything hurtled down, down, down.

"Hang on, Wally!" Breeth's terrified face swirled to life in the wood Wally was pressed against. "I can save you!"

Her form leapt around the office, trying to create wings from the floorboards. When that didn't work, she tried to find something that would cushion Wally's fall. But there was nothing in sight.

"I don't know what to do!" she cried. Then she gasped. "Wally, Moore's Quill!"

Wally saw it glowing red in the corner, but the force of gravity had glued him to the ceiling. He was having trouble staying conscious. Fighting with every ounce of his strength, he crawled across the ceiling. He managed to grab the Quill, but he didn't have anything to write on. The wind made papers whirl through the air.

But then a single page fluttered to him like a butterfly. "Write on me!" Breeth screamed.

Wally dabbed the Quill in a glob of spattered ceiling ink and tried to think of a solution. Blood was rushing to his head. Nothing came to him. Why hadn't Graham prepared him for this escape as well?

Or had he? Wally remembered the last thing his brother had yelled to him.

"What goes best with Graham?"

Wally scribbled the answer.

24
TWO THIEVES

The gurgling had finally ceased, and Breeth was feeling like Breeth again.

It had taken her a long time to crack into the tentacle monster's tangled mind. When the manuscript she'd been possessing was swallowed into the creature's belly, she'd found nothing but nightmares. But by drawing from her experiences with the mouse thing, she had focused on monstery things—roars and slurps and snapping bones—until she was able to control the tentacles, one by one.

At first it was freeing, having so many appendages. But then she'd discovered that the more parts a creature had, the more pain she felt. And she had feared another horrible death. But when Alfred Moore crossed over, his monster had vanished with him—sloshing back into the ink that created it. It hadn't felt like a death so much as an untangling. And the tentacle monster's pains and fury were laid to rest.

Now that Breeth was back to her old self, she felt a little restrained, only being able to stretch *four* ghostly limbs through the Manor instead of dozens of tentacles. But she felt good—good enough, in fact, to head into Kingsport with Sekhmet, who had recently returned to the Manor with a bump on her noggin, to help retrieve Arthur.

The Stormcrow Pub was barely more than rubble, but it didn't take Breeth long to clear the splintered boards to reach the Rook's office in the back. The trapdoor that led to the cellar was open. Sekhmet found Arthur sleeping on the floor next to his snoring father.

"Arthur?" Sekhmet said, gently touching the blood on his head.

Arthur barely stirred. It seemed he and his father had been knocked unconscious.

Breeth possessed a loose board and gently sat Arthur upright. She stroked his head with the board—this boy who had saved her from electrocution.

Arthur snorted awake and then rubbed his head. "*Garnett?*"

"He's gone, Arthur," Sekhmet said. "He and Alfred Moore crossed over to the other side."

"Oh," Arthur said, deflating. "Right." His eyes went wide. "And Wally? Did he make it out okay?"

Sekhmet hesitated. "After Moore disappeared, all of his creations returned to their original forms. Greyridge lost its bat wings and fell out of the sky." She hung her head. "Wally fell with it."

Arthur swallowed.

Sekhmet lifted her face and smiled. "Fortunately, he was able to grab Moore's Quill and transform the hospital into marshmallow right before it hit the ground. It was a soft landing, if a bit sticky."

Arthur grinned. "That kid's a *genius!*"

"You should tell him yourself," Sekhmet said.

Wally took that opportunity to descend the stairs into the cellar.

"Wally!" Arthur said, running to his friend and embracing him. Then he pulled away. "I thought you were dead! Why didn't you just come down with Sekhmet?"

Wally smiled. "Consider us even for abandoning me in Weirdwood."

Arthur looked like he wanted to strangle his friend, but instead he hugged him again.

Sekhmet picked up the piece of paper lying on a cask lid. "Where's Huamei's Claw Quill?"

Arthur turned in a circle, patting his pockets and searching the floor. "I don't know. It was right here."

Sekhmet stared up through the trapdoor. "Someone knocked you out and took it."

"Who?" Arthur said, rubbing his head.

Sekhmet sighed. "I'm guessing we'll find out sooner than later."

Harry snorted awake, then squinted and cradled his head. "Did I get knocked out again?"

Arthur helped him to his feet. "Let's get you to an inn, Dad."

* * *

The sun rose on two thieves, a swordswoman, and a suspicious shudder in the shop fronts, as the four traveled back to Hazelrigg.

The people of Kingsport were finally creeping out of their homes to clean the streets and move on with their lives. On the corner, a newsboy hocked copies of the *Kingsport Gazette*, whose headline read of a tornado that had swept a flock of ravens and a squid from the sea. People were already explaining away the monsters, and the part of the Veil that wove through Kingsport was becoming whole again.

"How ya feelin', Arthur?" Wally asked.

"Mixed," Arthur said. "I just led my hero through his greatest adventure yet. But Garnett will never pick up a sword again." His breath fogged in the morning air. "Still, it feels right, I guess. It was time for the Gentleman Thief to take one last bow to Kingsport. By saving it for real this time."

Sekhmet threw an arm around Arthur's shoulders. "Garnett Lacroix will not be forgotten. By us at least."

Breeth studied the people of Kingsport, who would never realize that two thieves, a Novitiate, a fictional character, and a ghost girl had saved their lives.

"Poetic justice," Arthur said with more pep in his step. "I wonder where the Merry Skeletons are now. Are they still causing mischief in the Mirror City? Or did they disappear with their creator, moving on to the afterlife?"

Sekhmet winced. "They probably vanished like the rest of Moore's creations."

Arthur's head hung heavy, but then he smiled. "Maybe Gus, Tuck, and Mim are currently in the *Punderworld*."

Sekhmet giggled and pushed him. "Terrible!"

"Yeah, boooooooooo!" Breeth said. "And I don't mean a ghostly boo."

For the first time, Wally laughed out loud at one of Breeth's jokes. Unfortunately, Arthur thought he was laughing at his terrible pun.

"Y'know, Cooper?" Arthur said. "I think I'm done with being a thief. It's time to pursue a new career."

"As an author?" Wally asked.

"Yeah! How'd you know?"

"I've known since the day I met you. I was just waiting for you to figure it out."

Arthur smirked. "The moment of revelation came when I realized it's much easier to write about a sword fight than it is to actually be in one."

Sekhmet snorted. "Why do I feel like I already tried to tell you something similar in the Mirror City?"

"Arthur only learns stuff when it almost kills him," Breeth said. "Or if it can get him rich."

Wally laughed again, and Arthur looked to the shuddering shop fronts, trying and failing to lock eyes with Breeth. "Is that the ghost girl? Whatshername? Breathe? Breeze? Briefs?"

"*Breeth*," Wally said.

Arthur smoothed his hair. "Does she think I'm cute?"

Sekhmet rolled her eyes. "He's only asking because he can't get attention from anyone with a *pulse*."

Breeth studied Arthur's face. "He's better than a tentacle monster, I guess."

Wally laughed again.

"What?" Arthur said. "What did she say?"

"Nothing," Wally said, fighting a smile.

Now *that's* cute, Breeth thought, but kept it to herself.

Back in the Manor, Amelia told them that she'd returned Moore's red-veined Quill to Huamei's family. She'd explained to Huamei's mother that her son had died trying to restore honor to his ancestors. But Amelia could not explain why one of Huamei's claws was missing. She did not notice the look exchanged between Arthur and Wally.

"In any respect," Amelia said, "the war with the dragons has cooled to a simmer for the time being." She opened a door onto a hallway made of silver. "Now, if you three would follow me . . ."

"Four!" Breeth said.

Amelia led Wally, Arthur, and Sekhmet to the War Room while Breeth creaked into the ceiling. Lady Weirdwood sat in her waxen throne, looking as starry-eyed and alert as ever.

"You know," the old woman said. "I only have so many days left in this old skin, and some were robbed from me by that vile Scarab." She eyed Arthur. "Amelia tells me you were the one who knew that that golden insect originated in the Temple of Kosh, allowing Pyra to mix up my antidote. How did you obtain this information?"

Arthur breathed deep, steeling himself. "I brought that Scarab into the Manor, ma'am. If I'd known that it would poison you, I would have thrown it into the gutter. As for where I got it . . . I don't want to get anyone in trouble."

"It was my brother," Wally said. "Graham Cooper. He gave Arthur the Scarab."

"I see," Lady Weirdwood said. "It sounds like your brother might be a problem for my Manor."

Wally stared at his feet. "I hate to say it, ma'am, but yes."

Lady Weirdwood smiled. "It also seems you've been released of your duties to look after him."

"Ma'am?" Wally said.

Lady Weirdwood nodded to Ludwig, who handed her a case of pink crushed velvet.

"Wilberforce Cooper, I hereby invite you—"

Wally cleared his throat. "It's, um, *Wally*, ma'am. Bit of a miscommunication."

Lady Weirdwood raised her eyebrows. "Very well. *Wally* Cooper, I hereby invite you to join Weirdwood Manor as a Novitiate. You would begin training as a paladin immediately."

She opened the case, revealing two golden fists that could slide over Wally's own. Sekhmet and Arthur beamed behind him. Wally seemed to have slid into shock.

"Amelia tells me you're quite good at fisticuffs," Lady Weirdwood said. "And finding solutions to tricky situations. I would like you to join us as a war planner in training. Perhaps you can help that brother of yours see reason and get him on our side."

"I—I," Wally began, then cleared his throat. "I'm honored, ma'am. Truly. But I didn't do anything. It was all my friend Breeth." He pointed toward the ceiling. "She's a ghost."

"Ah, yes," Lady Weirdwood said. "The Fallen Warden's victim. I have some news for her too, but in good time. Mr. Cooper, does it matter where our talents come from? You made a friend, and that friend helped you. Had you not formed this bond, your city might have been lost. Besides, I think you sell your talents short."

"She's right, Wally," Breeth said. "You came up with the plot to stop the evil author *and* saved a smelly baby *and* realized hospitals can be ticklish. Oh! *And* you're good at charades! Decent, at least."

When Wally still didn't move to accept the golden fists, Lady Weirdwood closed the case. "Think on it a minute. As for Breeth . . ." The old woman looked up at the ceiling, and Breeth shifted her position so they were looking right at each other. "We have identified your killer. And Arthur here already brought him to justice. Mr. Benton?"

"Who, me?" Arthur said. "Right . . ."

Arthur looked in the wrong spot and told the ceiling everything that he'd discovered about the Rook, including his fate at the talons of his own Mirror counterpart.

"My killer is . . . dead?" Breeth said. "But—but . . . I didn't ascend."

She would never get to avenge her death. Never see her parents again. The ceiling groaned with her sadness.

Wally cleared his throat. "Breeth was hoping her killer's death would let her, um, *move on*, ma'am."

Lady Weirdwood sighed. "That means there is yet unfinished business that Breeth must resolve before she can . . . move on." The old woman looked at the ceiling again. "Breeth, I want to help you get to your parents. In the meantime, we would love to have you stay on as our honorary librarian. There are some books we can't reach in our Bookcropolis. Your possession skills would be ideal for the job."

Breeth felt too shattered to answer.

"She'll think about it too," Wally said.

Lady Weirdwood nodded and stood with a grunt. "Approach, Sekhmet."

Sekhmet blushed bright and stepped up to the waxen throne.

Lady Weirdwood picked up a blue sword and held it up, as if to knight her. "I think it's about time you end your career as Novitiate."

Sekhmet did not kneel. "I cannot accept this promotion, Lady. I missed all the clues about the Fae-born. And to be honest, I still don't feel settled about my time as Warden."

Lady Weirdwood smiled, a twinkle in her eye. "The world is overstuffed with heroes who would break the rules in order to be promoted. You have striven to follow every rule ever since a poor decision on your part cost the life of your mentor, Rose." She nodded at Wally and Arthur. "When these two thieves showed up, you decided to break the rules again. But this time I believe you were judicious in your decisions. You broke the rules, not to serve yourself but because you thought it would save more lives."

Sekhmet bowed her head. "We lost Huamei."

"Yes, we did," Lady Weirdwood said. "But you were also facing a threat unlike anything we've seen. All of our Wardens combined would have struggled to take down Alfred Moore and his dragon-bone Quill . . . And for that, I really must insist that you accept this Wardenship."

Sekhmet nodded solemnly. Lady Weirdwood swore her in.

When they were finished, Arthur cleared his throat and stood tall.

"I haven't forgotten you, Mr. Benton," Lady Weirdwood said. "Unfortunately, I cannot extend the same honor I gave your friend. You made a difficult situation worse with your antics, and you lied. You have a long way to go before I would consider you to be Novitiate material. Besides, I'm told you have a father in Kingsport to watch after."

The color went out of Arthur's face. This was clearly the last thing he was expecting. But he swallowed and nodded.

"Still," Lady Weirdwood said, "you deserve commendation for your final heroic act." She held out her hands and Weston handed her a book. "This appeared in our Bookcropolis early this morning. I present you with the final installment of Garnett Lacroix. Within its pages you'll find the text of your grand adventure. We plan to make copies, and the book should be distributed to Kingsport's bookstores as early as next week. Your hero will not be forgotten."

Arthur took the book and traced the silver lettering on the cover. *The Adventures of Garnett Lacroix and His Merry Skeletons: The Monstrous Hospital* by Valerie Lucas.

Lady Weirdwood smiled. "I figured Miss Lucas was due some credit for all her hard work."

"Thank you, Lady," Arthur said and wiped a tear from his cheek. "Does this mean I have to leave?"

"I'm afraid it does," Lady Weirdwood said.

Arthur gave Wally a searching look. "Are you going to stay?"

Wally hesitated, then looked at Lady Weirdwood. "How long do I have to decide?"

"You have as long as it takes Amelia to escort Arthur back to Kingsport," she said. "Then this Manor will head west. It seems the Rook was funding the Order's efforts to fight us in the Mercury Mines. Now that those funds have dried up, they've grown desperate, using a train to collect Fae-born for a twisted traveling zoo."

Arthur's eyes went wide at this. Then darkened. Breeth didn't have to read minds to know what he was thinking. Arthur Benton wouldn't be a part of that adventure.

Amelia opened the door and gestured out. The boys took one last look at Lady Weirdwood before exiting. Sekhmet gave Arthur a small wave goodbye. Breeth couldn't tell which of them looked more miserable.

* * *

"This is it," Amelia said, taking the handle to the entrance of the Manor. She looked at Wally. "Are you staying or going?"

Wally glanced from Arthur to Breeth, who inhabited the front door.

"I could sure use a good lock pick to help me feed those orphans," Arthur said sheepishly. "Y'know . . . if you want to."

"And *I*," Breeth said, "could use someone to talk to and translate everything I say. It turns out no one here speaks ghost creaks."

Wally placed his hand on Arthur's shoulder. "I'm sorry, Arthur. I'm going to stay."

Arthur swallowed and nodded.

"Thank you for your service, Mr. Benton," Amelia said. "Take care out there."

She opened the door.

Kingsport was not waiting on the other side.

Instead, a desert stretched to the horizon. Golden dunes rose and fell under a blindingly bright sky.

"What's this?" Amelia said, her eye wide with shock.

A hot gust of air blew sand around their feet. The three stared into the desert, baffled, until the door to the forest room burst open.

"Amelia!" Ludwig said. "You are needed in ze Var Room."

Amelia slammed the front door shut. "What's happening? What's wrong with this door?"

"Ze Scarab laid eggs," Ludwig said. "Zey are scrambling the Manor's doors. Ve must make an expedition into ze lower levels of the Abyssment and catch zem."

Amelia touched her eye patch. "Glycon help us."

Arthur looked at Wally. This was bad. But it also meant they were both still part of Weirdwood's adventures.

A smile crept across Arthur's lips, and it was mirrored on Wally's.

AFTERWEIRD

Charlie limped toward the Stormcrow. In his pocket was the letter that had been waiting for him when he'd woken up at the hospital, a line of stitches in his side. That big black bird had gotten him good, but his chain mail had saved his life. The doctors said he'd be as good as new in a week or two.

The Stormcrow Pub had been all but destroyed. But every member of the Black Feathers had descended from the four quarters and were working to restore it. While some repaired the hole in the roof and replaced the front windows, Disembowelin' Joe was digging a hole. Next to it was a coffin. Charlie didn't have to ask who was inside. The Rook was to be buried in the pub he loved so dearly.

Charlie thrust the letter toward Joe. "I need you to tell me what this says."

"Oh," Joe said, wiping sweat from his forehead. "Charlie. New Rook wants to see ya."

"*I'm* the new Rook, you idiot," Charlie snarled. "I was second-in-command."

Joe looked at the rook-painted door with fear in his eyes. "I don't think so."

Charlie stomped to the back and pushed open the office door. His eyes went wide. Liza was sitting at her father's splintered desk.

"Oh good," she said. "Charlie."

She was holding that evil Quill, sleek and black and veined blue.

Charlie steeled himself. If he could survive being lanced by a giant talon, surely he could wrestle a pen from a little girl.

He stepped up to the desk, casting a shadow over her. "I never heard the Rook nominate his daughter." He cracked his knuckles. "Seems to me he'd prefer you remain safe and sound outside of the business."

"You didn't know my father like I did," Liza said, unflinching.

She wrote something with the Quill, and her eyes flashed a dark yellow. Black feathers fluttered across her face. For a moment, Charlie wasn't sure if he was looking at a girl or a monster. A monster that could pierce right through his chain mail. Charlie stepped back, trembling.

"Now," Liza said, setting down the Quill and retaining her human shape, "are you going to be my bodyguard? Or does this need to go another way?"

Charlie composed himself, knelt, and muttered the Black Feathers' oath. Then he held out the letter, unable to keep his hand from shaking. "Someone sent me this."

Liza took the letter and read it. Concern crossed her brow.

"What's it say?" Charlie asked.

Liza sighed. *"To whatever vile scum decides to take the Rook's place as head of the Black Feathers—Your gang will no longer use children as thieves. You will release them with adequate pay or else face the same consequences that befell your previous boss. Signed, LW P.S. You may tell the children that they have Wally Cooper and Arthur Benton to thank."*

Charlie stood. "We're ignoring that, yeah?"

"No, Charlie," Liza said, crumpling the letter. "I happen to agree with this. We'll let the kids go. With back pay."

"But . . . Arthur Benton. He killed your father."

Liza's eyes flashed yellow again. "What?"

Charlie told her the events on the night of the attack. When he finished, Liza's mouth was drawn taut. Almost beak-like.

"Very well," she said, collecting herself. "We'll deal with Arthur when we find him. For now, we have more pressing matters."

Charlie's forehead wrinkled with concern. "What's the plan . . . boss?"

Liza picked up the Quill and spun it between her fingers as she walked to the waxen woman the Rook had kept in the corner.

"My father spent the past few years trying to tear down something called the Veil so he could resurrect my mother," Liza said. She drew her fingers down the woman's cheek and smiled, lips sharpening. "I'm going to finish his work."

ACKNOWLEDGMENTS

First, thank you to John Cusick, who brought together this ragtag expedition. To Michael F. Stewart, who provided the necessary survival tactics, and to Russ Uttley and Sacha Raposo for all of the maps and books and sage advice. To Eric Deschamps for giving this volume a cover worthy of the adventure and to Katie Klimowicz for making me look more presentable than I actually am. And of course, to Anna Earley for capturing uncanny sketches of the flora and fauna we encountered along the way.

Extra executive thanks to Paul Pattison for funding the expedition and making sure we had the tools required for such a long and complicated journey. To Christian Trimmer for shining a light on our efforts and deciding the world deserved to read about them. To Brian Geffen for weaving complex spells to untangle the haunted wood and to Rachel Murray for hacking through the thorny stretches. To that roguish pensmen Christian McKay Heidicker for using his wit and wordsmithery to aid me in creating an accurate and entertaining record of these true events. And finally, thank you to Luke Minaker, who showed me the hidden entrance to Weirdwood and answered all of my magical, historical, and anthropological queries.

I'll see you all on the next adventure.

Keep reading for a sneak peek at
the next **WEIRDWOOD** adventure.

amie Hoxer's creature paintings were a smashing success.

"So *haunting*!" one person said of the flock of were-bats. "So realistic!"

"Wouldn't want to find one of *these* in my bathtub," said another of the copper spiders.

"This one looks like it could step right out of the canvas and sniff my hand!"

The woman was looking at the cloud fox. Jamie's favorite. She had sweated over its lightning bright eyes, its sleet teeth, over every hair on its nine tornado tails until the fox's portrait exuded a stormy *grandeur*.

"Oh! And look at this one! You could roast marshmallows on those horns!"

Jamie appreciated the praise buzzing through her art show. But she was starting to feel cramped in the crowded art gallery. So she stepped past her painting of the flaming bull and outside to get a breath of fresh air.

The evening was lit in pinks and oranges, the clouds rising like an eternal fire into the sky. Jamie was about to take a contented breath when something caught her eye across the street. Nailed to a telephone pole was a poster advertisement.

Come see! Come see!
Our ZOO OF MADNESS!
Creechers Unimaginationable!
Cheeper than a punch to the gut!
AT THE FAREGROUNDS

Jamie wasn't sure which part of the advertisement was worse—the spelling or the handwriting. But it struck her that it had been some time since she'd seen an actual animal. So she turned her fancy shoes down Main Street and headed toward the fairgrounds.

***

The zoo looked pasted together with spit and glue. The big top tent was ragged and patchwork, the cages lopsided and spotted with rust. Even the barker was rough around the edges.

"Letcherselves in, lovies and gents! Feast yer peepers on our *Zoo of Madness*! You'll swear yer dreams have sprung a leak!"

The man was tall with a round belly and an ill-fitting suit. His pant cuffs bunched at his ankles while his sleeves rode high on his arms. Scraggly gray hair hung greasy from under a frayed top hat, and his teeth were as brown and mottled as a tin can left beside a creek.

Jamie handed the barker a coin and then jerked back when a monkey shot out from under the man's top hat and, grinning, held out a ticket. Jamie smiled and took the ticket. Someone had sewn little gray wings onto the monkey's vest.

The barker grinned his rusted teeth. "Mind your hexpectations, Miss. They's about to be *reversified*."

Jamie joined a long queue of people, which slowly crept within the U of lopsided cages, circling the blood-colored tent. The visitors who'd seen the creatures had fallen completely silent, and Jamie couldn't tell if they were disappointed or awestruck.

Several minutes later, she reached the first cage and saw the unicorn. A rush of excitement bloomed in her chest but then quickly wilted away when she remembered that unicorns didn't exist. She squinted at the horn, which she assumed was made of tin, searching its base for signs of dried glue. She couldn't spot any, but the poor horse's head hung heavy, as if unable to bear the horn's weight.

Next came the goblin. It sat hunched in the corner of its cage, staring at the straw-strewn floor with slimy eyes as the zoo's visitors pointed and gawked. The goblin's chest and arms were dry and cracked, like someone had pasted dead frog skin to a malnourished child. This, thought Jamie, was in poor taste.

The third creature was meant to be some sort of basilisk. But clearly it was just three dead animals in one. Someone— that man with the awful teeth perhaps—had cut a rooster in half, glued a snake to its abdomen, and then stitched bat wings to its back. Finally, they'd arranged the body parts so that they resembled a single sleeping creature.

Jamie flinched when the basilisk seemed to *stir* in its sleep. But she excused the movement as the workings of an automaton, manipulated with cranks and gears by a remote operator. The only other possible explanation was that she'd been wrong about the glued horn and the pasted frog skin. That these creatures were actually . . .

But no. That was impossible.

Jamie reached the stifling heat of the last cage in the row and her face fell slack. She blinked at the thing, her pounding heart trying to decide whether to beat out of fear or excitement.

It was a flaming bull. No. It was *her* flaming bull, somehow escaped from her painting back at the art show. The bull's head swayed back and forth. Its molten eyes dripped tears of ember while its beard smoldered like a forest fire.

"Keep it moving!" a zoo-goer shouted. "My son wants to see the fire bison!"

Jamie blinked at the flaming bull several more times before snapping back to herself. She quickly left the line of zoo-goers and headed straight toward the ticket booth. But when she passed the scab-colored tent, a sound stopped her in her tracks. It was a mournful sound, and it echoed deep in the well of her memory. Trembling, she parted the tent's entrance flap and poked her head through.

Inside was a muscular woman with stone-gray skin. Her boulder-like biceps rippled as she tugged on a rope, which stretched taut into a giant *hole* that hung in the middle of the air. The hole was impossible. Like a tear in reality that looked onto an infinite cloudy sky.

The gray woman continued to grunt and pull on the rope until a net appeared in the hole. It seemed she had caught a cloud. Wait . . . It was too *fuzzy* to be a cloud. Jamie's heart sank when she saw the creature's scrunched tornado tails, its rainstorm eyes, its sleet teeth trying to chew through the netting . . .

It was her cloud fox.

You'll swear yer dreams have sprung a leak! the barker had said.

This hole seemed to be an entrance into Jamie's own imagination.

A hand smacked down on her shoulder, making Jamie jump and whirl around.

"Yer misplaced, Miss," the man with the rusted teeth said. He pointed a well-chewed thumb over his shoulder. "The beasties is *hindways* of ya."

Jamie noticed for the first time that the barker's eyes were almost entirely colorless. Like a shark's eyes.

She pointed a shaky finger toward her creation. "I . . . I don't know what's happening here, but that fox is *mine. I* painted it."

The man's eyebrows arched up his forehead. "Didja now?" He glanced at the gray-skinned woman. "Hear that, Astonishment? This here lady's the one we've got to thank for our current fount of wealthitude."

"I'm alerting the authorities," Jamie said, moving to step around the man with the rusted teeth.

The man matched her step, blocking her way. "Now, why would I let you leave when your imachination's so *valuating* to us?" He spoke so close, Jamie could smell the rot of his disintegrating teeth.

She looked over his shoulder and found the big gray woman blocking the way behind.

"*Silver Tongue!*" the man bellowed.

A moment later, a slight woman stepped into the tent. She was as thin as branches, and her skin was so pale, Jamie could see the blue of her veins showing. Her eyes were also colorless.

"Let's make our patron comfortified, shall we?" the man said.

"Sure thing, Rustmouth," Silver Tongue said in a voice as cracked and sugary as crème brûlée.

She pulled a flask from her belt and took a sip, a silvery

substance dribbling down her chin. "*Ah!*" the woman said, refreshed, then smiled liquidly at Jamie. "*Why doncha tie yourself up, cutie?*"

The words shrieked in Jamie's ears like metal scraping metal, and she found her hands involuntarily obeying the woman's commands, picking up the rope.

"Just think!" Rustmouth said. "With a bona fide *artiste* around, our humblish zoo can order up dreamity creatures on demand! Heh heh."

Jamie Hoxer continued to bind her own wrists and ankles against her will. And all the while, her cloud fox—somehow freed from canvas and paint—whimpered like a mournful summer storm.

THE THIEF AND THE NOVITIATE

Weirdwood Manor soared through the Fae like a lost balloon as the Novitiate tried and failed to tap into his magic.

Wally Cooper crouched behind a frozen bush, searching the courtyard for movement. Icicles dripped from the Manor's eaves while snow erased the sky. An icy wind froze the sweat on his arms and back. If the Manor didn't soar to a warmer pocket-world soon, he worried he might shiver to pieces.

Something caught Wally's eye—a wisp of steam coiling behind the stone fountain. Sekhmet might have been a master of hiding, but she couldn't keep her flaming swords from melting the snow.

Using his teeth, Wally tightened the straps on his gauntlets and then crept from behind the bush and crept through the howling flurries. Halfway to the fountain, the pressure in his ears shifted, and the blinding white of the sky disintegrated to murky green. The icicles dripped as the air grew thick, and the snow melted like butter in a hot pan.

Wally brushed the slush from his shoulders and loosened

his collar, adjusting to the swampy atmosphere. He sloshed the rest of the way to the fountain where he'd seen the coiling steam . . . but all he found was a single sword with a thorn-designed hilt laying on the ground.

"*Oh no*," he said.

He heard the splash of a footstep behind him and whirled, raising his fists just as Sekhmet's other sword came slicing down. The blade sparked off of his gauntlets and deflected into a bush.

"Good!" Sekhmet said, rolling past him and scooping up her other trainer sword. "You made a mistake, believing I'd always have my weapons with me, but at least you stayed alert!"

Wally raised his gauntlets as she came at him again.

"Widen your stance!" she said, and struck—*Kling!* "But stay *flexible*." She struck again. *Clang!*

The last hit woke a sickening pain in Wally's left fist, but he swung with his right, trying to execute a sonic punch that would knock her flat. Sekhmet feinted back as smooth as smoke, throwing him off balance.

"Remember, *creativity* fuels magic," she said. "Not strength." Before he could block, her left blade swept in and tapped his bicep. "It's not *here*." Her right blade tapped him on the temple. "It's *here*. Watch."

She closed her eyes and whirled her swords, sparking them together and sending out a flurry of flaming butterflies that Wally had to extinguish with his gauntlets before they singed his eyebrows.

"Hope that didn't tire you out!" Sekhmet said, and came at him again, giddy with the thrill of the fight.

As she drove him backward through the courtyard, the sky shifted again and again—from mossy green to swirling gray to salty blue. The air howled with wind, then roared with waves, then grew stale as a desert. In the brief silence, Wally tried tapping into his magic—arranging his stance and fists like Sekhmet had taught him and waiting for that *feeling* to come alive in his chest.

He swung again . . . only to feel his gauntlet whistle harmlessly through the air.

Sekhmet laughed. "Lady Weirdwood may as well have strapped *sponges* to your fists for all the good those gauntlets are doing you!"

They continued to fight as the sky curdled with clouds.

Thunder rumbled. Lightning struck one of the Manor's spires. After a downpour of rain so thick Wally could barely see his own swinging fists, the sky froze over again, encasing the courtyard in ice. The next time Sekhmet feinted back, Wally lunged forward as far as his feet would carry him, hoping to get in one measly shot. But his feet slipped on the ice and flew out from under him, his face smacking the frozen ground.

Wally rolled over and stared at the sky's shifting colors. A raw bruise spread across his cheek.

Sekhmet tapped his throat with her trainer sword. "*Dead.*" She clasped his arm and hauled him to his feet. "Final lesson of the day. Always pay attention to your environment."

Wally removed his gauntlets and flexed the ache out of his fingers. "The ground *froze* beneath my feet."

Sekhmet smirked. "I'll make sure to send a note to the Order of Eldar, requesting they never fight us anywhere *icy*."

"That's not what I meant."

"I'll tell them not to fight us anywhere *unpredictable*, then," she said, holstering her sword. "But that's going to eliminate most of the Fae."

Wally rubbed his bruised cheek to hide his embarrassment.

She pointed to his chest. "Before you even *think* about swinging, you've got to feel that magic rise up in you."

Wally touched his sternum. "What does it feel like again?"

Sekhmet shrugged. "The Wardens describe it all kinds of ways. A burning. A *tingling*. A fountain of stars. To me, it's like drinking a glass of iced tea on my grandma's back porch."

Wally had never felt anything like that. Not for the first

time, he wondered if Lady Weirdwood had made a mistake bringing him on as a Novitiate.

Before he had come to Weirdwood Manor, Wally had been a thief, taking from others in order to survive. But now the Wardens were giving him an opportunity to save people instead. To protect them against dangerous Fae-born that slipped into the Real through Rifts in the Veil—like murderous dolls or scythe-taloned birds or tentacles the size of ship masts.

Wally Cooper's life suddenly had purpose. And he didn't want to lose that.

"Don't worry," Sekhmet said, throwing her arm around his shoulder and guiding him back toward the Manor. "You and I have nothing but time to train until the staff figures out how to exterminate those Scarab larvae. You'll tap into your magic long before your first official mission."

It had been a month since the Manor's Abyssment had become infested with Golden Scarab larvae. The mechanical insects chewed on the roots, making Weirdwood hurtle from pocket-world to pocket-world—the Fae's many different realms. This was what made the weather in the courtyard about as predictable as a baby's temper.

"Focus on your drills," Sekhmet said, clapping Wally on the shoulder. "I'll see you out here tomorrow morning. Clock time, not sky time."

She vanished down the western passage, and Wally massaged his sore fists. The sky had finally settled, gleaming with crystalline branches that stretched toward purple stars.